I0663209

Manitoba Tea & Tarot Mysteries

MAGIC, MAYHEM & MURDER

JANUARY BAIN

Magic, Mayhem & Murder
ISBN # 978-1-913186-15-9
©Copyright January Bain 2019
Cover Art by Erin Dameron-Hill ©Copyright July 2019
Interior text design by Claire Siemaszkiewicz
Totally Bound Publishing

Published in 2019 by Totally Bound Publishing, United Kingdom.

MAGIC, MAYHEM & MURDER

Dedication

This book is dedicated to all those who enjoy small town magic combined with a whodunit. It is my very great pleasure to offer a book that comes straight from my heart. Memories of my early childhood greatly influenced the creation of this story, making it the book I feel born to write.

As always, thanks to those involved in the process, my incomparable editor, Rebecca Baker Fairfax, and the amazing team at Totally Bound Publishing. You guys are the best.

And to my darling husband, thank you for being the man of my dreams.

Chapter One

The most beautiful thing we can experience is the mysterious. It is the source of all true art and science. — Albert Einstein

Thirteen years ago

"Will she let us stay?" Tulip's eyes widened, her nose and cheeks reddened by the freezing wind. My triplet shivered, wiping her dripping nose on the back of her red mitten. I straightened the collar on her worn jacket and tucked the thin scarf around her neck. The snow was falling more heavily now, already filling in the tracks the three of us had made walking from the street light to the front stoop, the warning still ringing in my head. *'Don't knock until you've counted to a hundred if you know what's good for you.' Twelve, thirteen, fourteen...*

"I'm not sure, but if we're really, really good, she might. At least for tonight," I interrupted my counting to answer her.

"Yeah, don't you be backtalking her like you did to Mommy," Star said, staring accusingly.

"I never did that!" Tulip's bottom lip started to quiver.

"Hush, no one is at fault," I said. If she started bawling, I didn't know how long I could hold off. My throat had a lump in it big as a baseball. *Thirty-one, thirty-two, thirty-three.*

Star screwed up her face but held her tongue, though only after I gave her my sternest older-sister look. I'd been born at one minute to midnight, making me the oldest sister by a full day. Not that birthdays were ever celebrated, though we'd had eight already. Mommy said we were too much trouble on a regular day. No way was she holding a two-day party for a trio of brats.

I tugged the paper sack holding all our possessions closer to my chest, thinking of the one precious book and the half-box of Pop-Tarts Mommy had tucked inside for our supper. Maybe Granny would have a toaster or a stove element to warm them up? Or maybe she might have some juice or pop? My throat was dry. Even water would taste good.

Star stamped her feet to stay warm, her pink running shoes leaving an intricate pattern from the soles as she packed the snow. Her scarf had icicles forming from her warm breath hitting the frosty air and her cheeks shone bright red. No frostbite—not yet anyway. But the wind was picking up, blowing showers of ice crystals off the roof and onto our bare heads.

Sixty-six, sixty-seven. I glanced across the open field between Granny's house and the house next door, visualizing wolves coming out of the evergreens of the thick forest and circling the town. We'd been dropped off on one of the coldest days of the year. Minus forty-seven, according to the loud man on the radio in our old van. I'd caught the name of the town on the welcoming sign leading in. *Snowy Lake, population 1259.*

I was proud to be the first one to learn to read, first one to do most things. Then I could help my little sisters, when they'd let me.

Eighty-nine, ninety. I was shaking now, could barely keep from kicking at the door with my foot. But a promise is a promise. If Mommy came back and saw me doing wrong, I'd get a swat for sure. *You know she's not coming back, right?* a small voice inside me piped up, making tears well. *No! Don't ever say that.* Hard as times had been, Mommy loved us deep down inside. *She's coming back. One day.* When things were better for her, she'd be back. She promised. And if I kept my solemn promise to look after my sisters, then everything would be okay. It had to be.

"Okay, let's not forget who we are. The awesome McCalls. Okay, time's up."

Just as I reached one hundred the back-porch light came on, a beacon in the darkness, spotlighting the three of us huddled in the dark.

"Land's sake alive, what are the three of you doing outside waiting in the snow?"

I spoke up, holding out the bedraggled piece of paper with the slightly smeared ink. "Granny Toogood, my mommy said to give you this."

If she was surprised at me calling her Granny, she didn't show it. She took the offering and read it with an intense expression. I peeked at her while she read. Dark curls gleamed around a soft face. She was wearing a nice pair of blue slacks with a matching blouse over a slim body, no stains or holes. *She must be rich.* She was shorter than Mommy, too. When she glanced down at Star, Tulip and me, the expression in her blue eyes was kind, as though she was very sure of something. I liked her immediately. I badly wanted her to like me, too. Then maybe she would feel obliged to help my sisters.

"Well, let's get you all inside then," she said, refolding and tucking the letter into her pants pocket.

I waited until my sisters had clamored in the doorway before I glanced back at the forest. The pack of wolves had vanished.

Chapter Two

Present day

"Mrs. Hurst called. She wants a reading today. And don't forget it's our turn to host the Northern Lights Coven," Star yelled out from the kitchen of the Tea & Tarot café where she was supposed to be watching a batch of apricot jam simmer. Seven to one she had her head buried in that dog-eared notebook she dragged around, working on yet another song.

At least Mrs. Hurst liked our apricot jam, her only saving grace. I wasn't alone in thinking that. No one in town could handle more than a small dose of the old curmudgeon, who managed to find fault with even the most perfect of sunny days. I paid closer attention as Star added, "Oh yeah, and Judith Finch wants a stronger love potion. Says the last one's not working."

"She needs a heck of a lot more than a love potion if she wants to capture Laurence's attention—the guy's ten years younger and headed for parts unknown," I muttered under my breath, sorting through the newly arrived assortment of crystals, tarot cards, seer stones, spell books, fragrant incense cones, tiny drawstring velvet bags — nice, royal blue this time — and dozens of tiny fancy jars for housing sweet-smelling unguents for the tourists.

Tulip, my presumed helper, had drifted off as per usual. She was busy clicking away on her laptop. My daily prediction — if it wasn't for me and my military maneuvers, the Tea & Tarot café would fall into utter ruin. At least I had the meeting of our coven to look forward to. Life being what it was in Snowy Lake, it required a lot of female support.

"Who do you think you were in another lifetime, Charm?" Tulip took that moment to look up from her ceaseless blogging to ask another of her inane questions. *Okay, maybe not fair.* A lot of people counted on her to make sense of their dreams. Oh, and she was darn good at reading omens in clouds. *Has a nice following too.*

"Probably Cinderella. Looks like I came back as a drudge yet again. Must have liked it so much last time, eh." I softened my complaint with a smile directed at my triplet and hurried into the kitchen to make sure the other hapless McCall wasn't leaving the jam to scorch.

"Star!" I yelled. There she sat perched on a stool, ubiquitous pen in hand, dreamily gazing off into space. The fruit she was meant to be tending was giving forth its essence of sunshine and happiness, the fragrance waltzing through the air, making my mouth water. Okay, a mid-morning snack of a fresh muffin with apricot jam was in order. I was also the self-elected quality control officer of our fine establishment, hence my curvy hips.

"It's fine." She rolled her eyes. "I just stirred it. It's almost ready to go. Just needs the pectin added. And the jars are in the oven, sterilized and ready for filling, thank you very much."

"Good," I grunted. I took the cheery red oven mitts with the white hearts embroidered on the backs, reached into the oven and brought out the huge black roasting pan full of steaming hot jars. I placed them on the counter on clean tea towels, ready for service. Hmm, she'd even remembered to place the lids and inserts in a pot of hot water on the back of the stove. *Will wonders never cease?*

"Okay, you stir in the pectin and I'll line up the jars. Ladle sterilized?"

"Yes, ma'am." Star saluted, knowing full well it rankled.

"We've only got today to set things in order," I chastised her. "Granny's coming home tomorrow and I want everything properly done and in place. She's worked hard enough for us over the years — time we made her days easier." Even though at sixty-five she appeared to have the energy of a bulldozer, I didn't take chances with my family.

"You'll get no argument from me."

"Yeah, right!"

Star was nothing but a conflicted bundle of nerves and energy. Uncertain of which direction her life should be headed — Nashville, LA or stay. *Well, join the club, missy. Every thinking, breathing human being feels that way, at least some of the time. I should know. I can read minds.* Or at least so far as to help someone find things. Images and the like, but I sensed their longings too. And we weren't so different, we humans. Well, except for Mrs. Hurst, who I sincerely wished would stop the readings already. Her mind would try a saint. All the positive energy I directed her way seemed to get lost in some gigantic black hole hovering over her starched hair.

A soft chirp of greeting alerted me to company. Ling Ling, our gorgeous white Himalayan with pretty apricot-colored ears, pranced into the room, tail high and waving like a victory flag. Star reached down and stroked her soft fur, to be rewarded by loud purring.

"Someone needs to take baby Ling Ling to the *V.E.T.* at three. It's on the calendar." Star pointed to the white board I'd attached to the wall to keep track of everything and anything to do with Tea & Tarot and family.

Ling Ling shot across the linoleum as if a horde of berserker fleas were after her, nearly colliding with the doorframe before her fluffy white tail vanished.

"Now you've gone and done it! You know she can spell, right?"

"Yeah, sorry. I'll find her and take her."

"Good luck with that. Best reschedule and keep quiet about it this time." I shook my head at my sister's forgetfulness. She flipped me the bird for my trouble. "Okay, let's get at it. I'll fill the jars and you apply the screw tops as quickly as humanly possible. I don't want one speck of dust finding its way inside."

"Ah-h sure, but first, what do you think of this?" She picked up her scribbler. "I'm calling it *The Ballad of Snowy Lake Johnny*. Here goes." And with that lovely lilting country and western voice of hers, she sang, "*A sweet, wild man came a' callin' – told me he'd keep me from fallin'. He said my heart was safe in his hands. He'd be my man and my biggest fan.*"

"Star!" No luck interrupting—I was serenaded with the next verse.

"Then Sara Jean turned his eyes sweet blue. And though he'd sworn to love me true. He turned his back and left me dry. For a new woman who made me cry."

When she got to the chorus, she began singing with entirely too much glee, *"Snowy Lake Johnny's a sweet, wild man. He turned my head and warmed my bed. All before we found him dead."*

"You know, that chorus might be considered rather incriminating in the wrong circles, sis."

"What do you know?" *Instant anger at my proper consideration. Whoops. Should have prefaced it with a compliment or three.* But no one could flounce out of a room like Star. I thought I knew the back of her better than the front.

I got down to work. In short order, the jam was ladled into its fancy jars and properly sealed, left to set overnight on bright yellow-checked tea towels. I'd apply the jars' decorative labels as soon as I printed them. With a final look of satisfaction at my lined-up soldiers, I rejoined my siblings in the café that doubled as a storefront. A half-dozen cozy round tables with stools took up one side of the cramped space, including the small booth for readings, while our sundries for sale were laid out on a series of shelves and took up the other half. Upstairs, one suite was rented out and I lived in the other one. Being one day older gave me jurisdiction over Star and Tulip, who still lived with Granny Toogood in her house situated three blocks away on Moosehead Drive.

"You know, the saskatoon bushes are ripe. Anybody want to go picking later?" I asked, pretty much knowing the answer.

Star groaned the loudest. "I hate mosquitoes. This year they're as big as dragonflies, I swear."

"Two words. Bug spray."

"Yuck. I hate that stuff. I'll smell like a chemical factory."

"Better than smelling like a homeless person with no access to soap, which is what we'll be if we don't step up our game and bring in more income."

"We do all right." Star got that mulish look. "We've paid our own way. And I was hoping that maybe I could take a little loan and head to—"

"Absolutely not! Every red cent goes into this café to keep it on a sound footing. Maybe one day we'll even be able to franchise it, have a string of cafés all across Canada."

"That's your dream, Charm, not mine."

Tulips looked up from working on her blog. "I have one word for you both for making a lot more money — edibles. We could learn how to add marijuana to our muffins, brownies, slices and cookies. And sell them for *three times* as much. We should perfect the process now, before the October seventeenth deadline and the law makes it legal. We could beat everyone else to the game. Advertise online. If I mention them on my blog, it'll bring in tons more traffic. In a year we'd all be filthy rich. I've been researching how to make cannabutter, proper dosages — everything. Even ganja-bread houses for Christmas. Just say the word and I'll start the experiments rolling. They'd fly off the shelves like hotcakes."

"Don't you mean fly off the shelves like *potcakes*!" Star quipped.

"No! Absolutely not!" I was equal parts horrified and stunned.

"Charm, Mrs. Hurst is on the phone again," Tulip said, trying to get my attention.

I hadn't even heard it ring in my shock at her suggestion. Had she forgotten our family history?

What hard drugs had done to our parents? And wasn't marijuana a gateway drug? I had no idea, but I wasn't taking chances with my family, even if it did look like a harmless leaf. Belladonna also looked harmless, but it most certainly was not. Beauty aid or agonizing death. *Go figure taking a chance with it.* I was up on those things, my love for reading Agatha Christie mysteries my favorite pastime in the precious hour before sleep.

My fingers trembling, I took the old-fashioned phone from Tulip. There was no point in relying on cell phone service in Snowy Lake. Half the time it didn't work, so why pay for it? One less expense was a good thing.

I cleared my throat before speaking. "Charm here. What can I do for you, Mrs. Hurst?"

"I must see you right now! My pearls—left to me by my grandmother Doris on my mother's side—they've gone missing. And I'll just bet Suzanna's the guilty one. Never trust a maid that smiles. Always trying to hide something."

"Suzanna wouldn't do that." I rubbed at the sudden pain in my neck, watching my mid-morning snack vanish. I still needed to bake my favorite muffins— lemon glazed. *Who says muffins don't require icing?* The lady in question, however, only lived one block away from our café, which was part of the problem. What was that quote about familiarity breeding contempt? Make it double—no, triple—in Mrs. Hurst's case. "Okay. Come right on down. I don't want you blaming anyone else. I'm sure you just misplaced them."

"Well, we'll see about *that*."

We most certainly will. My gift—tracking anything down—would sort it out. Now, if only my gift included giving a customer an automatic side order of niceness, we might have been getting somewhere.

True to form, Mrs. Hurst was pounding on the front door not two minutes later. Even on our one day off, I couldn't afford to ignore her needs. She was one of our best customers.

"Is that apricot jam I smell?" she asked, bustling through the doorway, making the windchimes rattle with concern. I barely had the time to unlatch the screen door. *No idea how she does that.* Most times the tiny angel figurines sang out to announce a customer, not screamed their disapproval to the high heavens.

She didn't give me a chance to reply, but motored on. "Because if it is, I want to place my order right now for a dozen jars. No, just a minute, make that two dozen, if I get a proper discount." She waggled her thick eyebrows at me to make her implication clear. I got it. *Generous as she is nice.* "I'm going to send some back with my niece who's coming to visit tomorrow. She can dole them out to the rest of the family."

"Your niece Georgia?" I inquired, leading the way to the back corner and the small booth there, with its midnight-blue fabric canopy. We preferred to take turns doing readings in private. Tulip was the best at dream interpretation, Star at tarot and me at tracking down lost articles. Star, our resident glitter-mistress, had added one extra-large gold star over the opening, of course.

Our patron was in fine form that morning. Her impeccable navy-blue shirtwaist dress kept her ample figure constrained and her starched crown of dyed-black curls was aligned in rigid rows. Her wolf-like gray eyes kind of spooked me, I admit. The woman was always looking for fault or something to pick at. She sat down and placed her hands palms-up on the small wooden table. She was rumored to be the wealthiest person in Snowy Lake, though she never had many customers in her store. *Must be selling her antiques online.* Used furniture would do better in Snowy Lake.

"I'm in a hurry. Let's get on with it."

"Just think about what it is you lost."

"I *know* what to do."

"Of course," I murmured, ignoring her impatience. Taking a deep breath, I laid my hands atop hers. I took another deep breath, then released it, letting go of anything clutching at my mind.

I closed my eyes and waited. Out of the darkness, an image appeared, unfocused at first then clearer as it coalesced into something recognizable. A thick strand of soft white pearls. *Where are you?*

The image expanded outward and upward like a camera aperture opening, exposing a set of dresser drawers and a bit of beige carpeting. Cold chills crept up my forearms, adding a queer vibration. I shivered and pulled my hands away from hers with dread. Other vibrations were coming across the channel that had opened, unstoppable even though the connection had been severed. The sensation slammed into me with such force that I grasped the edge of the table to keep myself upright. This was new. Sure, I'd always gotten a few bad vibes off her—I think everyone did, according to gossip I tried to ignore—but nothing this intense.

"They've fallen through a crack at the back of your dresser between the carpet and the wall." My lips were stiffened by dread, the words coming out odd and squeakily.

"You're sure?" she asked, her tone skeptical, her beady eyes boring into mine.

I worked at keeping calm, not wanting her to see the state I was in. She was like a feral cat chasing down her prey. I shivered. "As sure as I can be."

"You don't mind waiting, then, until I check before paying you? That will buy you time to consider a proper mark-down for the jam."

I squirmed at her condescension, sweat tricking down my sides. *Such a lovely old soul.* But it did keep my mind off the unwanted experience.

"No problem. Same deal as always." I pretended nonchalance, uncertain of what had just occurred and praying it never happened again. A few negative vibes were one thing, but this had been something far more powerful. And scary.

"And deliver the jam soon as it's ready. Oh, on second thought, I'll take a jar now."

I gave a curt nod. She got up and I dimly heard her ordering Star to bring her the jam. I stayed in the cocoon, chewing on my thumbnail. Was something bad going to happen? I'd never had a premonition of such magnitude. They were usually more along the lines of someone calling then the phone ringing a minute later, and it being them. This, whatever it was, had no sense of direction, just an overwhelming sense of foreboding. *Okay. Shake it off.* I had stuff to do.

Chapter Three

After grabbing a bunch of recycled white ice-cream pails with the handy wire handles from under a counter for the berries, I bolted out of the café's front door. I stopped short then poked my head back inside. *How can I have forgotten?* It must have been the conversation about those darn edibles. I ignored the other, darker, part, one of my mottoes being, *don't think of something and it will go away. Eventually.*

"I'll be back by dark. Lock this door. If we start selling on our one day off, we'll never gain it back. And I expect everything perfect for Granny's homecoming — you hear me! And don't forget, we still need more peanut butter cookies and chocolate cream cupcakes for tomorrow's 'Eh Neighbor Festival. Oh, I'm working the dunking booth from one till two, so you'll have to do without me."

Why had I agreed to that? Now I'd be a drowned rat for the better part of the afternoon. *For the sake of the town's Christmas budget, that's why.* But least I didn't have to kiss a mule like the postmistress did. She'd raised fifteen hundred dollars already, which was quite impressive for our small town. Dunking a McCall didn't rate nearly as high.

"Aye aye, Captain. And be careful, Montana Jones spotted a huge black bear when she was out picking yesterday." Tulip's easy-going grin was quickly followed by Star's piercing stare. Though the pair were identical in appearance, they were nothing alike, personality-wise. And I was odd girl out, having been spawned from a separate egg — or universe, apparently. We don't even look related. The twins were fair, tanned beautifully and had light blue eyes, while I was ebony-haired with violet eyes and naturally red lips. Granny Toogood liked to say I reminded her of Elizabeth Taylor and Snow White. *Now if I just had seven little people to help...*

I didn't catch Star's mumbled words, which was probably for the best. I gave a quick look both ways down Main Street, admiring how everyone had gotten onboard this year with the new town council to give their storefronts old-world charm. Flower boxes, red cobbled pavestones, antique street lights with hanging plants, wrought-iron benches with silver plaques complementing the business that had donated them, and bright red barrels for trash gave the town a look I declared perfect.

Swinging my pails, I headed for my rusted Cherokee jeep — AKA Thor — that I'd bartered off an old trapper last year. Once I'd thrown the pails in the back, I gunned the motor and headed for the edge of town, a few blocks away at the end of Main Street and Sixth Avenue. Snowy Lake was a compact town and had added only a few more residents over the past decade, and had lost about the same. I turned onto the narrow trail leading into the forest.

I bounced along the rutted path, accompanied by the pail's metal handles jingling merrily from the sway of the ride, the jeep's worn-out suspension groaning and squeaking from the effort. The lack of a radio didn't faze me. I let out a lusty chorus, thinking of my second favorite country and western singer next to my sister, the one and only Johnny Cash.

"We got married in a fever, hotter than a pepper sprout. We've been talkin' 'bout Jackson, ever since the fire went out. I'm goin' to Jackson, I'm gonna mess around. Yeah, I'm goin' to Jackson. Look out Jackson town."

Singing was one way to alert the black bears I was in their territory, though that didn't mean I don't carry my own brand of homemade pepper spray made from extra-hot chili pepper essence, concocted on the kitchen stove last winter.

I pulled off to the side of the trail near my favorite picking area, switched off the ignition and jumped out of the jeep.

Ah, nature. A bald eagle flying overhead suited my mood to a T. He wheeled majestically against the soft blues of the mid-summer sky, his white crown proof of his continued reign. Tucking my pant legs into my boots—I really hated blood-sucking ticks—I sprayed myself with bug repellent and strode over to the first saskatoon bush. The dry grass rustled with my movements, and I sneezed loudly from the assault on my olfactory nerves. Three *loud* sneezes. My nose was going to be red as a beet. Taking a second to swipe at it with a tissue, I pulled my high ponytail tighter at the base and surveyed this year's crop that I'd been keeping an eye on for weeks. *Aha, beat the bears to them this year.*

Making sure the pepper spray was latched onto my belt, I got down to the sticky business of removing the plentiful bounty. I kept up the singing to alert the wildlife — it was better than an airhorn — changing from *Jackson* to *Sunday Morning Coming Down* by Kris Kristofferson. Though Star would have had a field day with some of the drug-reference lyrics, I loved the lonely old tune by the poet bard.

"Cause there's something in a Sunday, makes a body feel alone. And there's nothin' short of dyin', half as lonesome as the sound. On the sleepin' city sidewalks, and Sunday mornin' comin' down."

Less than two hours to fill four pails. Unbelievable. I'd have gallons of the tart deep-purple berries by day's end. This year's harvest turned into our best-selling brand of jelly would bring in a sweet chunk of cash. I lugged each pail back to the jeep as I filled them, not wanting to accidently knock them over and spill their precious contents into the dirt.

There came a loud snapping of branches. *Darn it, unwanted company.* My fingers grasped at the aerosol spray bottle at my waist. I waited for another sound to alert me to the direction of the intruder. The sun in my eyes, I squinted to survey the landscape, swiveling my head back and forth.

There.

I caught the movement of a humongous upright creature headed straight for me, plowing through the thick undergrowth and overhead canopy as though he had just one intention — to do me harm. I didn't care if it were a huge black bear or the legendary Bigfoot. Either way, I'd strike first, with the sharp knife hidden in my boot if it came to that. I sprayed the noxious substance from the hip, directing the wide stream from my belt holster.

A loud grunt of surprise sounded. "Aww, *why* did you do that?" More moans of human agony followed.

Oops.

Out of the bushes stumbled a very large man — not Bigfoot, but darn close. Dressed in a black windbreaker, black jeans and extra-large combat boots, he wore a very nice black Stetson, accompanied by a full-on grimace. And oh my, when he pinned me with a look from his haunting brown eyes under that spectacular bad-boy hat, my insides somersaulted. *Wow.*

"Oh, my goodness! I'm so sorry! Thought you were a black bear. If I'd known you were — well, *you*, I'd never have sprayed."

The tall hunk of a man was too busy flushing his face with a water bottle to give me an answer. I waited, chewing on my lower lip and wishing I could just sink into the ground. But who rumbled through the bushes in such an obvious way? A bear, that was who. A land predator unafraid of humans and wanting to take a bite right out of me.

"Ma'am, I was coming to warn you. There's been a bear sighted not far from here. I heard you caterwauling and thought you might be in trouble. Didn't expect to be pepper sprayed for my trouble."

I looked around warily. Maybe it was time to head back to town and bring a group of people to pick berries another day when I could assign someone to keep a lookout. I had filled four buckets. Not too shabby.

Wait.

What did he just say?

"I do *not* caterwaul. I was singing. And it sure beats crashing through the bush like Bigfoot."

"If you say so, darlin'." Was that a twinkle in his eyes? The rest of his handsome mug remained inscrutable, launching another fussy crop of butterflies into my body, looking to land. He came closer and the acrid

25

stench of the protection spray on his clothes made my eyes water in sympathy. *Oh, my*.

He caught my grimace. "Not so pleasant an odor to be around, I agree. I'm Constable Ace Collins, by the way."

"As in RCMP?" My voice came out in a high-pitched squeal. Darn it. *Of all the people to mace, how did I manage a lawman?* He must have been new to town or I would have heard about him by now. News traveled faster than the speed of light here. Not bad, considering light traveled at 299,792,458 meters per second and took eight minutes and seventeen seconds to reach us from the sun. I did love odd facts.

"I apologize." I gave him my best I'm-so-sorry face. "But with you thundering through the bush, I really thought you were a bear. Heck, you're big enough to be one."

"And you are?" Nary a hint of a smile on that stern face. I'd bet he had all the perps ready to surrender. One look at those extra-wide muscular shoulders and granite jaw and they'd give up.

"Charm McCall. My sisters and I run the Tea & Tarot café on Main Street."

"Well, Charm McCall, I think we'd best get a move on. There's the bear now." He pointed at an advancing lumbering shape, just visible out of the corners of my eyes.

"Oh, shoot!" Survival mode clicked in. *Run. Never play dead with a black bear – they think you've decided to become a high-protein snack.* I made the jump into the jeep in record time. An explosion of activity on my right proved the lawman had similar quick wits. I fired the motor, slamming the vehicle into gear.

"Hang on!"

We bounced along at breakneck speed for a couple of insane minutes before hitting the main road back to town. I eased up on the gas petal and glanced over at my passenger. He looked a tad pale.

"Are you all right?"

"Yeah, sure." He prised his fingers off the dash and straightened his hat which had slipped forward. "You always drive like that?"

"Nah. Only when a bear wants a chunk of my hiney." I glanced over at him and caught him checking me out. He looked to be in his mid-to-late twenties. *Yup. Perfect.*

"You should come back to the café. Have some coffee and a dessert on the house. I owe you—ah—for the rude response to your trying to help me."

"Sorry, not today. Maybe another time."

Disappointed, I made the turn onto Main Street. The odor of pepper spray dissipating, I could detect a different fragrance underneath. A fresh woodsy scent. *Nice.* Smelling good was always a plus.

"Where can I drop you?"

"At the detachment. I'll go back for my truck later. I need to check in anyway."

"Okay." I turned off at the Clip Joint with its oversized scissors perched on the roof. It had quite the history, what with the strange artifact having fallen to the pavement in an ice storm years ago. They had been fastened more securely since, thank goodness. The hairstyling establishment was situated next to ours and did a brisk business. I pulled into the first driveway on the right. "Do you like country and western music?" I asked as he scrambled out of the front seat.

"Yeah, sure." He gave me a quizzical look, closing the noisy passenger door. Twice. It never latched on the first try.

"Great. Come by the Boots & Lace tonight. Men's night. First drink's free. And my sister Star's singing, which is an awesome treat."

"You've got more family in town?" He rested his hand on the top of the jeep's open window ledge. He bent down to peer in at me, his handsome visage filling the space to an alarming degree.

"I'm one of three triplets. Oldest one by a day, so I'm in charge."

"I'll just bet you are," he muttered.

"Excuse me, I didn't catch that."

"I said I'd love to attend."

"Great! I'll introduce you to the town. Is this your first posting?"

"No. Spent three years in Vancouver after completing my master's in criminology."

"For real? They send a man with your credentials to our part of the world? No offense, officer, but Snowy Lake isn't a crime hub. What did you do?"

"Apparently my outstanding attitude towards helping others in law enforcement who didn't see the full picture wasn't the bonus I'd hoped it was."

"Not the first time someone got demoted for knowing too much. Do I detect a little good ole' boy in that southern drawl of yours?"

"Guilty as charged. Spent my childhood in Lexington, Kentucky, before my parents moved myself and my two brothers to Canada. Father's a university prof and mother's a scientist, specializing in virology."

"Impressive. Well, tomorrow's the 'Eh Neighbor Festival, which means you can get back at me for the pepper spray. I'm scheduled for the dunk tank."

"Really?" A genuine smile appeared. "What time?"

"Ah, one till two."

He looked entirely too smug now.

"You know, I could have taken you back to your vehicle." I narrowed my eyes, thinking of a return trip to deposit his sweet hiney in the vicinity of the big black bear.

"No, thanks. I value my neck."

And with that parting shot, he swaggered, all tall and well-built, to the detachment front entrance, exactly like Marshall Raylan Givens of the television hit *Justified* that Granny and Auntie T.J. insisted on buying all the seasons of on DVD. *Show-off.*

I made an abrupt U-turn, enjoying the cloud of dust my oversized wheels flung at the low-slung building that housed the town's entire single-digits police force, then sped the short distance home.

Picking up a pail of berries in each hand, I banged on the front door with my boot. Tulip opened it. "There's two more in the jeep," I grunted, pushing past her to deposit the fruit on a customer table.

Star strolled in, already dressed for the evening's gig at the Boots & Lace.

"You look nice," I said, admiring the short-fringed white cowgirl dress and red leather boots.

"Ya think!" She twirled, making the fringe dance.

"Get all the baking done?"

"Ah, about that—"

I groaned loudly. "Don't tell me."

Tulip came back in with the other pails of berries, darting her glance back and forth between us as she caught the vibe.

"I'll stay and finish the cookies."

"Did you burn a batch again?" I pinned Star in my sights. "If you did, *you* get to stay and finish. Not Tulip."

"I don't have time. I have to get over to the hotel. Jerry called and said he needs help with the sound check."

"And your family doesn't?"

"It wasn't my fault. I got busy with a customer and — "

"I told you to keep the café closed." Star never listened.

"You said we needed the money! And the person bought more than hundred dollars' worth of crystals and tarot cards. Even a top-of-the-line spell book." Star's expression turned murderous, like her song about Snowy Lake's Johnny.

"Star." I shook my head. "Okay, get out of here. Tulip and I'll handle it."

She gave me a final stab with her angry eyes, stomping out of the front door.

"Her heart was in the right place," Tulip muttered, only driving the guilt deeper.

"Yeah, I know. Come on, we got cookies to bake and berries to clean. And I want to see at least one of Star's sets tonight. I invited someone."

"Really. Who?"

"New constable in town. Ace Collins. Just arrived."

"Nice. Must have been later this afternoon then." Tulip glanced at the clock on the wall, a particular favorite of mine with its cheery image of a rooster crowing about the time. "Last update I got from Auntie T.J. was four-thirty. An hour ago."

"Probably took a nap. I'd expect a call anytime."

As soon as I'd said it, the phone rang.

Auntie T.J., short for Tegan Jane, lived over on Telegraph Road, next to the town's library. I loved her house, all gingerbread styling with fancy touches like embroidered cushions with old-fashioned sayings that warmed the heart. She was Granny's younger sister by a decade, and from Tulip's reaction, it didn't take a psychic to know she was calling.

"Auntie T.J. Sure, Charm just told me."

"Tell her she's slipping," I teased. I lugged the berries into the kitchen. If I worked like a banshee, I could finish in time for a quick shower and catch Star's second set.

Three sweaty hours later, berries lay in the cooler and a humongous batch of peanut butter cookies was stacked in clear plastic trays.

"You want to do the Kismet Spell?" I asked Tulip.

"Nah, not much energy left. You do it."

"We thank you for this bounty of the sacred earth. May this food be safe and nourishing to all who consume it and bless them to optimal health, gifting them energy, vigor and well-being." I sent my positive intentions out into the universe, visualizing the stream as a circle of love, enjoying the tug on my spirit.

"Shoot, we didn't get to bless the jar of jam Mrs. Hurst rushed off with." I frowned at Tulip, not liking the omission.

"I'll be fine, Charm. I'm heading home to change. See you there." Tulip tugged off her apron and flew out of the café. I crept step-by-step up the back stairs to my suite and glanced at the closed door of Ivana's. One step creaked under my foot and I cringed, stopping mid-movement. I prayed.

No such luck. A door flung open and our tenant stood there, hands on her curvy hips. Her wild red hair gave the impression of sinister movement similar to the famed Medusa, even when she stood still. Her gray eyes pinned me to the wall and I swore a spark leaped from her to land on my shirt. I absently brushed at it. She was in her early thirties and someone I never wanted to annoy. I thought she was related to Russian mobsters—at least she alluded to it often enough, once she'd downed a few shots of vodka. Of course, everyone loved her. *Smart.*

"Ivana, how's it going?" I asked, my throat tightening. There weren't many things I was afraid of, but Ivana Petrov? *Right up there with Bigfoot.* Her broken and clipped English just made her scarier.

"Not so good."

"Oh?" The skin on the back of my neck crawled. "What's the matter?"

"What have I done for such insult! You didn't think to invite *me*. Best friend and bosom neighbor." She was under the delusion it was all true. She struck once at her heart over her spectacular rack with a closed fist, as though she'd chosen to be martyred at dawn in the courtyard.

"Well, you're always invited to everything. You know that." I was going out on a limb there, but it seemed the best course. Ivana had a reputation she'd worked hard to maintain, perhaps without knowing it — rabble-rouser. And in a town known for practical jokers, that was some feat. Snowy Lake was isolated from the rest of the world, especially in the dead of winter when we were connected only by dangerously icy roads, or our tiny airport that expected a passenger to leave their firstborn as collateral, so we were adept at making our own home-grown entertainment.

"Star sings like sweet bird of paradise. Thank you for formal invite." She was all smiles now, and *that* I trusted even less.

I let out the breath I'd been holding. I should have been used to her dramatics by now — she'd been our lodger for six months — but I kept waiting for the other stiletto shoe to drop. *And stick in my head.* "I'll be ready in twenty minutes. Want to walk over with me?" There was no place in town we couldn't reach in under fifteen minutes.

"I accept." She slammed the door behind herself to punctuate her remarks.

I opened the door to my small three-room apartment, wishing I could curl up on the comfy, oh-so-soft suede couch for a long, long nap. Instead, I dashed into the bedroom and tore off all my clothes, tossed them into the laundry hamper, jumped into the shower for a five-minute scrub then out again for a quick application of makeup.

I lined the lashes around my eyes—my best feature, in my humble opinion—with black kohl and mascara, followed by a quick dusting of translucent powder to my face and slicking gloss on my lips. A blast of the blow dryer and I brushed my waist-length hair to a shine, holding the waves back with a gold hairband. *Yup. Granny's right. Snow White.* No matter how much time I spent in the sun, I ended up the color of alabaster. I sighed. Just once to be tan and blonde and three inches taller, like my gorgeous sisters. I'd have to make do with being a brainiac, or so my sisters loved to tease me.

I checked the clock by my bedside. *Yikes. Two minutes to dress.* Ivana was not a patient woman. Pushing aside three-quarters of the choices in my closet, all ideal for working in the café or gallivanting in the woods, I found it. My favorite red dress. *Dare I?*

I shimmied my way into it and smoothed the silky fabric over my hips. The skirt flared to my knees— perfectly respectable in case any of Granny's friends ratted on me—and covered just enough of my ample assets up top to catch a man's eye. How long had it been since I'd had a boyfriend? It didn't warrant thinking about. *Too depressing.* In Snowy Lake, my sisters got all the attention, especially Star, who was perfectly named.

A loud knock sounded on the door. Time was up. *Shoes.* I scrambled in the back of the closet, pulled out my one pair of black high heels and slipped them on, balancing myself against the wall, then hurried to pick up my purse and dashed for the door before Ivana broke it down. Finances were tight this month and the woman was as strong as an Amazon.

"Why are you out of breath?" she asked suspiciously. She'd chosen a tight neon orange number that covered some of the important bits, with her hair pulled into a flattering updo. Even the orange looked good on her as long as I didn't stand next to her. It just needed someone to wear green and we'd mimic the one stoplight located at the end of Main Street.

"I'm fine. Let's go."

The Boots & Lace dancehall was right around the corner. As soon as we exited the back of the café, the heavy thumping of the drums and boots on the wooden floor reverberated up the soles of my thin strappy shoes and into my bloodstream. My step lightened.

The press of hot bodies, the fragrance of freshly popped corn and the promise of cold beer permeated the air of the honky-tonk when we stepped inside. If a person's pulse didn't quicken, better call the coroner.

I leaned over and yelled in Ivana's ear over Star's singing on stage about a cheatin' Lothario, her voice enthralling the crowd as usual. "You get us a table and I'll get the beer."

She nodded and plowed a wide swathe through the crowd. I almost expected to see neatly stacked rows of dancers on either side of her as she barreled her way on by.

At the bar, I ordered a couple of bottled beers and a large tub of popcorn from Darcy. While waiting for my favorite ginger-haired bartender to assemble our order, I swayed to the music, getting my bearings. Not that I could see much. The place was being hijacked by at least a quarter of Snowy Lake's residents. Our town grew by a substantial number in the summer, aided by a clever advertising scheme that touted an opportunity to pan for real gold in the creek running through the south side of town, where just enough specks of the color were found to keep the interest ongoing. I suspected Auntie T.J., a huge supporter of all things local, of tossing pieces of fool's gold into the creek in the dead of night.

"There you go, sweetheart. No charge for the popcorn for such a pretty lady." Darcy placed my order on a tray, added a charming smile and waited for me to fork over the cash. I dug in my purse and handed him a twenty. While he made change at the till, I scooped up a handful of buttery popcorn and swept it into my mouth. *Yum.*

"Evening, ma'am."

I started, choking on the mass of fluffy kernels, and took a quick gulp of beer.

"Howdy, Sheriff," I said with a cheeky grin, looking up, way up, at Constable Ace Collin's ruggedly handsome mug. He'd dressed in a pair of faded jeans that hugged his trim hips and a white western-style shirt opened at the top button to expose the smooth skin of his massive neck and chest. He eluded a quiet confidence and the air of mystery that intriguing males managed so effortlessly.

"I'm a constable. Though sheriff does have a nice ring to it." He had to lean in close for me to hear him over the boisterous crowd. The fragrance of cologne drifted past my nose. I breathed it in. I had no idea of the brand, but it made me take a second, deeper whiff.

"You collect your vehicle all right?"

"Sure. Just had to use an airhorn to drive the monster away."

"Auntie T.J. uses the bagpipes. Works really well. On bears *and* humans."

He chuckled, pearly whites flashing against tan skin. He rubbed his freshly shaven chiseled jawline. *Show-off.* He'd left the hat at home tonight. His thick dark hair gleamed under the lights, swept back from his forehead. Yup, Johnny Cash was in the house. My body tingled with anticipation.

"Tell me why you haven't introduced me to this sweet hunk of Mountie, Charm? Didn't I change your diapers enough to warrant some proper respect?" Auntie T.J.'s voice squealed in my right ear, triggering instant tinnitus. She wouldn't have changed a diaper if her life had depended on it.

"We didn't arrive in town until we were eight. I think we were well past the diapering stage."

"Whatever. So, what's your name, handsome? Always wanted me a *big* lawman." She elbowed past me, dipping her head back to stare up at the newest member of our community, then thoughtfully licked her lips for emphasis in case her words weren't clear enough. I rolled my eyes, wishing I could vanish through the wide-board barn-style floor.

"Better enjoy your last night of freedom before Granny gets home and reels in that hiney," I muttered to my aunt. Granny Toogood was a bastion of decency and fair play who I'd relied on to keep the peace on more occasions than I could count. She was tough to boot.

Auntie T.J. pretended she didn't hear me, but Ace raised one speculative eyebrow in my direction.

"Come on, sugar, let's dance!" My aunt tugged on her new-found partner, dragging him like a towboat drags a capsized ocean liner before vanishing into the crowd.

I made the sign of the cross on my upper body, praying he could dance.

I picked up the tray and wormed my way over to Ivana, depositing the beer and popcorn on the table in front of her.

She mimed her thanks, picking up the beer still in the bottle and blithely ignoring the tall glass provided. *Two kinds of women, those who like to be outrageous, and those who don't.* While she tilted her head back and let the cool amber fluid flow down her throat, garnering the glances of all nearby males, I poured mine sedately into its glass.

"I have new duty," she shouted over the din, setting the half-empty beer on the table with a determined thud.

"Yeah?" Mildly curious, I paid her half a mind while scoping out my aunt manhandling her big Mountie around the dance floor like a prize ox. Ivana had gotten us a prime location. I didn't want to know what she had done to get it. I nodded at Star singing on the raised stage. The white fringe of her costume glowed against her tan skin, her blonde hair curled into long coils and bouncing when she moved. My feet just couldn't resist the music of the two-step, tapping out the beat under the table.

"My mission—find Charm hot man."

I sputtered out the beer I'd just taken a sip of, wiping my mouth with the back of my hand. I waved her off, shaking my head vigorously. "No need. I'm fine. No hot man, please."

"No man?" She pouted, her eyes narrowing dangerously. Then her face lit up with a new understanding. "Woman then, yes?"

"No!" I shouted. "Definitely no hot man or hot woman for me. Stay out of it. Please."

37

The band had reached the end of their song, news I wished I'd been party to ten seconds earlier. *Now* it had gotten so quiet I could hear a mouse fart.

Mr. Hunky Lawman eased into a chair beside me, a smile tugging his mouth upward, exposing dimples that didn't quit. "Well, ma'am, that's good to know."

Ivana's eyes widened. *Yeah. I get it. He's hot.*

"If I try not to sizzle, will you do me the honor of the next dance, Miss McCall?" Out of the corner of my eye, I watched Ivana's eyelashes flutter, her hand clutching at her chest, exposing more cleavage.

"Yes, of course," I murmured, my body tilting to its hottest setting. *Ever.* Granny would never forgive a lack of manners, though, and I had best rely on safe protocols and keep a proper six inches between our bodies. The sooner I introduced Constable Ace Collins to Star, the better.

On the dance floor, I barely came up to his chin when he tugged me to his broad chest. He tucked my hand into his far larger one that threatened to swallow it whole, pulling me into the slow waltz step, his other hand searing the flesh of my lower back. I gritted my teeth. And Star and her country band would have to line up a romantic song next. He danced with casual flair, making it easy to follow his lead. *Unfortunately. Better if he danced like Bigfoot.*

"I had no idea Snowy Lake was such a thriving community. Nice to see so many people out and about on a Thursday night."

"Oh, that. It's just because my sister Star's band's here."

"That's your sister? Nice voice." He didn't glance over at the stage, where she crooned about crying over lost love, but held my gaze instead.

"You staying in town for a while?"

"If you'll have me."

I nodded. "I'll introduce you to Star between sets."

He shrugged. "Sure. Any other relatives in town I should know about? Parents?"

Raw emotion surged, but I tamped it down, shaking my head. As the years had gone by, I'd given up the hope of ever seeing my mom again, no matter how much good karma I'd tried to create. It just wasn't good enough. "Long gone."

"I'm sorry to hear that." His eyes darkened with empathy, making me swallow a mouthful of saliva.

"It is what it is." I shrugged. "You?"

"Both parents live in Winnipeg. Divorced, though they live side-by-side in a duplex on Academy Road. Go figure. Got two brothers, Stone and Mick. My younger brother Stone's working on a degree in computer engineering at the U of M and Mick's even younger — training to be an RCMP officer in Regina."

"Sorry about your parents splitting up. It usually sucks for the kids."

"Yeah, well, it was after we'd all left home, which made it easier." He shrugged, letting it slide off his extra-wide shoulders. "A little harder when you're eight." *Hmm, excellent hearing as well.*

"You cope. Learn to make the best of it. Granny Toogood took us in. We're the lucky ones. At least we didn't land in the foster system."

"I hear you."

The press of bodies swaying romantically around us while we danced in our oasis of proper decorum left Ace and I the odd ones out. When the song ended, I hightailed it for the table, waving off a chance at a second round of torture.

Star put her guitar on its stand and bounded down the short flight of steps from the stage, fringe and curls flying.

"Star, I want you to meet Constable Ace Collins." I leaned in close to shout in her ear. I crossed my fingers that such enticement as this fine specimen of a man would keep Star in town.

Star put out her hand and Ace took it. But instead of shaking it like a normal person would, he laid a smooch on the back of it, giving her an admiring glance from his chocolate-brown eyes. She blushed under the overhead florescent lights, her eyes sparkling with merriment.

"Charmed, m' lady."

"Nice to meet you too. Has anyone told you how much you resemble Johnny Cash?" she purred, earning a dimpled grin from Ace. *O – kay. This might have worked too well.*

"A time or two. May I join you?" he asked, though I'd already extended the invite. Oh, such a real dream guy, not that I was into that sort of thing.

"Of course." Star gave him the sweetest look imaginable, sitting down next to him, legs crossed toward him. "So, when did you mosey into town, Sheriff?"

I rolled my eyes.

"Just today. Got a call about a black bear on the way and stopped to have a look around. Ran into Charm and – "

"And I pepper sprayed him," I finished. He gave me another of those long looks that made my heart stutter.

"What? How *could* you?" Star's exaggerated horror was well played.

"I've already apologised for thinking he was a bear."

"Or Bigfoot," he added with a wry smile.

"Charm." Ivana shook her wild hair, the ends spitting in my direction. "Not nice to do that to such *big man*. And you know what said about man with big foot, eh?" She laid a hand on his forearm, squeezing as if checking for something. *For heaven's sake, he's not a slab of beef.* And I wasn't touching for all the tea in China the comment about a man with big feet.

"Anyone know what's keeping Tulip?" I took a sip of beer, noting Ivana had just about finished hers.

"Maybe new boyfriend?" Ivana's eyes gleamed with interest. Ivana went through men like no woman I'd ever met. *No one with a big enough foot? Okay. Not nice, Charm.* I blushed at my own audacity.

"I'll get some more beer," I offered, getting up. Ivana worked part-time at the local beauty salon, which barely covered her rent—probably why she was a month behind. I wasn't complaining, envisioning her Bratva brothers climbing out of the woodwork and through the windows to warn me to lay off their sister. Plus, she was good enough to cover in the café when both my dear sisters went AWOL. She didn't drive too much traffic away on a good day.

"A pitcher this time, Darcy," I said at the bar, once I'd gotten his attention. "Everyone's thirsty tonight." He nodded, busy filling orders. But he bumped mine up the queue, pouring it right away.

"Thanks. Have you seen Tulip?"

He shook his head, taking my money then handing me the change. I carted the golden-colored nectar back to our table and plunked it down in the center, rivets of moisture condensing and running down the sides of the see-through pitcher. A loud disturbance near the entrance grabbed my attention. I scanned the area, my skin twitchy with heightened nerves. The crowd separated, revealing my errant sister barreling her way toward our table. *Oh boy, now what?*

Chapter Four

"I got here as fast as I could!" Almost out of breath, Tulip held her hand to her heaving chest. "It's Mrs. Hurst. She's gone." Tears flowed down her reddened face, dripping off her chin.

"What? What are you talking about?" The black force-field from my earlier reading with the woman came back with a vengeance, darkening the edges of my vision.

Ace got up, took Tulip's shoulders and directed her onto a chair. "Tell me what you saw?"

"I went over to see Mrs. Hurst, to deliver the rest of her jam—she, she didn't answer the door. I didn't want to leave it outside, so I went in the back door to put it on the kitchen table. I took the key from under the mat. And there she was." She hiccupped. "Dead." Tulip dropped her face into her hands, large sobs shaking her slender shoulders.

"Why did you take it to her tonight?" Confused, my brain sought answers. "I was going to deliver it tomorrow, properly labeled." At least we had given it the green light of the Kismet Spell, except for that jar she'd taken earlier. That still plagued me.

She lifted her tear-stained face to me. "She called the house and left a message it was an emergency and she needed it right away. That's why I'm late. I don't know why she needed it so soon, but you know how she is. Oh my goodness, it was awful. Her face — it was all blue and her tongue—" Tulip shuddered and closed her eyes.

"Have you called nine-one-one?" Ace asked.

"No. I just ran straight here. I didn't know what else to do." Tulip shook her head, her eyes widening with more emotion. I jumped up and pulled her to me, hugging and soothing her, rubbing circles on her back.

"It's okay. I've got you."

Ace stood up. "I'll deal with this and call it in. What's the address?" He pulled out his phone, frowning when he discovered there was no cell service. He looked at me, a question in his eyes.

"Mrs. Hurst's house is at edge of town on Ring Road. Huge Victorian-style white-framed house with black trim."

He turned to leave and I gave Tulip a look. "You okay if I head over there?"

She nodded, and I handed her over to Star. I chased after the long-legged Mountie, catching him outside the door. "I'm going with you."

I didn't give him time to object, but climbed into the passenger seat of his white SUV with its RCMP logo, *To Serve and Protect*, decaled on the rear bumper and buckled myself in.

Frowning, he fired up the engine and pulled into traffic.

"I was led to believe this was a quiet little town."

"Yeah, well, we have our moments. But murder — that almost never happens."

"What makes you think it's murder?" The look he gave me pinned me to the seat.

"Don't know for sure." I swallowed my worry. "But with what Tulip said about the state of her body, it seems possible. Turn here." Maybe I should have said something to Mrs. Hurst about the dark energy? A terrible unease filled me at the thought that I might be partially responsible by not warning her. Nervous adrenaline rattled my body.

A few more tense blocks and he pulled up in front of the town's only mansion. A couple of lights were burning behind the front living room drapes and in the wrought-iron sconces decorating the gingerbread-house-style entrance.

"You wait here," Ace commanded, reaching into the back to unlock his gun from its case. He hadn't worn it on his person, being off-duty. I grimaced. This was *my* town. Not his. I disembarked the police vehicle alongside him.

I shivered, the midnight air giving me instant goosebumps. Hugging my arms around myself, I strode after Ace. We marched around the side of the house, past the display of fragrant fuchsia-colored peonies in full bloom and down the path to the back door. It stood wide open, attesting to Tulip's wild flight. A halo of light spilling from the kitchen carved out a half-circle on the ground. Crickets chirped, the night air thickening with apprehension.

Ace stopped, listening. "Stay put," he ordered. Drawing his gun, he slipped through the doorway.

I waited all of ten seconds. When no shots rang out, I crept inside. I hadn't spent years reading all those Agatha Christie whodunit books for naught.

I gave the room a full appraisal from left to right, spotting the two boxes of apricot jam that Tulip had delivered stacked on the countertop. An opened jar of the sweet nectar was splattered across a red placemat on the table, the glass resting on the edge, still oozing jam down onto the floor in thick gobs. My view drifted downward and I spotted a leg lying at an awkward angle on the floor near a chair. I caught Ace's stern glance and hugged myself tighter. Ignoring him, I moved slowly around the perimeter of the table, bracing myself. Mrs. Hurst. Blue face with swollen tongue lolling out, just as Tulip had described. *Oh-oh.* A blue face was worrisome. An abandoned spoon lay by her side as if she'd dropped it mid-tasting. Fear chilled my heart. The poor woman didn't deserve this ending. No one did. Her limbs were all twisted at weird angles, as if she'd gone into convulsions at the end. Awful. Disturbing. And frightening.

"Don't. Touch. Anything." Ace was in full Mountie mode.

"I know! I'm not stupid."

His look said that statement was not proven either way. Yet.

"Wait here." He left to go through the house— checking for intruders, I supposed. Obviously having found none, he rejoined me and set his gun aside.

Dimly aware of Ace using the house phone to call in the event to the late duty dispatcher at the detachment, I turned away, finding it an invasion of the woman's privacy to stare any longer. I shook my head in dismay. Who or what had killed her? My heart thudded. What if she'd choked on the jam? The very idea was too horrible to contemplate, with me taking such pride in the preserves. *Maybe it was something natural, like a heart attack or stroke?* Because if it had been murder, there'd be a lot of suspects. The woman had managed to piss off just about everyone in the town at some point in her life.

Chapter Five

"I want you to think of your heart's desire." I gave Judith Finch a thick pad of paper. The middle-aged woman, with the nervous habit of saying everything twice, had tracked me down, demanding a refund on the love potion or another way into the heart of the man she'd set her cap on. Her potent perfume stifled me in the tiny enclave separating us from the rest of the restaurant. Half as much scent would have done the job twice as well.

"Write it down. Just a few words will do."

She bent her dark head over the lined pad, her mouth working, miming the words.

"Okay, now circle the first letter of each word, ignoring any that begin with a vowel. How many letters do you have?"

"Three. Three."

"Good. I want you to think of how to combine those letters to make a magic sigil."

Her quizzical expression while she tilted her head had me adding, "Make them into one drawing. An abstract figure. Like a logo maybe. Any which way you like."

Ah. Comprehension dawning, Judith gave me a broad smile. "Then what do I do? Then what?"

"You need to charge the sigil. Focus all your energy on it while staring at it. Any extreme emotion works. Then, look at it once a day, letting it slip into your subconscious. You can even burn it if you like. But whatever you do, keep it private and show no one. Clear?"

"Sure, sure. Thanks, Charm. Thanks."

Star popped her head in, nearly making me fall over backward from my cheap diner chair. "You should tell Judith the best way to charge a love sigil is by having an orgasm."

"Really? Really?" The woman's dark eyes rounded, her mood brightening.

"Yeah, that'll work." I shot Star a bolt of fire with my eyes, sending enough energy to load twenty sigils.

She grinned and danced off as the chimes sang out over the door to the café, announcing a new customer.

I waived my fee for the reading, aware that not much could help a heart yearning for the love of a particular person if said person was not right for them. I sighed.

"Morning, Charm." Ace touched the brim of his Stetson when he caught sight of me exiting the magic cave. He sat down at a table, nodding at Star's inquiry about coffee, and took off the spectacular hat. He reached up and placed it on the rack.

"Howdy, Sheriff." I didn't wait for an invite but plopped down across from him. Dressed in his RCMP uniform, all official, he'd turn heads anywhere. What would the red serge look like on him? *Best guess? Pretty darn amazing. Maybe we should have a parade?*

He shook his head at me, his expression grim. My stomach dropped into the floorboards.

"I knew I shouldn't have let Mrs. Hurst take that first jar of jam before I spelled it."

His eyes widened. "You put a spell on jam?"

"Ah—yeah. The Kismet Spell. I want to give all our food the energy to keep people healthy and happy."

"Doesn't seemed to have worked in this case."

"No." I looked away, chewed on a thumbnail. "It didn't."

"Did you see Mrs. Hurst earlier in the day?"

I stilled, frowning. "Yes, she was here."

"I have to investigate this properly, Charm, it's standard procedure. Mrs. Hurst was seen leaving your café in the morning."

"Then why ask like that?"

"Like what?" His brow knitted.

"Like I'm going to lie to you?"

He sighed. "It's the way we're taught to formulate our questions. No offense meant."

"No offense taken."

His eyebrows rose at my short reply. "I suggest you don't take up poker. You'd be lousy at it."

"Anything else?"

"We're sending the jam in for testing. I just wanted to give you a heads up."

"I can assure you, *Officer*, it's of the finest quality and ingredients!" My heart slammed and my lips froze in anger. How dare he?

"I'm sure it is. She might have choked, of course, or had a stroke or heart failure while eating it. The coroner didn't find any other wounds. We won't know the cause of death until his report is concluded. That could take days. But I'm here to suggest—strongly—you not sell any more of that brand for now until we know the deal."

"I think you should leave."

He retrieved his Stetson from the hat rack by the table, smoothing the brim with his extra-large fingers. "It wasn't my intention to offend. My sincerest apologies."

I nodded, but was unable to force even the briefest of smiles, I crossed my arms over my chest, watching him stroll from our former haven. The door chimes turned traitor as well, singing out gaily to announce his departure. *Frickin' man.*

Star joined me, topping up my coffee. "Ace is just doing his job, you know."

"Yeah, I know." I took a large sip of the strong brew. "Just don't like aspersions cast on our product."

Her forehead creased with concern. "What if something did go wrong?"

"How? It was made under ideal conditions." I crushed my lower lip between my teeth. But if even a whiff of a scandal about our jam got out, we'd be finished.

"I need to find out more." I held the cup in my two hands and took another sip. "If someone doctored our jam, then we need to be proactive."

"What do you mean? How's that possible?"

"Ever read Agatha Christie?"

"You know I haven't. I like my cowboy or rancher stories, with lots of steamy heat."

"Well, this could be bad for us if I don't start my own investigation. I need to get to the bottom of this before it goes south. If it turns out Mrs. Hurst was murdered—"

"You think she was murdered? Tulip said she did look really awful. I hate to think that's what a normal dead person looks like." Star shuddered.

I checked the rooster clock about to crow the hour and finished the last of the coffee. "We need to set up for the festival. And I've got that darn dunk tank thing this afternoon."

"Yeah, going to buy a few balls myself. I've still got a pretty good arm. I just might be the first to dunk your hiney." Star's eyes gleamed.

"Yeah, better line up. There's a few waiting to have that honor. I'd be putting Ace Collins at the top of the list after yesterday's bear spray incident, hot new sheriff or not. Not to mention Judith will probably sling a few if this new idea for a sigil doesn't pan out."

"You driving off possible suitors with pepper spray while I was gone, granddaughter? I didn't teach you very well now, did I?" A melodic voice rang out behind us and I span around with a leap of joy. *Finally!*

"Granny! I didn't hear you come in. You should have called us. I'd have picked you up from the airport." I rushed to embrace her, the fragrance of lavender emanating from her soft skin soothing my frazzled nerves. I released her to allow my sisters to hug her too. She was looking serene, an invincible sage who saw the world for what it was, and though she found it lacking in character, she made it spin just fine in her sphere. Did I imagine a hint of tiredness about her eyes? We had to step up our game.

"Elsie gave me a lift. She left her car there on purpose. I've already been home."

"Sit down," I urged her, rushing to prepare a pot of tea. Earl Grey, her favorite.

"Just a quick cup. We've got a festival to set up for, sweetings."

I fixed a pot, added a slice of lemon and bore it back to the table where a flock of magpies — my hyperactive sisters — were haranguing Granny about all the events that had occurred since she'd been gone. I caught the last bit of spilled information about Mrs. Hurst from Tulip's lips and tried to catch her eye. *Enough already.*

"Tulip!"

"I found her. It's my story to tell."

"It's not a competition, sweetings." Granny sighed. "How are you holding up, Charm?" Her soft blue eyes met mine.

"I'm fine." I gave a quick look around to make sure there was no customer within earshot. "But our new local constable thinks our jam might be at fault." I hadn't meant to share the worry, but when Granny was around, I never could seem to help myself. She'd sleuth it out soon enough. It was her way.

"That's why he was here just now." She frowned.

"Yes. And we both went to Mrs. Hurst's last night."

"So, you saw the body?" She held the teacup in both hands and blew on it to cool it enough to drink.

I nodded over the tight lump in the back of my throat.

"Terrible thing." Granny shook her head. "I've known Anne Hurst for decades. A misunderstood woman and a very unhappy soul."

Star choked on her coffee and I patted her back absently. Granny continued her tribute. As much as she hated cussin', she hated speaking ill of the dead more. The practice had become ingrained and was maybe not a bad thing, even if it did set us at odds with the rest of the world on occasion.

"She wasn't born to the big house and money. I knew her as a child. She came from humble beginnings and made her own way in the world. There's something to admire in that."

Star rolled her eyes, but Tulip sniffed and blew her nose.

"Not much to admire about Auntie T.J.," I said. "Playing handsy with our new Mountie like he's her prize ox."

"Big one, is he? And a southern gentleman, I hear. We'll all have to bone up on our southern expressions. They'll go well with our Canadian expressions, eh." A twinkle glinted in her soft blues. "I'll have a word." And it would work as well as last time. Not. At. All.

I picked up the empty tray. "I've got to cart the treats over to our booth before ten. I could use an extra pair of hands," I hinted.

"Go — all of you," Granny directed, shooing us out. "I'll manage the café. Won't be many customers with the festival about to start, anyway."

"Shoot. I've got to make sure the apricot jam is safely hidden away until we know more." Brother, the trouble that new Mountie had brought to town. *Not his fault*, the fairer side of my brain intervened. *Yeah, well the timing is piss-poor, at best.*

Fortunately, the jam in question was still in the back. The fancy jars with their decorative labels looked the epitome of wholesome, the nectar inside gleaming golden in the sunlight. I shook my head. *Crazy.* And that included our new lawman. I would vouch for our product any day.

I opened a bottom cupboard, stacking the jars way in the back. No point in making things worse by not following standard procedure. Constable Ace Collins had been here one day and was already proving the biggest thorn in my side. I didn't have one iota of sympathy left for the bear spray incident now. We were more than even. The man had insulted my cooking, and *no one* got away with that.

Straightening, I picked up a large plastic-covered tray of assorted cookies then hurried out of the back door, headed for my jeep that I'd parked there to make the process easier. The fairgrounds were on the outskirts of town near the high school and too far away to schlep the cookies on foot.

My two fellow triplets trooped after me, handing off the trays to store on the backseat. "Meet you there." I waved to them and turned the key to start the motor. Nothing. *No, don't fail me now, Thor.* A quick prayer, a love pat on the dash and the motor turned over. *Pays to be nice to man-made objects.*

Breathing a sigh of relief, I directed the jeep into traffic and followed the lineup of vehicles headed to the fairgrounds.

The decorating committee must have worked all night. Flowing white banners, bunches of colorful balloons and streamers dancing gaily in the breeze all screamed funfair. The biggest banner, *Welcome to the 'Eh Neighbor Festival*, was strung over the road from two hydro poles. *Oh boy, I wouldn't want the job of shinning up there.* If one of the volunteer firemen spotted that infraction, it guaranteed a bruhaha of major proportions. *But, not my problem today.*

I disembarked and picked up two stacked trays. I'd need to make a few trips, but Tulip and Star should be along shortly if they ever got their act together. Grumbling to myself, I slammed Thor's door closed with a determined foot and strode over to our waiting booth set in the middle of the action. The delicious fragrances threading the air enticed me. I took a deep, appreciative breath. The odor of fried treats, pizza, the barbecue pit with meat roasting on the spit — a glorious bouquet of flavors that made my mouth water in anticipation. My stomach rumbled, agreeing wholeheartedly it was past eating time. My step quickened.

After stacking the trays on the ten-foot counter that ran the length of our gaily painted booth — glittery gold stars on a midnight-blue background courtesy of Star — I got down to the work of setting up. With my sis being one of the main attractions, singing with her band at regular intervals all day long, we were going to be hard-pressed to cover all the bases. And then there was that darn dunk tank thing right after lunch…

I glanced over to where a community crew was finishing up the money-maker, filling the large steel tank below the drop chair with ice-cold water. Shuddering, I took a sip of the hot coffee I'd packed and nabbed myself a chocolate chip brownie cookie from the tray. Between nibbles, I sipped more delicious coffee.

"I'd offer to take your hour, but I've discovered I've been signed up for my own slot, called 'get the new guy'. Not certain my heart can take an hour of being shocked by freezing water."

I'd missed Ace's arrival. "Wait until they add the buckets of ice."

"They do that?" His dark brown eyes widened in dismay.

Touché, Constable. I snorted. "Not usually, but I could always have a word with them. When's your shift start?"

"Can't wait to get your chance at soaking me, eh."

"No way I'd miss that opportunity, Sheriff. So, low man on the totem pole gets corralled for the job. You could always bow out. You have an investigation to run, after all."

"I can give up an hour for the good of the town."

"I teach a self-defense course on Monday nights. Any chance of you giving up another hour to show us a few of your tactical techniques?"

He gave me a quick glance.

"Why, is that a look of surprise in your eyes, Officer?"

"No, no, I think that's great." He shrugged. "Sure, count me in."

"Ah, are there any new developments in the case?" I asked, casually. "Want a cookie?" I gestured at the tray.

He shook his head. I squinted at him and he picked one up, the same kind as mine. At least he had good taste. He took a bite.

"Good cookie." He took another quick bite, swallowed and continued. "It's early days. Not entirely certain if we even have a murder on our hands yet. Other explanations are entirely possible. There was no sign of a struggle, other than by the victim when she fell to the floor. Seizures have many causes, anything from a brain tumor to a blood clot. Perhaps a drug interaction. Won't know until I get the results of the autopsy."

Goosebumps erupted all over my body. My worst worry was the blue skin that I hesitated to mention and draw undue attention to. I'd read *Sparkling Cyanide*, and blue skin was a hallmark of a drug that caused an agonizing death. Had someone put cyanide in Mrs. Hurst's food or drink? And if so, who? The list of suspects was not going to be short. I needed to take this seriously, *now*, before fingers got pointed. My gut said it might be up to me to solve. I knew the town. I could interrogate people without them realizing my intentions.

"When was she last seen alive?"

"In the morning, leaving your place. Did you get along with Mrs. Hurst? Not finding too many people in town who speak well of her. And most just clam up when her name's mentioned."

"Ah, sure. We got along for the most part. Not an easy woman, but she's—was—a good customer," I self-corrected. "Always buying our jam in bulk. Loved a good discount." I made myself chuckle as if I found it charming. *Not.* "What are you getting at?"

"Nothing really. Just making conversation."

"Yeah, right. Okay. Straight goods. She was not well-loved, though the evidence is entirely circumstantial that she sold the soul of her firstborn to the devil. She never had a kind thing to say about anyone. Ever. But you didn't hear it from me."

"Hmm. Why did she come to the café yesterday morning?"

"She'd lost something. Wanted my help." I glanced at him, taking in the chiseled jawline and the brooding Heathcliff eyes. He wore faded jeans this morning, hanging off trim hips. A red T-shirt stretched tight over his Bigfoot-sized chest. The shirt was neatly tucked into his pants, buckled with a silver engraved buckle with a bull image engraved on it, along with the year *2015*. Had he been a rodeo bull-riding champion?

"Why would she think you could help?"

I sighed, letting out a long hiss of air between pursed lips. This was territory I didn't want to get into. *Like a cop would ever understand.*

"My sisters and I all have areas of expertise. Star's a wiz at the tarot card readings and Tulip divines dreams for clients."

"And what is your gift, Charm, other than the obvious?" He leaned in closer, pushing a strand of hair that had broken loose of my hastily constructed braid behind my ear. His eyes locked with mine and my heart stuttered. I was suddenly glad I'd taken the time to apply a light floral scent instead of yesterday's bug spray. Oh, and a bit of makeup.

I looked away first. I took a gasp of air, my eyes searching into the distance. "I'm a tracker. I help people find things."

"What does that mean exactly? A tracker?"

"It means I see visions in my head. Then I can tell people where they lost something!" My anger at being grilled boiled over. *Great.* Now he'd think I was certifiable.

I chanced a glance. His brown eyes had widened and in the depths swam curiosity and surprise. But no condemnation. At least, not yet.

"What did you see that morning?" He kept staring at me and I chewed on my bottom lip. Nervous, I wanted to step back, but an invisible force pinned my feet to the ground.

"I saw her pearls. She'd lost them and was blaming her maid." I shook my head at the loathsome idea. Suzanna was a good person and it was terrible that she'd been slandered. "They were behind her dresser in the bedroom."

"That was all you saw?" Why was a Mountie taking me seriously?

"I—yeah, that was it." No way was I going there, to the dark force I'd experienced surrounding the woman.

That would sound crazy. I crossed my heart automatically with a gesture for forgiveness for lying and opened my eyes to find him still staring at me.

"You're certain?"

"You believe me—about my being able to track?" *Misdirection works wonders.*

"Why shouldn't I? The world constantly amazes me. So much we are never made party to, just being human with our limited capacity. Besides, I'm a big fan of Brian Green's theories. I've read *The Elegant Universe*—twice. Also, *The Hidden Reality*, *The Fabric of the Cosmos*, *Icarus at the Edge of Time*." He ticked them off on his fingers as he named each one. "Oh, and I've watched all his PBS television specials. And I'm also partial to Michio Kaku's *Parallel Worlds*. Oh, not to forget Carl Sagan and Kip Thorne."

"Me too! Hard to choose between them. Are you for real?" A lawman who read books about our amazing universe by a Pulitzer Prize finalist and by other great names in physics? Something we had in common, a love of reading and big ideas. *Note to self, tread lightly and don't underestimate this guy.*

"Yeah, not much else to do during a cold Canadian night in the dead of winter. But I'll have to do more than dunk you in the water tank if you breathe a word of this to my staff sergeant." A killer smile accompanied his joking threat.

"If you *don't* dunk me, I promise not to tell." I returned his grin, adding, "And a belated welcome. It's nice to have another certifiable bookworm in Snowy Lake. I'm just waiting for the geniuses of the world to invent the ultimate equation that explains everything. Someone needs to pull another Einstein."

The look he shared with me was priceless. It paid to have read any book I could get my hands on. Our librarian was eclectic — I'd give Miriam that distinction — bringing in books on a variety of subjects meant to expand Snowy Lake's residents' horizons.

"Truce?" He held out his hand.

When I took it for a quick shake, my world literally imploded. A bright light flashed across my mind and coalesced into an image. *Oh, boy.* I was sunk.

Chapter Six

"Sorry I'm late." Tulip steamed up to our booth, trays of treats stacked in her arms and looking harried beyond belief. "Ivana was in a state this morning. Something about not being invited personally to the 'Eh Neighbor Festival."

Ace raised his eyebrows quizzically, as if he found the information surprising. "Ivana?"

"You really don't want to know. If I don't personally invite her to *everything*, she throws a hissy fit." I shook my head. "Must be a Russian thing. I mean, everyone is invited to the festival. It's a public event, for heaven's sake."

"Well, explain that to her, please," Tulip muttered, setting her trays in position on the counter. "Granny calmed her down with an offer of tea and cookies, but I'd expect to hear more about it later."

"You remember to bring the cash box?" I asked.

"Shoot. Another trip to the café." Tulip made an about-face and took off at a gallop.

"I'll catch up with you later." Ace gave me a last lingering smile, leaving with a quick stride. The view going was as nice as the one coming, but I had no time to linger on how fine the man looked in his jeans. I had plans to make. Getting back into Mrs. Hurst's house before it was considered a crime scene and taped off — my first priority. Maybe something there would incriminate a person or two and narrow the field from the whole darn town full of suspects.

Mrs. June Smith, the only woman in town who insisted on being called Mrs. at all times, strode up to our booth just as I'd taken a big bite of a peanut butter cookie. I smiled cautiously over the mouthful of crumbs.

"You have something on your lip, dear."

I mumbled my thanks, grabbed a napkin and set the cookie aside. Her determined look this morning said she was staying for a visit. Okay, she'd cornered her quarry fair and square.

"I heard your sister Tulip found the poor woman while delivering jam." She shook her head. "Terrible thing." Her eyes gleamed with interest under her white sunhat. The banker's wife wore a simple blue sheath dress, her brown hair tied with a matching bow at the nape of her neck. She was in her early fifties, with her two children having moved or escaped to Alberta. Her oldest daughter, Alison, had suffered for years under the illusion she had to be perfect, even changing universities in her misguided effort to obtain the best grades possible for her mother. She was so desperate for them. I remembered being told she'd cheated on a test in high school and her mother had hotly contested the accusation against Alison, getting the black mark expunged. I expected that if I searched for a top ten list of control freaks, I'd find Mrs. June Smith's photo and stats.

"Yes, it is. She was such a *wonderful* contributor to our town. Why, just the amount of coin alone she spent at the café is going to be sorely missed." I looked away and picked up a clean rag and, praying I wouldn't be struck by lightning, systematically wiped the counter free of any speck of dust that might have landed in the last ten minutes.

"They say she was found in a terrible state, blue in the face and everything. Did you notice anything amiss, dear? Killer leave any clues at all?" *Other than a body?* Of course, she knew I'd been there. *Duh.* But even for a town busybody, she had an inordinate amount of interest in this case. Almost ghoulish.

"I can't say." I made the gesture of buttoning my lips with my fingers. "But I really need to take a quick break. I left something back at the café. Would you be able to help me out?" Her eyes glazed over and she took a step backward. "Just for a few minutes until Tulip gets back? You can take a half-dozen cookies for your trouble. I know Fred loves the peanut butter ones."

She stepped forward again. "Sure. Anything to help out."

"Thanks. I won't be long." I sashayed right out of there.

Thor and I made Mrs. Hurst's former residence in record time. *No sign of activity. Perfect.* I half-ran to the door and twisted the knob. *Locked.* I scrambled for the key and came up empty. *Darn it. Maybe a window?* I hurried around the back and tried one not visible from the street. Shoving hard at the half-frozen latch corrupted by coats of thick paint, I slowly eased the window upward, grunting and groaning with the effort. Darn thing was about as cooperative as a four-hundred-pound Sumo wrestler. Wiping the sweat from my brow with the back of my hand, the day growing hotter by the second, I looked round for something to stand on.

Spying a shallow wooden rain barrel under a water trough, I dashed across the yard to the garage, quickly dumping the container's contents on the grass along with a load of dead mosquitoes. Once I'd rolled it over to the window, I turned it bottom-side up and stepped onto it, praying it could take my weight and had not rotted out. From there I fish-tailed myself into the open window.

It took me a moment to get my bearings in the dim light. It was a back storage room, by the looks of the shelving and supplies. I crept to the closed door and listened. *All quiet.*

I opened the door then stepped into the hallway. My best bet was an office or the space where she'd kept her records. The first room turned out to be the laundry room, the second a pantry. I kept moving, listening to the tick tock in my head, and tried a third room. *Bingo.* Her office, complete with a computer situated on the lone desk and a gunmetal gray file cabinet snugged up beside it.

I rushed to the desk and rifled through the bills and correspondence with hands that trembled slightly, to my dismay. I tried not to focus on the violation of a dead woman's things. An invisible force was pushing me to do this, and a sense of disaster loomed if I didn't get answers, *now.*

Nothing stood out. The file cabinet was next. Everything was neatly labeled in vanilla legal-sized folders. *Nice system.* When I had more time, I'd consider adopting it. I read each label, trying to think what might reveal something of note. *Ah, her banking records. Those should prove helpful.* I pulled that one out and set it aside on the desk. I skimmed the rest of the folders but found nothing of interest. *Hmm. What else?*

A sound of nails scratching and scrambling on hardwood came. I whirled around, glimpsing a streak of something huge out of the corner of my peripheral vision. The monster landed on the desk beside me with a loud ominous thump. I stumbled backward, certain I was about to be attacked.

"Meow."

Larry, her cat. A swoosh of breath left my body of its own accord. I reached out and ruffled his furry head.

"Hey, Larry, you trying to give me a heart attack or what?"

He responded with his usual motor-like purr, his massive head bumping against my hand for more scratches.

"No one looking after you, big guy?"

The huge fluffy Maine Coon responded with a plaintive yelp, his golden eyes full of indignation. *Guess not.*

"Okay, I'll get you something to eat in a sec," I promised.

"MEOW. MEOW. MEOW..."

"Okay. Okay. I'm coming right now. Stop your kyoodle." I grabbed the folder and tucked it under my shirt and into my pants to keep it secure.

Larry jumped down, tail up, expecting me to follow him right into the kitchen. Of course, I did. I stopped dead in the doorway though between the kitchen entrance and the back hall, the rubber soles of my running shoes squealing on the tiled floor.

A woman had died in this room yesterday. I looked over to the spot, still seeing her lying there in my mind's eye. I blinked. When my vision cleared, the image was gone. *Oh boy.* Taking a deep breath, I hurried on wobbly legs to the cupboard where Mrs. Hurst stored her cat food. I'd fed Larry before when his 'owner' was away, and in anticipation of some Fancy Feast, he danced around my legs to speed up the whole darn process.

Working rapidly, I popped the small tin open, dumped it onto a saucer then placed it on the floor in the tray provided. I dumped the contents of his water dish and refilled it from the tap.

"That's better, eh. Who's going to take care of you now, I wonder? I don't see you and Ling Ling getting along." I sighed. *Poor little man.*

Too busy to respond, Larry kept his head buried in his food dish.

"Too bad Mrs. Hurst didn't keep a diary or something. That would help me enormously."

No response except sounds of serious noshing down.

"Okay. I got to go, big fellow. I'm sure Mrs. Smith is ready to lop off my head by now. Or maybe use one of her daddy's pistols on me." Her father had been a big-time collector of weapons, from the Civil War onward. "I'll look in on you later. Okay?"

Wincing, I noted that the jar of jam had gone from the table. It pained me to think of someone looking for bad things in jam I prided myself on. I let out a shuddering breath. Okay. I flicked a glance farther down the counter, seeing the two stacked cases were still in place. *What a shame if all that effort goes to waste as well.* Swallowing my anger, I gave a last perusal of the kitchen and turned to head out of the door. Larry had a cat door and would be fine until I found out what the deal would be. Worst-case scenario, Ling Ling and Larry would have to make friends. Or at least call a truce.

I crashed right into a brick wall.

"What on earth?" I stumbled backward. A pair of strong arms kept me from tumbling to the floor.

"Are you all right?" The low growly voice, full of resonance that enticed me on a whole new level, turned my head on the spot.

"No." I breathed in his woodsy fragrance just as our eyes locked. In horror, I stared at our new Mountie, his body heat stored from the morning sunshine emanating through his shirt and into me. Suspicion filled his chocolate-brown eyes.

"What are you doing here, Charm?"

Good question. I prayed the folder I'd hidden in my clothes didn't show. "Nothing. Well, except feeding Larry." *Thank you, Larry. Our home is now your home, buddy.*

"Larry? Oh, the cat." Larry was still heavily involved with his feast, declining to acknowledge an interloper during mealtime. But I did note his ears flicking backward to keep tabs on us.

"You can let me go now," I suggested, tugging at the arms that pinned me to his rather broad and awesome chest. Maybe he was a weightlifter too?

"Oh—yeah."

Strange. His tone was breathless, as though he'd run all the way here.

He belatedly let me go.

"So, I'd better get back. Mrs. Smith, the banker's wife, is watching the booth for me."

"Nice of her."

"Yes, she's a real sweetheart."

His eyes darted to mine and I smiled as though I had a mouthful of stolen whipping cream.

"Why are you here?" I asked pointedly. Mrs. Smith could wait another minute.

He flushed, not meeting my eyes, but I caught the surreptitious glance toward the counter.

"No! You are *not* doing that!"

"Just doing my job. I have to take in the rest of it. We have to be certain."

"You have no call to do that. If the first jar turns out fine, all this will be wasted." I crossed my arms over my chest, giving him a full-on glare. "You'll destroy our business."

"I promise you confidentiality. Nobody will know except the authorities."

"Yeah, right. Do you know where you're living? In Snowy Lake rumors travel faster than the speed of light. Everyone will know by suppertime. Guaranteed."

"Well, they won't know from me."

"And that's supposed to make me feel better?"

"I don't want to fight about this—"

"We're not *fighting*. It's the truth."

He pressed his lips together, looking about as comfortable as an animal caught in a trap. I almost felt sorry for him. *Almost*.

"Do what you have to. Just don't expect me to agree." And with that, I hightailed it out of there. New item on the agenda—teach the lawman a lesson.

I ran down the sidewalk, my runners slapping. I scurried into my jeep and gunned the motor. *Tick tock.* The noise in my head was ratcheting up and meant my solving what had happened to Mrs. Hurst had become of paramount importance.

At the fairgrounds, I parked in one of the exhibitors' parking spaces to jump the queue of out-of-town vehicles lining up to pay for public parking, and pulled the folder out from under my shirt. *Hmm. How to disguise it?*

After tugging the sheets of printed paper from the marked folder, I turned the cardboard cover inside out, then shoved the papers back inside. Untitled, it could be anything. I could then study the pages during downtime at the booth — that is, if we got some. The fairgrounds were fast filling up, meaning a busy day lay ahead. At least we'd make money until rumors began flying. Sighing, I guessed there was nothing to be done about it. I exited and locked Thor then hurried across the parking lot to our stall.

"Finally! I thought you'd gotten lost." Mrs. Smith's expression was sour enough to turn sweet butter rank.

"I'm so sorry. Please, take a dozen. My small way to make up for your inconvenience."

"Harrumph."

But she got down to the business of helping herself and was soon on her merry way, minus the sour look. *And us minus a few loonies in profit.*

The sound of the band starting up their first set drew my full attention. Star was decked out in a red leather minidress and white cowboy boots today. She looked hot enough to set the world on fire, which I prayed she did. She deserved it for all her hard work. Just why couldn't she be a success from Snowy Lake instead of warmer climes?

Oh – Oh.

Snowy Lake's Johnny strolled by with his new fancy girlfriend holding his hand, headed for the grandstand. And Star. *Oh fudge.* It was intervention time. I dashed from the booth, running full-tilt for the stage. Maybe I could catch her eye, keep her from making the biggest mistake of her life.

But her higher vantage point gave her all the fuel she needed. The band fired up and the first song started, sung by a scorned angel.

"A sweet, wild man came a' callin' — Told me he'd keep me from fallin'. He said my heart was safe in his hands. He'd be my man and my biggest fan."

I tried windmilling my arms in an effort to abort the song. *Please let her see me!*

"Then Sara Jean turned his eyes sweet blue. And though he'd sworn to love me true. He turned his back and left me dry. For a new woman who made me cry."

When she was about to sing the chorus, an energetic presence nudged at my elbow and I looked up to see who it was. Ace Collins, our snoopy new Mountie. *Oh, double fudge.*

"Snowy Lake Johnny's a sweet, wild man. He turned my head and warmed my bed. All before we found him dead."

"Nice song," he deadpanned, shooting an inscrutable glance my way. It was not just pouring raindrops, but broken glass.

I cleared my throat. *Busted.* "Yeah, she wrote that not long ago about a man who broke her heart. All make-believe, of course. You know — metaphors and that kind of thing. Songwriters write figurative. Not meant to be taken seriously," I said, not meeting his eyes.

"Hmmm."

Snowy Lake Johnny had vanished, along with his new girlfriend. But I spotted someone else I desperately wanted to grill — ah — chat with.

"Excuse me." I made my excuses to the sheriff and darted a zigzag line through the burgeoning crowd for Suzanna.

"Hey, Suzanna!" I gave a yell. Fate seemed to be having her move away, not toward me.

She turned around, her face quizzical, and waited for me to catch up. Dressed in jeans and an embroidered peasant-style blouse, she looked pretty that morning, her curly dark hair caught up in a clip with tendrils framing her elfin face.

"Hey, Charm. What's up?" she asked.

"I need to ask you a couple of things?"

"Oh, yeah. I heard about Tulip finding Mrs. Hurst." She shook her head, making her curls dance. "Terrible thing. Guess I'll need to find another job. Not much call for maids in this town. Hopefully I can get on at the Snowball Inn."

Hmm, she didn't seem too cut up by Mrs. Hurst's passing. But again, not many would be.

"Did Mrs. Hurst have any visitors yesterday, do you know? Were you working?"

"Yeah, I pulled a full shift. And to think just a short while later…" She grimaced.

"Who did you see?"

"Well, she had a number of visitors. You know how she is. Calls people up and expects them to drop everything and attend to her needs." She covered her mouth with her hand, realizing, I imagined, that she'd just spoken ill of the dead.

"And?" I pressed, noticing out of the corner of my eye our Mountie friend, closely trailed by Ivana, getting closer. *Oh-oh, I have to get a move on here.*

"Yes, okay. There was the banker guy, Fred Smith. Boyd Thompson from Boyd's Wheels — something about a new car. And Helen Davis came by with a loaf of her homemade bread. And — oh yeah, her niece Emma came for coffee in the afternoon."

"That all?" *Four names. Not bad.* Emma would be the easiest one to talk to, her having been my best friend since kindergarten. And, duh, of course the fact that she had nothing to do with it.

Her eyebrows knitted together. "No, I forgot. Just before I left, Sean Blackmore dropped by. Mrs. Hurst seemed surprised to see him, though. Guess she hadn't ordered him to."

Okay, five. And Sean Blackmore was the most interesting of all. Why would a guy with no obvious connection to Mrs. Hurst visit her? Sean was married to Christine, a former Davis, a member of the other rich family in Snowy Lake. The two families had been voted on occasion to be the most likely to replace the Hatfields and McCoys. And Christine was a woman of legend in her own right, as jealous as Megaera, a spiteful entity from mythology who loved to punish infidelities of the marital kind most of all. Nothing like the wrath of a goddess to wreck a good day. And Sean was no angel, with his reputed fondness for women — not that I'd taken him up on any of his come-ons in the past. Even the one in high school where he'd used an airplane with a trailing banner to ask me to go to graduation with him. There was no accounting for why some men took such risks, though, now that he was married. The guy was lucky he hadn't ended up like Lorena Bobbitt's husband.

"I speak to you, Charm!" Ivana had outpaced the lawman. Amazing, when she had shorter legs and smaller feet.

I turned to face her. *Never hurts to be nice. 'Treat others like you want to be treated, sweeting, you'll be better for it.'* Granny's tutelage came in handy more often than not. "Ivana. Thank goodness you're here! I'm so sorry I forgot to call you and invite you to our little festival." I added a curtsey and nod for maximum effect.

It took the wind right out of her sails. *Perfect.*

"Okay. I buy cookies now?"

"Sure, sure. I'll be right there." Shoot, with all the shenanigans the booth was being neglected. Where was Tulip? I needed help if I was going to keep all the balls in the air.

"Miss McCall. A word."

"Could we head back first? No one's looking after our stall. We could be being robbed left and right." Hardly the case, when others would be watching out for us, of course. It was a small town thing. But it sounded good.

He nodded and fell in alongside me. No matter how fast I quick-stepped it, he strolled as if we were taking a walk in the park. *Show-off.*

The booth had a crowd lined up in front of it, obscuring my view. Where had all the customers come from? I breathed a sigh of relief when I finally jostled myself to the front of the line, excusing myself multiple times for cutting in. Tulip was in charge, packing up cookies and tucking money into her fancy Tea & Tarot apron. *Thank you, goddess.*

"What was it you wanted?" Of course, the Mountie was right behind me. Easy enough to tell, with his ridiculously large shadow dogging my every step.

"I think we should speak in private."

I rocked where I stood and pointed to the back of the booth, tugging open the curtain that obscured the interior from our customers. "In here." The space was awful tight, squeezed in as we were between boxes of cookies and cans of drinks. I chewed on my lower lip. His presence was using up all the darn oxygen. The guy really was bigger than life.

"Someone broke into Mrs. Hurst's by going in a back window. In the last couple of hours, at most."

My stomach dropped farther, if that was possible. Did I fess up or not?

"And?"

"Would you know anything about it?"

I swallowed. Hard. "Yeah, Larry was hungry. Poor little guy." *Twenty pounds of fat and fur, but who's quibbling?*

"And so you just broke in — an illegal act by the way — and didn't think to call the police?"

His expression was all lawman now. *Oh, boy.*

"I love animals. They're often nicer than humans. So arrest me." I gave him my best defiant look, holding out my wrists.

His expression shifted. I wasn't certain why. But his right cheek seemed to be developing a twitch, right above his deep dimple. *Aw, nice, a matching dimple on the other side.*

"I'm not here to arrest you, Charm, but to warn you. Don't try *anything* like that again. Ever. Understand?"

"Yes, Officer." I nodded politely, crossing my fingers.

He caught the action, his eyes widening. He grabbed my hand, rubbing the palm and making it tickle while he separated my entangled fingers. He held on even while electricity shot past my wrist and up my arm. I stared at him in dismay. Hairs prickled on the back of my neck while the fire continued on its merry path zinging all the parts of my anatomy.

"I'm not fooling, darlin'. If you interfere with my investigation in any way, I will throw your sweet butt in jail. No matter how beautiful or intelligent the woman attached to it is. Understood? Now say 'Yes, Officer' and mean it this time."

"Yes, Officer."

He let go. Free, I rubbed at my tingling hand, even more worried about other tingling parts that a lady simply cannot rub in public.

He turned and strode from our cubicle. *Finally.* I took a deep a breath. It beat passing out.

I slumped onto a lawnchair, absently picked up the folder with the sheaf of papers hidden inside and began fanning myself.

"Charm! I need you out here. Right now!"

The panic in Tulip's voice about stopped my heart.

Chapter Seven

I threw down the folder. Stumbling out from behind the curtain, my legs getting enmeshed in the fabric in my wild dash, I expected to see Tulip being held up at gunpoint. Instead, Auntie T.J. stood beside her like a Siamese twin, all righteous indignation.

"What's the problem?" I looked from my auntie's horrified expression to Tulip's imitation of an owl.

"I ran over as fast as I could." Auntie T.J. was huffing and puffing. My heart squeezed.

"What is it? Is Granny all right?" *Please, let it be so.*

"What? Yes, of course." She shook her head and my heart quit bleeding.

"Then what's wrong?"

"I was walking over to the fairgrounds, down my usual path past the café —"

"The short version, please. We have customers."

She shot me an instant glare that I was too strung out to react to before she began fessing up.

"A bus broke down."

"Okay. Then what?" I prompted her, not at all surprised. Our roads are infrastructure pay-no-minds when it comes to repairs. Sometimes whole pieces of machinery are lost to the boggy bits in springtime, never to be seen again.

"Well, you'll never believe who's on the bus."

"Try me."

Auntie T.J. leaned in as if her news was too potent to speak aloud. In the periphery of my vision, the crowd gathered at our booth leaned in as well, their faces filled with interest.

She stage-whispered right in my face, her hair crackling with as much indignation as her tone was. "A busload of...of...loose women. You know, *strippers for hire*. The kind of women who go from town to town and make trouble for the rest of us goddess-fearing women. Parading their wares to entice and entertain and nab all the attention and money of our local men."

Apparently, there was no bigger crime.

I sighed, rubbing the back of my head, where pain was blooming. I had too much on my plate for this. I had a possible murder to solve and a hot Mountie to keep in the dark.

"Well, I'm sure, soon as their bus is repaired, they'll be on their merry way."

"No! That's the thing. They're *broke*, according to Darcy. Went in brazen as can be and asked him for work at the Boots & Lace to pay for parts."

"And what did he say?"

"They're doing shows *all weekend*." The lament had to have been heard at the farthest reaches of the festival.

"Well, they need to make money, same as the rest of us." I used my eyes to point out the customers still waiting.

"But…but…"

"Don't take it so hard, Auntie." I patted her shoulder. "I'm sure things will settle down fine soon as they've made their money and are observing Snowy Lake in their rear-view mirror. Only two days. Surely you can manage."

"Don't you take that tone with me, missy! I changed your diapers and made sure you had a warm bed at night. Sang you lullabies and everything. I'm paid my dues. No Highfalutin' women are coming into *my* town and taking over, if only for two days."

"Nothing to be done about it. I'm sorry. You'll just have to turn the other cheek."

"I'll give them cheek all right! Why —"

"Tegan Jane, I need to speak with you. In private," Granny Toogood's strong voice intervened. No one ever ignored the call. *Halleluiah.*

I gave Granny a smile of thanks and stepped up to the sea of customers, trouble over. "Now, who's first?"

Two busy hours later and the lines had dwindled to a few stragglers. More than half our wares had gone. I sighed. We'd be busy tonight, baking a ton more. I checked the time — five minutes until my own D-Day, the dunk tank.

I'd been so busy I'd only managed a few quick, longing glances at the crowd obscuring Constable Ace Collins when he took the position of honor on the platform. Of course, we'd declared a truce — for the moment — but that didn't mean I wouldn't have hooted and hollered as someone else did the dirty deed. All that hot man flesh revealed by a bath of cold water…

The head honcho for the festival, George Simmons, his toupee barely up to the feat of staying on his perspiring scalp, came hotfooting it across the field.

"Charm! There you are! It's your turn. You ready?" He nearly slammed into our booth, right out of breath, and held on to the edge of the counter as if his life depended on it. *Where does he expect me to be? Maybe hiding out of sight to avoid the inevitable?* I mean, who really ran toward getting dunked as though it was going to color their world bright and happy? *Per – lease.* I said the word to myself like I was some kind of diva.

"Been here all along, Mr. Simmons. I'm ready to be sacrificed for the good of our town now. Lead away."

His pasty, sweat-covered face didn't morph into a smile, but instead remained less than pleased.

"You accepted the invite, Charm. Not like you had to."

Yeah. Right. With Auntie T.J. behind the nomination, I'd had a snowflake's chance in hades of avoiding it.

I took baby steps out from behind the counter, fussily arranging things for Tulip to continue her shift alone. Tulip gave me the thumbs-up. *Easy for her.*

"We need to hurry. The people are getting antsy for more victims, ah, sorry – volunteers." He tried false words of encouragement as I made some progress across the too-short distance separating our booth from the dunk tank. It didn't help that I caught the hot Mountie watching the proceedings with interest. As if I didn't have enough to do. I still hadn't had time to read Mrs. Hurst's banking file. But at least I had five suspects on my hit list.

I took the last ten steps quicker, determined to get it over with.

Sixty minutes later, half-drowned and having gained the dubious honor of raising the most funds of all the victims today, I sloshed back across the fairground to retrieve my keys. It was time for a hot shower and dry clothes. Apparently, it helped when others catcalled the throwers. In my case, it'd made them spend more of their money trying to knock me from my perch. My hit list had about doubled.

A series of snickers behind me made me whirl around, ready to tackle the culprit.

"Good thing I nominated you, eh." Auntie T.J.'s expression earned her a frown.

"Yes. You're such a dear."

"I am, aren't I? Now, get cleaned up. We have to do something about the strippers ASAP. We're all gathering at the Boots & Lace to have a talk with Darcy."

"You mean to string him up?"

"Of course not. Where do you get these ideas, Charm?" But I caught the dangerous glint in her eyes at the suggestion. And maybe it wasn't just Darcy hanging from a rope she was seeing in her mind's eye. "Now hurry. Time's a-wasting."

"I'm not going with you to harass Darcy. He knows what he's doing, just trying to help out some stranded women."

"I'm with Charm on this," Tulip piped up, busy packing a small box of assorted cookies for a customer. She gave me a wink.

Our auntie's expression imploded, her lips pursing and her eyes squinting, half-shut. "You'll regret this, I promise you both. And to think of all the things I've done for you." And with that she turned on her dressy platform heels and stomped away.

I breathed a sigh of relief. "Okay, I'm heading back to clean up, check on Granny and make sure we have supplies for more batches of cookies. We've been just about cleaned out today of peanut butter delights."

Tulip nodded, her hands occupied making change.

I slipped behind the curtain and found a plastic bag for hiding the banking folder, thrusting it inside. I'd have to read it in bed tonight at this rate.

Squishing my way across the parking lot, I almost missed Sean Blackmore coming toward me. *Perfect opportunity.*

"Hey, Sean." I tried for a fetching smile, though not certain I managed it with my teeth chattering from the chill of being wet.

"Charm McCall. Been in the dunk tank, I see. Still, can't hide all that beauty. In fact, your clothes being wet seems to have brought out a couple of your — ahem — best assets."

Eww, did he just say that? Sean was at his slimiest when he ran across a woman alone. He was dressed in too-tight dark-hued jeans, Hawaiian shirt with black and white pineapples stenciled on it and brand-new cowboy boots. His hair was molded into some kind of pointed swirl like the rooster he'd always liked mimicking.

"Well, a gal does what she has to. The town's always in need of funds for this or that."

"Hmm, true. I'm always encouraging people to donate for the cause, whatever it may be. I have a cause of my own at present." He popped one of his trademark mints into his mouth. *Double eww.*

"I'm sure, man like you. Why, both you and your lovely wife, Christine, are such great town supporters. By the way, Suzanna was saying you were one of the last people to see Mrs. Hurst alive. That you visited unexpectedly just before she left for the day." I leaned in closer to give a sense of conspiracy to the charge, fluttering my unaided eyelashes at him. *No point in wearing mascara in a dunk tank.* "I'd love to know what you and Mrs. Hurst have in common that made you visit her? You hiding something?"

"Really? That old lady?" Unease showed in his expression. *Good.*

"You hitting her up for anything, Sean?"

"Phttt. Mrs. Hurst was *nobody's* type. She was a pain in the—"

"Careful, Sean. My granny thinks it unlucky to speak ill of the dead."

"Well, anyway, no one in their right mind liked her. I gotta go."

"Why did you visit her then?"

"It was nothing. Christine asked me to stop by. Check up on the old lady." He looked away, crunching down harder on his current breath candy. The odor of peppermint tainted the air.

"Really?" Christine hated her as much as her adorable hubby did. There'd been a couple of screaming matches recorded for posterity on Main Street. He was definitely lying. *Still suspect number one, Sean.*

"Well, I gotta go." He began edging away from me. As much as I wanted to grab his arm, the opportunity was slipping away.

"Yeah, me too. I'd stay clear of the new Mountie if I were you, though." I found it hard to resist a parting shot.

"Why?"

"He's looking to question anyone who saw Mrs. Hurst the day she died."

"Why? Not like it's a murder investigation or anything." The look of surprise appeared genuine, though it was hard to say for certain. He'd had a lot of practice at lying—to his wife.

I shrugged. "Jury's still out."

"Well, the number of people who hated that old battle-axe would circle around a city block — twice. Could have been anyone." He gave a snort of disgust. *Nice man.*

"Well, I'd expect a call from Constable Ace Collins in the near future, if I was you. He seems very interested in the case. Got a master's in criminology and all."

"Yeah, well, I heard she visited *you* that morning. And the new constable's been seen sniffing around your pasture. You'd best be careful too, Charm." And with that he slunk away.

Is that a threat? I narrowed my eyes. Then a slight breeze blew across my damp skin, making me shiver uncontrollably. *Time to go home.*

I cranked up the heater in Thor two minutes later, my body too frozen for heavy-duty thinking. I rubbed my hands together, holding them in front of the forced heat vent. A rap on the window made me jump. Cranking the door handle to roll the misted glass down brought me face-to-face with the man at the root of all my recent troubles, Constable Ace Collins.

"You okay?"

"Sure. Why wouldn't I be?"

"I saw you talking with Sean Blackmore just now and neither of you looked too happy."

"I'm fine." Who is this guy? My new nanny? I'd never had a nanny or a babysitter who looked like Ace.

"Okay. Just checking."

"How did you know Sean's name already?" My brain was thawing out along with my body.

He shrugged, resting both hands on the window frame. I glanced at those fingers now, noting how wonderfully made they were, all strong sinew and tan from the great outdoors. "I make it my mission to learn as much as possible quickly. Important factor in doing my job. Blessed with an excellent memory for names and facts as well."

"Well, I'm fine, Officer. Now, if you'll excuse me…"

"Of course." He shoved off with his arms from the jeep and stood watching as I drove away.

I pulled in behind the café again and killed Thor's motor, hoping to avoid any conflict or Mountie surveillance for ten minutes, or at least long enough to shower and change clothes. And for once, things did go as planned. I slipped up the stairs unobserved.

Entering Tea & Tarot's kitchen a few minutes later, having hidden the file folder in my nightstand, I got down to the important business of checking supplies. The festival was a real money-maker and I had to be certain to capitalize on the opportunity. Running out of baked goods would eat into profits.

"Ah, you're back." Granny entered the kitchen, joining me as I made notes on my famous clipboard I was known to have a hissy fit about if it ever went missing from its assigned spot. I'd gone to the trouble of printing out all our standard supplies by recipe. Sure, I could print it out again, but I only updated the computer program bi-weekly and a lot of information would be lost by someone's incompetence. "I can see you got this well in hand. Good job as always, sweeting. How's it going at the festival?"

"Gonna have to bake tonight. We sold a slew of cookies today."

"I'll start on that right now. The café's virtually empty."

"No, you need your rest, Granny."

"I'm fine, don't coddle me." Her slightly sharp undertone shocked me. It wasn't like Granny to be short with anyone. Especially me. My entire body clenched with worry. What was up?

"Okay." I doodled a daisy chain in the border of the page.

"I'm sorry, Charm. I guess the trip took a bit more out of me than I realized. But I'll have a good sleep tonight in my own bed and be right as rain by morning." She gave me a cheerful smile and a pat on the arm.

I nodded, unconvinced. "I need to go and get five pounds of butter from the Grab-n-go. Be back in ten."

I pulled out a couple of twenties from the cash drawer and thrust them into my pocket. After kissing Granny on the world's softest cheek, I strode out of the back door and took a short cut through the alley to our local food store.

The Grab-n-go was quiet with everyone at the fair and I hurriedly scooped up the necessary pounds of butter. At the till, I paid for the supplies and waited while the cashier placed them in my green and black Grab-n-go recycle carry bag.

"Hello, Charm." My friend Emma Hurst came toward me. She looked sad today, her gray eyes red-rimmed. Even her shoulder-length red curls looked droopy, and I suddenly realized that in all the things I'd been doing, I'd forgotten she'd just lost her aunt. Maybe one she despised but, still, I should have been there for her.

I took her into my arms, hugging her tightly. She was a foot taller than me and thin as a rail. My arms circled her easily, too easily. She needed to eat more of our cookies.

"I'm sorry about your loss, Emmy. It sucks."

"Yeah, it does." She pulled back and swiped at her eyes with the back of her hand. "I know no one liked her. But still, she's gone and it feels weird. I think I feel worst because she wasn't well liked. I mean, who's going to go to her funeral?"

"I'll be there at your side. And others will go. You'll see. Do you need anything, for the wake or the funeral service?"

"Probably some food, I guess."

"I'll take care of it. Sandwiches and cookies? Lemonade?"

"Sure. You know, I saw her the day she died. She looked fine too. Full of it as always." Emmy shook her head, tucking her red curls behind her ears. "How can one die so quickly?"

"Must have been a stroke or heart attack." *Or poison?* The thought rose unbidden in my mind, but no way would I speak it aloud. We'd know one way or the other soon enough. But my money, from the vibes I was getting today, was on the latter.

I noticed the book bag slung over my friend's arm. "Shoot, I gotta renew my books. They're due today. We'll catch up later. Okay? I'll be up baking half the night, so come by if you feel like it."

"I'll see. Thanks."

I took the bag of butter from the clerk and hurried from the store, half running down the street to our local library, my third most favorite place in town, right after Granny's house and the Tea & Tarot café. The cozy chairs Miriam, the town's librarian, had strategically placed about the inviting space were just made to curl up in and read a good story. The overhead skylight let in sunbeams that warmed body and soul. So many happy memories called to me here. I had spent most of my childhood haunting the place and pestering Miriam. I pushed open the large glass door and hurried inside. *Aw, the lovely smell of musty books.*

"Hey, Charm, thought you'd be tied up at the festival today." Miriam looked up from sorting through some volumes, giving me a quizzical look. She was a short woman, nearly as broad as she was tall, blessed with the biggest heart and smile of anyone in town.

"I am, but I didn't want to pay any fines, so I'm here to renew until next week, okay?"

"Sure. And that reminds me, I've gotten something in for you from the Bookmobile today." She began rummaging around a cart, checking the titles on book spines.

I had a sudden inspiration. "Do you happen to have *Sparkling Cyanide* by Agatha Christie on hand?"

"Funny you should ask that."

"Why?"

"I loaned it out earlier this week. Your best friend Emma has taken a recent interest in Christie's backlist. Wonderful, eh!"

Awash with emotion, I stood and stared at the happy librarian. I had not seen this coming. Still, it didn't really mean anything, did it?

"Aha, here we go. Take a gander at this one." She handed me a book.

"Oh, you got it in!" I reverently ran my fingers down the glossy, futuristically designed cover, checking out Michio Kaku's coveted latest, *The Future of Humanity.* "Thank you! I really appreciate it."

"You're more than welcome."

"I have to get back and help bake cookies."

"No problem. I'll renew your books. You wouldn't happen to be baking any of my favorite triple chocolate macaroons?"

"Sure. Stop by later and we'll have some freshly baked for you." It hadn't been on my initial list, but it had just got added. I needed a whole lot of baking to get my mind off this weird day and a proper *thank you* was in order for my favorite librarian.

I hurried from the library, my feet pounding the pavement until I made it back to the café. How soon until we knew what killed Mrs. Hurst? It couldn't happen soon enough.

"Hey, Granny." I greeted her on the fly, racing to wash my hands to get down to work.

Three hours of slave labor later and the café had blossomed with all the tantalizing fragrances of a multitude of cookies. I took the last tray out of the oven, setting it aside to cool, and swiped at my perspiring forehead.

"There. That should get us through tomorrow at least."

"You talk about me working too hard, child. You need to slow down a bit as well."

"Granny, I'm young and strong. This is the time to work like a wild woman."

"You take on so much for someone so young." She shook her head, her expression filled with concern.

"I'm fine. Now, Miriam's coming by for a bag of the triple chocolate so make sure to save her some. I've got to go upstairs and check on something."

"Okay."

I ran up the stairs two at a time, locking the door for good measure. In my small bedroom, I pulled out the folder. I had to know if there was anything to my suspicions.

When I was tracing my finger down the rows of numbers, the first thing that stood out was how very well off the woman had been. I'd known she was rich, but this was more than I'd counted on. And fair sums were being deposited into her account each and every month, though she'd had no visible form of employment since her husband died ten years ago. Of course, John Hurst had been the first gold miner in the area and had made his fortune before anyone else knew of the find. She must have been living off the stock market and investing. But the regular cash deposits were odd. And the amounts had increased of late. Maybe she owned more property that she collected rents on and they paid in cash? Or maybe she was a darn drug dealer? *Yeah, right!* But it was odd. Worth investigating if this thing went south like I worried it was going to any minute. There would be receipts somewhere in her house for receiving all that cash if her business was legit.

A loud knock resounded through the apartment. "Charm. Are you in there?" More banging came on the door.

Sighing, I closed the folder and slid it back into the nightstand. With so many suspects, I was going to have to get completely organized about doing this thing right. Starting with taking notes. I grabbed a pen and paper from the drawer and quickly wrote down the five suspects, pausing over my friend's name. *No way.* Emma couldn't hurt a flea.

The knocking continued. "Charm, I know you're in there!"

I laid the pad aside and got up to answer the door. Time alone was the biggest threat to getting to the bottom of this thing.

As soon as I saw Star's face, I knew.

Chapter Eight

Star threw herself at me. "It's terrible. I'll never be able to show my face in this town again!" She moaned, holding on to me for dear life.

"Calm down. Nothing can ever be that bad."

"But everyone's talking about us. The coroner says it was cyanide that killed Mrs. Hurst. And it was found in our jam!" At that confession she burst into a flood of tears, drenching the shoulder of my formerly dry T-shirt.

Though I'd suspected, it was a different thing to hear the words spoken out loud, I admit. *Way different.*

"Who told you this?" My body filled with icy anger. Why hadn't that darn pesky Mountie prevented this? Kept his report private until the real murderer could be unmasked? I wanted to rip a piece off him now and if he'd been in the room he'd have been in for it. Big time.

She hiccupped, her tears slowing as she thought about it. "I remember, it all started with Sean Blackmore. He talked to just about everyone at the festival. People began to look at me and Tulip strangely. Then I overheard some people talking and found out what was going on. What are we going to do, Charm? This is really, really bad."

"Well, we know we didn't do it, right?"

"Yeah, that's true."

"Then we just need to prove who did."

"How are we going to do that?" Her tear-stained face made my stomach hurt, tied as it was in twisted knots of equal parts anger and worry. "No one will ever buy our jam again." A fresh flood of tears accompanied the wail.

"Don't be silly. I will get to the bottom of this, I promise you. The real murderer will be found out. I'm already working on it. And I've got a list of suspects that saw Mrs. Hurst on that final day. But I'll need yours and Tulip's help more than ever now. You'll need to keep things running while I investigate. I can use my analytical skill from reading all those murder mysteries."

"But solving a mystery is not like reading a book, Charm." Her eyes were still very worried, though I was trying my best to console her.

"I know. But I have other gifts as well. I'll tap into them."

"But you've always said they're kind of hit and miss. What if it doesn't work? And the café goes bankrupt? What will happen to Granny?"

"I'd *never* let that happen." A righteous thrust of ancient anger seared my mortal soul, and my fingertips lit up with white-blue sparks. Shocked, Star stepped back from me, looking at me as if she didn't recognize her own sister. I turned my hands over and stared at their familiar shape and contour. *Did that really happen?*

I shook my head. Must have been a hallucination brought on by the depth of my pain and despair. No one hurt my family, no one.

"Static electricity, nothing more, sis." I dismissed it, not wanting Star to worry. But her big eyes with their damp lashes proved that wasn't going to be so easy.

"What do you want me to do?"

Good. She was pulling herself together. "First thing. We need to show the world we're not afraid of this thing. That we know we didn't do it. And we must protect Granny at all costs."

Star nodded.

"Go and put a cold cloth on your face and reapply your makeup before she sees you. 'A McCall always shows the world their best face.'" I recited one of Granny's sayings.

She dutifully headed for my bathroom while I hauled out the pad of paper again. Now it was serious. I tamped down my anger and got to work.

Sean was still at the top of my list. But the others needed checking out as well. *Keep your friends close, but your enemies closer* came to mind. Much as I wanted to bash a certain Mountie who would remain nameless over the head with a frying pan, I needed his help. Gritting my teeth, I worked out a plan.

Star came back from the bathroom as I finished writing. "Good, let's go. You head back to the fair, do your sets, and I'll join Tulip at the booth. I want to talk with people. Mostly, find the suspects and get a reading on them. Can you do that? Pretend it's no big deal?"

She raised her chin defiantly, her blue eyes narrowing. "You bet. Someone's trying to frame us — that's not going to happen to a McCall." Star and I had often not seen eye-to-eye, but on this, we were united.

"Good. I'm proud of you." Darn it, her eyes were awash with tears again. But this time she swiped them away, blessing me with a tremendous smile.

"Okay, catch you later, sis."

I used the bathroom facilities myself, making sure my own appearance would pass muster with a crowd seeking any signs of weakness, then rushed down the stairs and into the café, as fast as my feet could carry me. "Granny, I'm off to work the booth with Tulip. You need anything?"

"No. It's been quiet. Oh, there's Tegan Jane sprinting across the street. You know, for an old gal, she sure can move fast."

No, you don't. I raced out of the front door of the café, intent on stopping one of the town's biggest gossips.

"Charm!" Auntie T.J. grasped her sides, wheezing and out of breath, apparently having run all the way from the fairgrounds. We met on the sidewalk, nearly colliding.

I grabbed her shoulders. "Now you listen here, Auntie, I will not have you upsetting Granny. She's been through enough. Do you hear me? Do not tell her about this coroner's report, or so help me, I'll spill the beans on the New Years Eve's party where you went after Granny's new boyfriend. And bedded him in the back room."

Her eyes widened to owl size. "You knew about that?"

"Yes. And if you want Granny to continue talking to you, you will keep quiet about this thing until I solve the mystery."

"What can you do about the case that the new Mountie can't?" she about hissed in my face.

"This is my town. I will get to the bottom of it. Just give me twenty-four hours."

"Phttt. You expect me to believe you can do that. What are you *not* telling me?"

"Never you mind. Do I have your word that you will not tell Granny?"

"Someone will. You can count on that. Best it comes from family."

She was right, whether I wanted to accept it or not.

"Then you go right in there and say you need her to drive you to see your friend Rose in Winterville. That she's not feeling well and that you need to see her today, to make sure she's okay. You need Granny to drive you because you're too upset. Tell her to close down the shop—no business today anyway—and take you. *Now.* I don't care how much you need to lie—just do it already. And make Rose play along. Stay overnight there as well. That should give me just enough time to get this thing figured."

She nodded, her face suggesting how unhappy she was with how her day had turned out. A twinge of guilt stuck my gut.

"You had nothing to do with Mrs. Hurst's death, right?" Auntie T.J. asked, not quite meeting my eyes.

I gave her a full-on glare. "Of course not, how could you even ask that?" Any guilt I had over blackmailing her vanished like a fart in the wind.

Hmm, blackmail. Wouldn't put it past the old bird.

I stomped off, making my way to the fairgrounds as quickly as a crow flies. Or a wolf taking down its prey. Strange. I hadn't envisioned wolves since my first foray into town, when our mother had abandoned us all those years ago, and I didn't like the reference any better now.

I joined Tulip, noting the lack of any customers at our booth. Bad news travels fastest of all. We'd replaced the strippers as the topic of conversation. *Lucky us.* It looked like I wouldn't be needing to bake any more cookies that weekend, or maybe for days to come. The thought made me swallow hard. This was so bad, but I couldn't waste a moment thinking about it or I was sunk.

"The Mountie came by looking for you."

"Good." I gritted my teeth. "I'd like a word with him as well. Have you seen Boyd Thompson or Fred Smith?"

"Haven't seen Boyd all day, but Fred walked by about five minutes ago. Headed due south."

"Hold the fort. I'm going after him."

"Why?"

But I didn't take the time to answer, hearing the darn clock ticking relentlessly in my mind again. *Tick tock. Tick tock. Tick tock.*

Of course, I didn't make it, getting confronted by the Mountie soon as I stepped away from the booth. *What special ability does he have? X-ray friggin' vision?*

"Charm. I need to talk with you."

His pleasant demeanour looked like it had headed south as well. I crossed my arms over my chest and gave him a full-on glare, double what I had blessed my auntie with moments ago. *And she'd better be headed for Winterville right now or so help me!*

"I take it you've heard the result of the diagnostics on the jam and on Mrs. Hurst."

"I have." My teeth began to hurt from the pressure. I eased up on the biting down.

"There was enough cyanide in the jar of jam to take down an ornery buffalo."

"Well, Mrs. Hurst was pretty darn ornery. I'm surprised it was enough." My sharp tongue was known for making a bad situation so much better. *Not.*

He took off his hat and rubbed the back of his neck then plunked his headgear down again, twisting his full lips into a grimace.

"I need to ask you some questions."

"Okay. And I need to speak with someone. Can I get back to you later?"

His eyes narrowed to slits.

"I won't be long. It's really, really important. And where can I go anyway? I promise, I'll be right back to talk. On this spot." I pointed to the space under my feet. "I just need five minutes. Have a cookie or three on me."

"Okay. I'll give a fellow science nerd a break. Just this once. But if you're not back here in ten, I'll be coming after you."

"Fine." I hurried off, aware every person at the fair was watching us intently. Heading toward the south end of the fair, I kept swinging my head back and forth, peering into the booths and games of chance, searching for Fred Smith, our town banker.

I spied him in deep conversation with Boyd Thompson. Somehow Tulip had missed Boyd, the owner of Boyd's Wheels, entering the fair. *But thank you, goddess.* Two for the price of one.

I skipped over to the shady tent set up as a place for people to take a break. Picnic tables lined the space. Most weren't occupied, and Fred and Boyd had one all to themselves.

"Hi, guys. How's it going?" I sat down beside Fred on the bench, giving the two men the sweetest smile I could paste onto my twitchy lips. My stomach roiled, not pleased at all with the outcome of this day.

"I'm surprised to see you, Charm. Have you spoken to the new constable yet? He's looking for you," Boyd asked, his tone nervous and annoyed.

It was all I could do not to scream that the sky was falling in. "Thanks. I'll catch up with him."

I reached across Fred the Banker to nab a few unshelled peanuts from the dish, clutching at his forearm in the process. When I closed my eyes, a vision came to the forefront of my mind. My first lucky break. Fred was thinking about recent events. He was feeling relieved, happy Mrs. Hurst was gone, but he had no idea how it had happened. He thought *I* had done it. I took a deep breath, feeling tainted by the unspoken accusation. Why was he so happy that Mrs. Hurst had been murdered? That didn't make any sense—he stood to lose business when her assets were divided up among her living relatives. Okay, who stood to gain by this? Following the money trail usually revealed the culprit. I ignored that this would again point a finger at my best friend. Surely others would benefit from the estate as well?

"You okay, Charm? You look a little pale," Boyd asked.

"Sure, I'm fine." I unshelled a peanut like I had not a care in the world, popping the nut into my mouth. I chewed and swallowed. It tasted like dirt.

I stood up and groaned. "Oh, actually, not feeling quite right here." I swayed, praying the right man came to my aid.

Fred leaped to his feet, steadying my elbow with his hand, repeating, "You okay, Charm?"

Well, Boyd was no gentleman, I'd give him that. He continued sitting, watching the show, munching on peanuts. It explained his three divorces, though. He also had an iffy reputation as a car dealer out to make a buck any way he could—probably to pay all that alimony.

"Yes, I'm fine now, thanks. I should be going."

With a target on my back, I stepped away from the men.

"Do you think she did it?" Boyd asked Fred while I was still within earshot, further endearing himself to me.

I stomped back to our booth.

The lawman waited, standing straight as an arrow beside Tulip, who was busy chewing on her fingernails, a habit she'd given up years ago. Right then, what I wouldn't have given for a quick stress releaser. I didn't smoke and didn't drink, which didn't leave much except burying myself in a good book. *Later*, I promised myself.

I strode right up to him, my fingers twitching. "With a staggering two billion trillion possible Earth-sized planets orbiting a sun-like star in the visible universe, you just had to walk into my backyard."

"Not much choice, darlin'," he said with a chuckle, tipping his hat back to observe me with a half-grin. "I go where I'm needed. So, about that little talk? Here or down at the station?"

"Here's fine. Come on." I led the way back to the curtained-off partition of our booth.

I gestured for him to precede me.

"After you," he said, sweeping off his hat and stepping in behind me.

I sat down on a chair and he did likewise. *Face-off.*

"Did you spread the rumor about our jam being poisoned?"

"As it happens, I did not. But it's not a rumor." His voice turned solemn. "Now I need to know who had access to the jam?"

"It was perfectly fine before Mrs. Hurst took it. The adding of cyanide must have happened after it left our place. She had a string of visitors that afternoon. Any one of them could have laced it with the poison. I'm working on it. I'll figure out who did this. You can take *that* to the bank."

"I will be the one investigating this, Miss McCall. It's my job." The stern look accompanying the warning did not sit well with me.

"I know this town. I can find out more in an hour than you'll find out all day long. In fact, I already know one suspect who didn't do it. The banker, Fred Smith. I've been able to rule him out."

"Really? How's that?"

"I have my ways." I gave him the benefit of a piercing stare. *Don't think you can push me around.* I just needed to get close to each of the suspects, then I would know who to focus on to find the proof they did it, the old-fashioned way. *Having visions doesn't play well in a courtroom. Go figure.* At least a good segment of the rest of the world had clued in. Visions were real. I had them enough to know this for certain. Tested and approved.

"You need to be more specific. Are you ruling them out with facts, or something intangible like a feeling, that will not hold up in a court of law? Big difference."

I looked away. Knowing I was right and proving it were going to be very different things. Nice of him to point it out.

"So, am I under arrest?"

"No. Like you said, anyone could have laced the jam with the poison. But I must caution you not to leave town. Oh, and I'm sorry what this will do to your business, especially if you weren't involved."

"If I wasn't involved! I'll have you know that I would *never* do such a thing. Why, you…you…" Granny's no cussin' rule was a royal pain in the butt.

He gave me a steady look from his incomparable deep brown eyes, their liquidness drawing me in like a siren to deep water. What was the male version of that image? Maybe a Triton? Whatever he was, it should be labeled friggin' dangerous. "Careful. You don't want to be insulting a lawman just doing his job. But if you discover some facts about this case, you'd best be sharing them with me straight away. Sooner this is resolved, the better for your business. I don't want to see you or your family hurt in anyway."

"Too late. Business was booming this morning. Now look at it. Not a customer in sight." I sighed. Taxes were due in two months. Worry about having the money in time sent chills of anxiety down my spine. I bit the inside of my cheek, the instant pain taking my mind off it.

"I'm sorry to hear it. Anything I can do, don't hesitate to ask." He stood up, hat in hand.

"I think you've done quite enough."

With him standing, his virile presence filled the tiny space to a suffocating level. When had it gotten so hot in here? My breath caught in my chest. The look in his eyes was mesmerizing, sending a different kind of chill racing through me.

"I'd hazard a bet there's not a straight man alive in Snowy Lake doesn't have a crush on you, Miss McCall."

"Sorry, that crown goes to my sister Star, Officer. I'm just the town science nerd."

"You're a lot more than that, darlin'." He placed the Stetson back on his head, giving it a tweak with his fingers as a silent salute and exited the tent with a final shot. "'If at first an idea does not sound absurd, then there is no hope for it'. Albert Einstein. Be where I can find you later. We need to talk more about how you ruled out Fred Smith."

"If you can find me, have at it," I muttered, quieter than I wanted to. But I had places to go, things to do, people to grill. No time to hang around the café waiting for *him*. I had until tomorrow to get a handle on this thing before Granny came home, probably towing Auntie T.J. behind her Buick.

Chapter Nine

I watched the Mountie walk away, drawing the attention of every female worth her salt — and pepper. He made his own straight and narrow path, walking like a cyborg of a lawman right through the thinning hordes of late-afternoon fairgoers. For most people, the red carpet rolled up at six p.m. anyway, the supper hour in Snow Lake. I'd bet Ace Collins never let up. But on the plus side, I didn't think he'd ratted me out. There were too many gossips in this town to do that.

Okay. Time to check out Helen Davis.

"Can you hold the fort, Tulip? I gotta see someone."

"Don't you mean hold the booth?"

At my stare, she flushed. "Okay, lame. Go. I want to hear Star sing again anyway. Oh, and Charm, if there's anything I can do, just ask, okay? I know what you're up to — couldn't help but overhear when you talked with the Mountie behind the curtains, so just say. I'll do whatever I can to help."

I rushed forward and gave her a hug. "Thanks. I needed that."

She gave me a further nod of encouragement, and I was off and running. Helen Davis' house was on the edge of town and I made it in three minutes flat, even being stopped by our one traffic light. Crazy. But I hit it all the time and I'd swear someone hid in the bushes watching and activated it soon as they saw me coming. *I know. Not paranoid or anything.*

I parked in Helen's driveway. Knocking on her front door, I admired the profusion of day lilies blooming around the house. Her charming ranch-style house boasted a curving patio-stone walkway and raised-brick flowerbeds. Not so much stooping to do at Helen's compared to Granny's, with her right-on-the ground profusion of semi-annuals.

"Why, Charm, how lovely to see you. How's your grandma doing? Come on in, dear." She held the screen door open for me and stepped aside to let me pass.

She wasn't the type anyone would pick for a murderer, either, but still, I had to check it out. Maybe she knew something. Anything.

"Would you like some iced tea, dear? I made a pitcher this afternoon. I'd offer you some homemade bread and jam, but I know your Granny insists on the six p.m. dinner hour and I don't want to spoil your appetite." Then she realized what she said and turned red to match the strawberries dotted all over her apron. "I'm sorry to hear of your troubles about your jam. And poor Mrs. Hurst." She tsked-tsked. "Terrible thing. At least she must have gone quick. Cyanide is known for that."

"How did you know that? And iced tea would be nice. Thank you."

"You're not the only one who reads in this town, dear. I do love a good detective mystery myself."

"Suzanna said that you took Mrs. Hurst a loaf of homemade bread the day she died?"

"I did. Come, let's sit in the kitchen. I've got to keep my eye on dinner. Got a pot roast simmering on the stove."

I followed her through to the back, admiring her home. Immaculate as always. I sighed. I needed to get down to some serious housecleaning myself, if time ever permitted. Generally, I found it easier to visit outside my apartment than invite anyone in. But if I did ever want to have a guest over, say, like a male visitor, I needed to get busy. *Now where did that idea come from?* I gave my head a shake. I needed to keep all my wits about me if I was going to get to the bottom of things.

"Extra sugar, dear?" she asked, taking the pitcher of iced tea from the fridge.

"No, thanks. So, you were saying about the loaf of bread?"

"Yes. I used an overnight recipe. Makes it easier in the morning. Just pop it in the oven. Easy peasy."

"Smart. And?" She set a glass of iced tea in front of me, placed the other on the table and sat.

"Well, all her money can't buy her a loaf of real homemade bread, now can it?"

I shook my head. "She was lucky to have a friend like you."

"Well, I wouldn't go so far as to say we were friends. But I like to think that good karma is returned. I like to pay my way forward. Not take any chances." She gave a hoarse cough, taking a swallow of her tea to ease her throat. Her faded blue eyes watered and she blinked a few times.

"You okay, Helen?"

She waved me off. "Doc Watson's been fussing about, but I'm fine. Just a silly cough that won't go away. How's everyone in your family? Star sure has been making the news lately. That girl's blessed with the voice of an angel."

"Yes, she is." A jolt of worry made me sit up straighter. Star was looking more and more ready for the big time. Problem was, I wasn't ready for the changes that were coming. Not the time to be dwelling on it, though. "Did anything seem different at Mrs. Hurst's? Was she upset or anything?"

"No. She was actually in a good mood for a change. She'd found some pearls she'd lost. You know, I've been all through this with that nice Constable Collins. Perhaps he can help you, Charm?"

I started at the use of *his* name, a wave of unease washing over me, and it was all I could do to stay seated. "Perhaps. But if you could do me one favor it would help me a great deal?"

"Of course, dear, whatever you need. I don't believe you had anything to do with Mrs. Hurst's unfortunate demise." She shook her head. "You had nothing to gain and everything to lose putting the poison in your own jam. I think someone's setting you up."

"Yeah, me too. Hope you shared that thought with our new Mountie?" I made myself ask the question.

"I did. What is it you need me to do?"

"I'd like you to visualize Mrs. Hurst — what you saw at her house yesterday — while I hold your hands."

"You don't think I'm involved?" Her hand fluttered to the neckline of her housedress, her expression one of deep concern.

"No, of course not. But anything you saw might aid me in some way."

A network of worry lines crinkled across her skin. When had she gotten so old? And still trying to do for others. I shook my head.

"Sure. Shall we try then?"

I gave her a smile of encouragement, pulling my chair closer to hers. I took her cool hands in my mine, picking up on the slight tremor.

"Now, close your eyes and just think about being at her house. What you saw and felt. Go over it in your mind."

I closed my eyes, breathing slowly, waiting. A dismal, sluggish image began to emerge to me, much slower than normal, as if her mind was clouded by something. Instead of a color image, gray tones dominated. But when the picture finally came into sharper focus, I didn't see Helen should be seeing — I was seeing into her body.

Confused, I stared at the internal image. Not being an expert in anatomy, I was uncertain at first, trying to make it out. Were those her lungs? A large dark ominous area on one drew my full attention. It pulsed with an irregular beat. An invader. I reacted without thinking, attacking it with all my being, sending a death ray like in a video game. Awesome energy flowed through me and exploded into it. The evil monster turned a bright red hue, lit up with a huge charge of electricity. I focused as hard as I could on the villain, wanting instinctively to drive it out. Blow it to pieces. Grab a hold of it and force it to leave this good woman, all the while thinking I had done this before, a very long time ago in someplace that was far away from here...

I had no idea how long we sat like that, my hands electrified and clutching onto hers while I envisioned her cancer gone. The affected area on her lung went back to a healthy pink, all traces of the tumor vanquished. But when I sat back, overcome, she was staring at me with the oddest expression on her tired face. She raised one trembling hand to her chest.

"What did you do, Charm?"

I gulped, unable to explain. "I don't know," I whispered, slumping back in the chair. I swayed a bit, a wave of exhaustion washing over me.

"Are you okay? Did you find out what you needed to know? Was I able to help?"

Then she didn't know. Maybe no one did, if no CAT scan or MRI had been taken. But I was dead certain I had just blown up her cancer and sent it to the great unknown.

"I wasn't able to see anything, sorry."

"But something else happened, right?" she pressed, the expression in her eyes wary and confused.

I shrugged, took up my glass of tea and gulped it down. *Better.*

"More tea, dear?" Her color was returning to normal and her eyes were brightening.

"No. I should get home."

"I'm sorry I couldn't be of more help. Please, come back and see me if you need anything. Anything at all."

"Thanks, I will." I went to stand and it took every bit of effort I had not to show my weakness. Gritting my teeth, I made my way to the front door, feeling more like a lumbering zombie than a human being. What the heck had just happened?

"You take care, dear. You're looking a bit peaked."

I nodded and made my way outside, the screen door slamming shut behind me. Taking a deep breath of fresh air, I used my stubborn willpower to make myself march over to Thor.

In the jeep, I reached for my water bottle, draining it in mere seconds. "So, Thor, I wonder what all that was about? Well, at least I know Helen didn't kill Mrs. Hurst. That's something, anyway."

I began to drive to Granny's house, then remembered she was with Auntie T.J. in Winterville for the night. I must have been a bit off if I'd forgotten that. I made a quick U-turn and headed back to Tea & Tarot. I'd rummage in the fridge and find something to eat. Suddenly starved, I cranked the wheel again, heading to the Grab-n-go to buy some decent food.

I picked up a basket inside the store and hurried down the first aisle to choose my purchases. Maybe I should have gone for fast food? My stomach rumbled alarmingly, screaming its need.

"Okay, okay." I grabbed a microwavable fried chicken dinner special and made my way to the till. The cashier eyed me, her lips pursed.

"So, you heard, eh?"

"Sorry, not sure what you're talking about." Her prissiness grated.

"The coroner's report. You telling me you haven't heard all about it? That no one has shared it with you?" My skepticism might have been verging on snarkiness.

"I may have overheard a bit about it."

Her expression screamed enjoyment at my discomfort and possible demise.

"Did you hear the part that I love to read murder mysteries and that this choice of weapon — poison — is a rip-off of *Sparkling Cyanide*?"

"Really. That's how they'll nail you? Oh my, why would you even admit to such a thing?" Her round owlet eyes grew wider still.

I rolled my eyes, grabbed the bag and gave her a politically incorrect finger. *Way to go, Charm.* Now Granny would be racing home just to admonish her granddaughter.

But at least my energy was slowly returning. I hurried back to Thor, almost prepared to eat the dinner frozen. Inside the Tea & Tarot, I popped the dinner into the microwave and stood by impatiently tapping my foot, waiting for the timer.

Ding.

Finally. I'd never lived through a longer three minutes in my life. I pulled off the cellophane with trembling fingers and dumped the steaming contents onto a plate. Picking up a piece of fried chicken, I attacked.

Ten minutes later, partially satiated, I sat back and consumed a second glass of milk.

I looked around. I needed to bake, take my mind off everything else. A hot Mountie, a dead neighbour and the oddest of all, a strange experience I could not explain. Was Helen even going to be all right? What if my actions had sent miniscule atoms of cancer all throughout her body? *No.* That couldn't happen. It had felt like such a good thing, that maybe she was now cured. But it would take days, weeks, even months before I would know for certain. An incredible ray of confidence rose in me that she was cancer-free. I would cling to that life raft.

In no time I was elbow-deep in brownie batter, singing along to the radio.

"'Fly me to the moon. Let me play among the stars — "'

"I would, darlin', but Jeff Bezos and his New Shepard rocket ship's only going up sixty-two miles."

I startled, shooting a quick glance over my shoulder at the intrusion. "Well, at a round trip lasting less than an hour, at an estimated cost of $200,000.00 US, making the trip worth about $3,000.00 a minute, I'll pass. Taxes are due soon. I'll have to put the moon trip off until they're paid."

"Okay. What about like George Bailey of *It's A Wonderful Life* fame, I lasso you something? An asteroid would pay off huge dividends."

"Now you're talking. A flying goldmine. Just need to invent the tether device first and we'll be all fixed. Those suckers can be worth trillions with their rare earths and valuable metals. Why, the platinum alone would be worth the trip."

"Not to mention the palladium, rhodium, iridium, osmium."

Oh, brother. This guy could make reading a dictionary sexy.

He came around and stood right beside me, filling my lungs with his tantalizing scent.

He leaned in closer, taking a deep whiff of the batter. *Don't breathe.* "Hmm, that smells nice. What are you baking?"

And before I could stop him, he'd picked up a spoon from the counter and dipped it into the batter, sweeping a large amount of my favorite concoction into his mouth. "Yum. Triple chocolate." He smacked his lips, grinning like a small boy getting away with things, and it was extra charming on a man as large as Bigfoot.

"That's going to cost you."

"I think I can afford it."

"Are you sure? I haven't said what I charge yet."

He leaned in closer, getting far too near my own for comfort. I reached up and swiped a bit of chocolate from the corner of his mouth with a finger, swallowing. *Hard.* Our eyes locked while I sucked the batter off the digit.

"You have the most amazing eyes." He reached out and touched my face.

On a sigh, I parted my lips to his. He slid his tongue into my mouth, rich with the lingering taste of sweet chocolate, but it was him tasting me in deep penetrating waves, stroking the fire within that captured my rapt attention. I'd never been kissed with such hunger and reverence. He branded me with every thrust of his tongue against mine. Our breaths mingled until I couldn't tell if it was his air or mine I inhaled.

Stop this, are you certifiable? What if someone walks in? No, I don't want this to end. Confused, overwhelmed by a thousand sensations and emotions, I finally found my voice.

"You don't kiss like a lawman." I turned away to hide my embarrassment at kissing a man I'd just met and picked up my spatula to scrape away at the sides of the bowl. Even if we'd had a lot of interactions today, none had been a bona fide date. For heaven's sake, it had all been about a murderer being loose in our town, and me being suspected of the murder. None of this made any sense. None whatsoever.

"And how does a lawman kiss?"

I shrugged, feigning indifference. "How should I know? But I'm fairly certain nothing like you. You trying to soften me up, Ace?"

"Is it working?"

I glanced up from overworking the brownie mixture, catching his intent interest in the subject, and made myself look away.

"Could you move back a bit? I need to get a pan."

He did as I asked, moving his hot bod out of my way and finally giving me some breathing room.

I poured the chocolate batter into the prepped pan, carefully spreading it to the edges. He popped the oven door open for me and I tucked the brownies inside to bake. I took a second to set the cute rooster timer by his bright red comb then turned to confront him.

"Okay. What are you doing here?" I focused on the comforting *tick tock* of the timer, finding it soothing to my jangled nerves.

"Don't you remember I said I needed to talk to you?"

"Sorry. Been a crazy day. Do you want some coffee?"

"Sure." He walked about the room as I fired up the coffee machine, picking up this or that utensil, then looking at it like it housed some odd mystery of the universe. Still in jeans and a white shirt, he looked absolutely nothing like any Mountie I'd ever seen. Now, a sexy actor playing a sheriff in the movies, that I would buy.

"Cream or sugar?"

"Don't think I'm sweet enough, darlin'?" he teased, looking up from inspecting a cookie press we used for larger orders, adding, "Black, thanks."

"If your objective is to get the suspect to relax enough to confess with idle chitchat, Officer, you're failing big time." My heart hammered, overcome with the severity of my predicament. I had to find the murderer to clear my name and keep a roof over my Granny and siblings. Pressure was building, and I didn't like it, afraid I'd screw up even more than I already had, kissing the man investigating a murder I was implicated in. Didn't he worry about the same thing? Or was he okay with it?

"Why? Do you have something you need to get off your chest, Miss McCall?" He pinned me with a look. He set down the cookie press and joined me, pulling out a chair and sitting across the small table I'd placed our cups of coffee on.

"No, I do not." I took a sip of the hot coffee, breathing out a sigh of contentment.

He followed my actions, the smoldering look in his eyes saying more than words ever could.

"So, you ready to tell me what you know about Fred Smith?"

"I know he didn't do it."

"And you know this how?" He took a sip from his cup and nodded. "Good coffee."

"Thanks. Consider yourself reimbursed for the kiss."

His eyebrows rose. *Good. Surprised you for a change.*

"Okay. So, Fred Smith?"

"Pretty much the same way I find things for people. I touched him and got a reading. I was fortunate enough that he was thinking about the case at the time. He thinks I did it." I ignored my fear.

"You touched him? How?" His eyebrows came together like thunderclouds, a tic developing in his cheek again. I froze, thinking a suspect would spill all they knew if this big guy was standing over them.

I gulped. "Just on the arm when I was reaching for something."

He nodded, still frowning. "I guess I wasn't clear enough last time. I'm the one investigating this case, not you."

"Couldn't you deputize me or something? I can help you. I know these people. They're my people. And my inside knowledge will solve it quicker."

His eyebrows rose higher, a look of astonishment replacing the anger. "No such thing as a civilian deputy."

"There must be some way. Look, this affects me far more than you. Our business of selling our baked goods is our livelihood. Surely you can make an exception?"

"It's my job to protect the citizens of Snowy Lake, Charm." He shook his head. "I need you to promise me you'll stay out of this."

"Or what? You'll arrest me?" Anger boiled over.

"I don't want it to come to that. But interfering, going around burgling people's houses, I can't allow that kind of lawlessness."

I pressed my lips tightly together to avoid saying something that could only worsen the situation.

He stood up, his frustration clear. I remained sitting, refusing to promise anything. I did not want to be shown a liar. I had to continue my quest. My family were counting on me.

"So that's it then? You refuse to listen to me?"

I shook my head, my mind churning.

I defiantly looked anywhere but at Ace, and the back door slammed behind him. With trembling fingers, I poured myself another cup of coffee. But it grew cold, untouched, as I stared into space.

Chapter Ten

Ding.

The brownies. I stumbled to my feet, grabbed a pair of oven mitts and pulled the tray from the oven.

Infuriating man. My anger grew as I whipped up a batch of chocolate buttercream frosting for the brownies while they cooled. I like everything iced, so sue me.

I went about boxing them up in groups of six, intending to carry out my plan no matter how annoying the edict from His Holiness was. Brownies were currency in Snowy Lake and the murderer would know they were fine to eat.

Picking up the stack, I exited the kitchen, heading for Thor. One night to solve the mystery before Granny came home and I couldn't afford to waste a second.

First up, Boyd Thompson. I drove toward his car dealership, Boyd's Wheels, keeping an eye out for Ace. The last thing I needed was him noticing me snooping around. I hoped my cover of brownies would divert suspicion, but our most recent interaction suggested not. His warnings hadn't exactly been unclear.

The lot was still open, as it was every Friday night. Boyd was the kind of man to know that as the festival closed, people would mosey on over to have something else to look at before calling it a night. A family was enjoying ice-cream cones as they drifted around the lot, followed closely by a salesman. I pulled in alongside Boyd's Lexus and switched off the motor. Grabbing a box of brownies by the string, I climbed out and took a deep breath. The odors of fair food lingered in the evening air, stirring up my hunger again. I promised myself a brownie later, though my pangs argued for one now. Hopefully I'd be having two or three in celebration of knowing the identity of the killer.

I hurried through the front sliding glass doors, intent on making a beeline for Boyd's office. I nodded at the employee coming out, whose eyes widened on seeing me.

"Evening, Shirley."

She smiled tentatively and kept walking away.

I entered Boyd's spacious office. The walls were covered with photos of him and different people, shaking hands over the buying of a vehicle. All locals. Boyd knew his audience. Everyone liked to be appreciated and hung on his wall of honor.

"Charm McCall." He looked up from his laptop and set his coffee cup down, his eyes alert and calculating. Of course, he'd have seen me coming on the lot monitor. "What a nice surprise. And you've brought me something, I see."

I handed the box of brownies over, the odor of his favorite almond roast coffee lingering in the air. "Your favorite treat, triple chocolate brownies with buttercream frosting."

"Mighty sweet of you."

"My pleasure."

"Did the new constable finally catch up with you?"

I nodded. "Yeah. He talk with you as well?"

"Why would he be interested in me? It was your jam that was laced with poison."

I swallowed down the sour bile and pasted a smile on. "He's talking with everyone who saw Mrs. Hurst on her last day. And that puts you squarely on the list."

"Yeah, well, I had a legitimate reason for being there." He smoothed his bad combover. "Mrs. Hurst was looking to order a new car."

"She get around to signing a deal?"

"Not sure that's any of your business. But as it happens, no. For the best really, now that she's gone."

"Yeah, not much call for the dead to drive."

He narrowed his eyes at me. "Was there anything else? I do thank you for the brownies."

"Thinking of buying a new vehicle myself."

"Ah, do you think the timing is right?"

"Why, because I'm also on the list of suspects?"

"I would say it's a bit more than that, Charm. I had a good reason for seeing Mrs. Hurst and I did not harm a hair on that dear lady's head. I didn't lace *my* jam with arsenic or cyanide or whatever poison you used."

"Excuse me." This was going too far. "'Dear lady's head.' Why, Boyd Thompson, I'm surprised *your* head doesn't explode."

"I have to ask you to leave my office now. I won't stand for this slanderous talk. I thought more of you than this. Why, if your granny was here, she'd be horrified at what you're suggesting." His eyes squinted at me, his mouth twisted up in a silly way. *Pompous idiot.*

My legendary streak of patience must have ended without my knowledge.

"Boyd Thompson." I stood. "Tell me what happened. Did you do something to Mrs. Hurst?" I moved around the desk. He was now standing as well, his expression wary. I moved in closer, grabbed his arm and closed my eyes to get a reading.

A vision came firing into my brain, making me shudder. I held on, trying to see what he was seeing. *Yes. Think about Mrs. Hurst…*

"Miss McCall, what do you think you're doing?" A thundering, commanding voice made me let go of Boyd and stagger backwards.

Oh-oh, crap on a cracker. Constable Ace Collins stood in the doorway, looking thoroughly pissed-off.

"Just trying to get to the truth," I whispered. Not able to look away from the outraged Mountie, I stood and stared, beyond horrified. Being found out so soon did not bode well for the rest of my plan. *Abort. Abort.*

"And what did I warn you of not even an hour ago?"

"To say out of your investigation. That you had it handled."

"I thank you, Officer, for coming by. I was just asking this woman to leave and she was not willing to."

"Are you wanting to press charges, Mr. Thompson?"

"*Charges!*" Equal parts horrified and angry, I crossed my arms over my chest and glared at the two imbeciles. I must have dreamed the kiss. This was as far from that divine experience as humanly imaginable.

"No, I just want her to leave."

"Good, then we see eye to eye. Miss McCall, if you would?" His Holiness held out a hand to me that I studiously ignored, making a point of walking around the desk and pushing past him to get into the showroom. The zing of electricity I got touching Ace did not help my mood.

I walked stiff-legged out into the warm July weather, enjoying the slight breeze that cooled my overheated skin. I spun round soon as I heard *him* behind me.

"You just had to follow me. Stalk me like...like...a darn Mountie!"

"Sorry, ma'am. Just doing my sworn duty."

"That Sheriff Taylor from *Mayberry* sh—stuff doesn't work on me."

"You couldn't use a bad word if your mouth was full of it."

"And that's a bad thing? The world is going to hades in a handbasket—"

"Now who's acting all Miss Goody Two-shoes!"

"Phhht."

"Back at you, Miss McCall."

We glared at each other, unminding of our audience.

"Okay, let's calm down."

"I am calm."

"I can see that."

"How about we sit in your jeep and discuss this? It will be less obvious than using the patrol car." He nodded toward the interested parties watching the sparks fly.

"Fine."

I crawled into my side and stared out of the windshield, not seeing much of anything except the color red.

"What were you thinking? Going in there after I explicitly warned you to stay out of my investigation?"

"I needed to know if he did it."

"And did he?"

I turned, venturing a peek at him. He genuinely seemed to want to know, under his very pissed-off Mountie look.

"Inconclusive. He hated her enough. They'd had some kind of long-standing beef. But I can't say for certain."

"I'll look into it. Now, will you leave this alone?"

I bit my lower lip to keep from saying the exact wrong thing. *One of my specialities.*

"Tell me how to get through to you? For such an intelligent woman, you can be so headstrong."

"Okay." I asked through stiff lips, "Do *you* think I did it?"

"What?"

"Do. You. Think. I. Did. It?"

He rubbed the back of his neck, then gave me a rueful glance. "Truthfully, no. I don't think you have murder in your heart. At least not for a townie." His look suggested for a non-townie I might be provoked into the act. He might be right.

A rap on the window right beside my face made me jump halfway out of my seat. I placed a hand over my heart, rolling down the glass with a few twists of my wrist.

"Tulip. What's up?"

"Ah, you're needed back at the café. There's an important meeting you should attend."

"A meeting?" I stared at her, noticing the high color in her fair cheeks and her slightly disheveled hair from sprinting across the parking lot. She must have run all the way, I couldn't see her little Volkswagen bug any where.

"Yeah, there's a consortium gathering to prevent the strippers from working at the Boots & Lace." Her expression suggested I needed to get with it. "I said they could meet at our place. Thought it might be good for business."

"You thought right. Good call." I couldn't have cared less either way about the strippers doing shows to anyone over the age of majority. However, it was best to insert ourselves in the midst of the fray and try to steer it if it went south.

"Can we finish this later?" I asked brightly as Tulip came around the back of my jeep to wait for Ace to step out.

"I think we are finished for now. You go to your meeting, stay out of my business and all will be well. Deal?"

I didn't dare look at him. I nodded once, the skin prickling on the back of my neck. I wasn't into his business. I was into my own and no one need be the wiser if he took it the wrong way.

"Okay then. I'll leave you to host that meeting. Sounds like it might contain fireworks, but I'm sure you can handle it. Call me if it gets out of hand."

I chanced another look and found him grinning widely at me.

I watched him climb out of my jeep, his tight gluteus maximus on display in his well-fitted jeans. Phhht, the guy was just too, too — what was the right word? *Yes. Just too much.*

Chapter Eleven

Before Mr. Too-Much made his vehicle, Tulip had jumped in beside me and I was directing Thor out of the parking space. I floored the gas petal in my rush to get back to the café before it was torn to pieces by a horde of angry villagers. A crowd with pitchforks as in Mary Shelley's *Frankenstein* came to mind. Not a reassuring image.

I parked out back and the two of us raced inside, finding the café filled to bursting with the human version of a noisy swarm of killer bees.

"Well, I say we need to let them know they're not welcome here. We should elect a group to go right over to the hotel right now and let them know that. Tonight." Harriet Stokes, one of the stylists at the Clip Joint, had the rapt attention of the women assembled in our café. At least some of the invited guests were occupied, munching cookies and drinking coffee, watching the antics as though they were at the drive-in movie theater our town boasted during the summer months.

I poured myself a cup of coffee, laced it with a jolt of cream and sat, nabbing a peanut butter cookie from a tray sitting open on the tabletop. Tulip had placed cookies on every available open space. Smart. Temptation would lesson suspicion of our products. Maybe this stripper problem would turn out to be a boom for us. Take the heat off, if nothing else. *Thank you, strippers*, I silently toasted them, munching on the cookie.

"Yes. We need to make it abundantly clear. It's *not* acceptable in Snowy Lake for women to remove their clothing for money," another voice spoke up from the back of the room.

I didn't bother to mention that that was already the case for a few women who'd chosen another way to make their daily bread in town, not wanting to stir the pot. I guess because they were *our* scarlet women, it made it okay.

"It's disgusting! Every time I think of it, my heart flutters. I'm going to have a heart attack or something and it will be on their heads. Mark my words."

I didn't bother to check who said it. It could have been any of a number of the women.

I stood. Time to wade in. "They need funds to fix their tour bus, right?" Every eye in the place turned to me. I tried not to shiver and pressed on. "How about we help them with that problem? You know, raise funds in a socially acceptable way for them?"

Silence.

"You know, that's not a half-bad idea. We could have a bake sale or something. You'd help with that, right, Charm? Tulip?"

I nodded. *More free cookies. Well, goodwill is priceless.* Harriet Stokes glared at the woman agreeing with me, but thankfully remained silent. A number of heads nodded. *Good.* It wouldn't be a consensus, but hopefully enough to push the idea through to a vote.

"We'll bake up dozens, and all the profit goes to the cause. Every last penny. That bus will be rolling out of town before you know it," I assured them.

Tulip added her voice. "Yes. We'll get right on it. Start baking tonight."

"I'll add a dozen loaves of my homemade bread," a strong voice rang out. Was that Helen? I searched the crowd, locating her beaming face behind a couple of other women. She shone, rosy with health. I breathed a sigh of relief. Maybe things were looking up in Snowy Lake.

I waded through the crowd, managing to get close enough to Helen to speak. "That's nice of you, to help out with your famous bread. I would love to spend a day with you learning your recipe."

"Least I can do. Sure. When things calm down, I'll set a day aside and teach you my method. It's as old as I am. A pioneer recipe from the eighteen hundreds that an ancestor brought over from the old country," she teased. "Though I must say I haven't felt this good in years." Her eyes twinkled as she looked up at me. "Must have been something to do with the iced tea and companionship we shared this afternoon, eh, dear?"

I returned her smile, praying the improvement to her health continued. "Maybe. Glad you're feeling better."

Tulip drew my attention by stabbing a fingernail determinedly into my shoulder blade.

"Ow. For heaven's sake, Tulip. What is it?"

She leaned in and whispered in my ear, "Emma needs to talk to you. She's in the kitchen and she looks really upset."

"If you'll excuse me, Helen, I've got some cookies to see to."

"Sure, dear. I'll bake bread tomorrow and deliver it to you in the afternoon."

"Thanks, I appreciate it."

I hurried after Tulip. *Now what?*

Emma looked upset when I rushed to her side, her gray eyes huge and bloodshot in her elfin face. Her red curls were haphazardly pinned up in a bun and her clothes were wrinkled as though she'd slept in them for days.

I hugged her, careful not to pull any readings out of her. Emma was my best bud and I respected her way too much to ever accuse her of anything nefarious. Like the Mountie said, I didn't have murder in me. Well, that went double for my sensitive friend.

"What's going on, Emma?"

"No one will do the eulogy for my aunt. No one cared about her. No one." Fresh tears threatened.

"I'm sorry. Everyone deserves a decent send-off."

"Will you do it, Charm?"

"What? Me? Are you sure I'm the right person? I mean, considering the way she died and all." I couldn't say it out loud, that I was under suspicion.

"Phhht. I know you had nothing to do with that. You'll prove it. Or that new Mountie boyfriend of yours."

"He's not my boyfriend. Just a guy working a murder case."

"Have you found anything out yet? Any leads?"

"I'm working on it. That is, when that Mountie will let me." I rolled my eyes.

"He sure has taken a liking to you."

"It's not like that. He keeps following me around, trying to keep me from learning what I need to, to solve the case. I could resolve the whole thing in no time left to my devices."

"I know you could. Anything I can do?"

"No, I'll sort it through. You've got enough on your plate. When is the funeral?"

"Not until late next week, at the earliest. I have to wait for the body to be released."

I nodded, biting my lip.

"Thanks, Charm, for doing this."

"Hey, you'd do the same for me." A final hug and she left through the back door. I didn't blame her for avoiding all the women I could still hear milling about in the front part of the café.

I sighed. What was I going to say about Emma's auntie that wasn't an out-and-out lie? Ah, Granny Toogood, of course. She'd lend a hand in writing it. But all that could wait, while solving the crime could not. I checked the time. Nine-thirty p.m. Still early. I'd ruled out Helen and Fred, and of course Emma. That still left Sean and Boyd. And I had just the ticket for seeing Christine and Sean if I hurried. The house speciality, triple chocolate brownies.

Picking up another small box of dainties, I dashed from the kitchen and hurried to my jeep. If I was lucky, I could catch them at home. But as I trawled past their large two-storey brick house, it was dark, just the porch lights on for when someone did come home. So, where had they gone? Friday night meant either the Boots & Lace, which I didn't figure Christine would appreciate, or visiting friends, which meant I would be out of luck. Best-case scenario, maybe they'd split up for the night and Sean had gone drinking.

The boot-stomping music spilling out onto the street from the honky-tonk suggested the crowd was in fine form tonight. I had no idea what I would find unfolding in the dancehall, but I took a deep breath and entered anyway. The press of heat and bodies and the aroma of popcorn and beer stirred my blood.

Darcy gave me a nod and came right over to the bar rail, where I'd managed to squeeze in between the regulars.

"Have you seen Sean Blackmore here tonight?"

He pointed to his left. "What you want to see him for, sweetheart?" His look suggested I could do a whole lot better.

"I need to see the man about a jar of jam."

Darcy's eyebrows near crawled up his forehead and he gave me a lopsided grin.

I took the beer he offered me and wormed my way over in the direction Darcy had pointed out, ducking and diving elbows and raised drink glasses. The crowd was mostly men tonight and I got my fair share of male attention since the stage act looked to be on break at the moment.

Oh, brother. Someone had beaten me to it. Constable Ace Collins sat just as nice as could be across the table from Sean Blackmore. And judging from their expressions, they were getting along just fine.

Dare I interrupt? Duh. And I knew just what to do. The crowded space was about perfect.

I pushed past another pair of drunken revelers, finally making my way to Sean's side of the table. Sidling up nice and tight to his barstool, I laid my hand on Sean's shoulder. He started, giving me an up-and-down look.

"Charm, what a pleasure. Sit on my lap if you like. All the chairs are taken. My gain, though."

"Thanks, I don't mind standing."

Ace's sharp look could have cut through glass. *Really. Closer to literally than figuratively. Just sayin'.*

"Miss McCall." He gave me a cool nod of acknowledgment.

I left my hand on Sean's shoulder, hoping Ace would get the point and ask the right questions. The sense of being on the same team came as a surprise, thundercloud expressions aside.

Sean patted my hand, then played a bit with my fingers. I managed to keep from gagging.

"So, Sean and I were just discussing winter activities."

"Hmm. You like to ice fish or skidoo?" I raised my eyebrows at Ace.

"Well, all I'm hoping for is to solve the mystery of who laced your jam with cyanide before the snow flies."

Sean shifted in his seat at the mention of Mrs. Hurst's unfortunate demise. I held on and closed my eyes, trying to tap into what he was envisioning. He was handing her a thick stack of money. Twenties, judging by the color. And quite recently. What on earth for?

"Before the snow flies, eh. You're sounding like a true northerner already, Constable," Sean said, wiggling his forefinger under my hand and tracing circles in my palm, in the age-old gesture of a man interested in being more than just being friends. *Too much.* I yanked my hand away.

The bank deposits from the folder I'd nabbed came to mind. Okay. Time to see a woman about my suspicions.

"Well, if you gentlemen will excuse me, I gotta run."

"But, sugar, we were just getting reacquainted. The night's young. Stay. Have another beer," Sean said with a pretend pout and an expansive gesture with his arms.

Was that a growl? I gave Ace a quick glance, but other than the scowl, he looked the same. I frowned, certain I'd heard something out of the ordinary.

"Sorry, another time. But thank you for the offer." I turned and made a beeline for the door. Or as much as one as I could manage through the horde of drunken, but happy, revellers. The sounds of raunchy music drew my attention before I could make it all the way out, and I turned toward them. A half-clad smiling female came prancing her way along the front edge of the stage my sister usually sang on, a come-hither look in her eyes as she licked her lips, signaling her intentions.

Hmm, how very thoughtful of Darcy to have put up a temporary steel pole for dancing and swinging capriciously on. *Hope it holds.* I watched the stripper reach for it, making me wince. I'd seen a lot of insta-poles fall from the ceiling at the exact wrong second, sending dancers on their keisters. It was a popular category on YouTube.

I finally made the street and took in a deep breath of fresh air. The full moon hung low and added its usual aura of mystery to the night. About now, what I wouldn't have given for a tourist's ride to the moon. Anything to take my mind off the insanity residing in Snowy Lake.

Shirley, Boyd's administrative assistant, was running full tilt down the street toward me. The look on her face told me the truth before she spoke. Something bad was in the wind.

"Charm, oh my goodness, something's happened to Boyd." Almost out of breath, she stopped and grabbed her sides.

I took her by the arms and made her look at me. "What, Shirley? What happened?"

"He's dead. In his office. Just now. I think he choked on one of your brownies. It's all down his shirt front and everything." She shuddered with horror.

"No!" My mind went blank with shock.

Chapter Twelve

"I have to find the new Mountie," Shirley said, trying to pull away from me.

I let her go and slumped back against the rough brick side of the building, barely feeling it digging into my back. This couldn't be happening. Not again. This would ruin us. *Ruin me.* But it made no sense. I'd used proper methods and perfect ingredients that I trusted. Placed the Kismet Spell. *Where could I have gone wrong?*

Shirley came out with Ace in tow not thirty seconds later, a small crowd streaming behind them. He nodded at me and moved closer as he caught my expression. "You okay, Charm? You look pale."

I waved my arms about. "Go. See to Boyd."

He called someone over. "Ivana will take you home."

"Okay, whatever."

Ivana took my arm, for once not accusing me of anything. "I get you to home."

I didn't struggle but let her lead me back to the Tea & Tarot, the moon taunting me all the way.

"What happened — not good, my friend. I make some coffee. We talk," she said, opening the back door of the café and turning on the kitchen lights. She bustled about getting the coffee on as I slumped down on a chair. The aroma of the fragrant brew coming out of the instant Bunn machine triggered something primal. The strong smell of almond roast in Boyd's office earlier. *Is it possible?*

I stood up, electrified by the idea.

"I have to go."

Ivana looked at me, alarmed. "Charm, that no good for —"

I raced out of the back door, cutting her off mid-sentence. I ran all the way to Boyd's Wheels, my lungs burning by time I made the car lot. A small crowd had beaten me to the punch, standing around the doorway. I pushed past them and reached the showroom without anyone stopping me.

Ace looked up as I entered Boyd's office, his expression changing when he caught sight of me standing there, wheezing and out of breath.

"Charm, I'm going to have to ask you to leave."

"Check the coffee pods. I noticed a strong odor of bitter almond earlier when I dropped off his favorite brownies." I studiously avoided looking at Boyd.

Ace frowned, his voice stern enough to freeze water into perfect ice cubes. "I will. Now you have to leave, or I will arrest you, Miss McCall. You're interfering with a crime scene."

At the mention of the word 'crime', my eyeballs seemed to take on a life of their own, pulling me towards the body of Boyd slumped in his office chair. Ace stepped in front of him, obscuring the body from view. But I had caught sight of him for a split second, and the blue tinge to Boyd's face gave the game away. Cyanide symptom. Chocolate frosting was smeared down his shirt front, leaving no doubt that he'd eaten some. *Oh boy*. Two murders in two days. What was Snowy Lake coming to? My nerves twitched, reminding me I would once more be a suspect. And this time, I'd bet my hiney I'd be called in for questioning.

I stumbled out of the room, not certain where I was headed. Just anywhere away from having death shoved in my face seemed a good idea.

"Charm. Are you okay?" Sean Blackmore put his arm around my shoulders, leading me away. "Let's get you home."

I didn't object to the help. *Home. Yes.* It was a good thing Sean was holding me up, my legs were as malleable as dough, ready to fold to the floor at a moment's notice.

"Thanks," I mumbled. The full moon was still visible in the Northern sky when we made our way outside, but right then, it looked different to me, as if it was saying, *'I told you so'*. It was strange, thinking the moon could talk. *Maybe I'm in shock?*

Sean led me to his vehicle, oozing platitudes. "You poor thing. What you need is a drink. I'll stop by the vendor and pick us up a six pack."

"I don't drink."

"Tonight, you do. Do you good."

He tucked me into the passenger side seat then hurried around to the driver's door.

Get out! A voice shouted in my ear.

A shiver of dread shot through me. *No.* Going anywhere with Sean Blackmore was a bad idea. I went to open the passenger-side door, but it was locked.

Sean slipped into the driver's seat and buckled the seatbelt. The smell of peppermint wafted in the air.

"No, I've changed my mind. I'll walk home. I need the fresh air to clear my head." I jerked at the locked door again, nearly yanking the handle off in my frustration. "Unlock the door, Sean, or I'm warning you, I'll scream."

"Relax, Charm. You're exhausted, overly emotional. Sit back and I'll drive you home. I'm just trying to be a friend here."

"I don't need any more friends. Listen, Sean, I'm not kidding around, unlock the door!"

"For crying out loud," he half-shouted, giving me a look of barely controlled rage. "I was just trying to help you. I wasn't good enough in high school to date you, and apparently, I'm not good enough now to help see you home safely. And half the town is now watching us have an argument." He slanted his head at the interested crowd observing us from not fifty feet away, still clustered around Boyd's Wheels showroom.

He was right. I'd never given him the time of day. And with so many residents of the town knowing my whereabouts, I couldn't be safer. *Right?*

"Sorry. I guess I overreacted. Such a shock seeing Boyd dead and all."

"Apology accepted." His mercurial mood change was discombobulating.

"But take me straight home. I don't drink and I don't intend to start. Deal?"

"Sure. Whatever you say, Charm."

Still leery, and ready to drop-kick Sean with one of my defensive moves at a moment's notice, I waited for him to pull into the alley behind the Tea & Tarot.

Unbuckling, I turned to offer my thanks, but he was suddenly right in my personal space.

He reached out and ran a finger down my cheek, making me cringe. "Do you have any idea how long I've wanted to get you alone, Miss McCall? For years and years. The only woman I've never been able to charm." He chuckled at his non-joke.

"Was Mrs. Hurst blackmailing anyone else in town, do you know?" I threw out a line complete with accompanying fishhook.

His hand dropped away, his expression tightening, the street lamp near our business turning his skin an ominous gray.

"What do you know about that? Did she have something on you too?"

Bingo. "How many people do you suppose she was blackmailing?"

"I have no idea. Not me, that's for sure." He turned his head away.

"Then who?"

"You should stay out of things that don't concern you. But I do know that Boyd hated her guts. Always going on about how she was sucking him dry. Getting a new vehicle each year for next to nothing."

"What did Mrs. Hurst have on Boyd?"

"No idea—he wouldn't say. How about that drink? We can talk more, get to know each other better." He'd regained some of his color along with the bluster.

"I'll take a rain check. I'm bushed. Thanks for the ride." I went to open the door of his Lexus and found it still locked.

"The door." I added steel to my tone.

"Ah, sure." He pressed the unlocking mechanism, and I scrambled out.

"You've been a big help, Sean. Oh, have you shared any of this with our new Mountie?"

"The stuff about Boyd? No. Why? I only told you because we're friends."

And because I wormed it out of you.

"Well, he'll be asking. It does fall under a lawman's purview."

"None of any outsider's business." The chill in his voice hinted at more animosity than the situation called for. Or maybe it was just a guy thing. Hot Mountie moving in on his supposed territory. *Eww.*

"Thanks again." I shut the passenger door and waited for him to drive away.

Exhaustion overrode any other concerns, forcing my weary feet to walk the short distance into the café then up the back stairs to my suite. It had been the longest day of my life. *Ever.* I face-planted on the bed fully dressed, intending to rest for a few minutes to gather myself. I woke instead to bright sunlight streaming through my bedroom windows, Ling Ling curled up at my feet, a white puffball. My awesome guard cat.

"Hey, baby Ling Ling, you finally showed up. Don't worry. I won't mention anything about you know who. Deal?"

She got up and stretched, moving up the bed to butt her head under my hand, insisting on her morning rubdown. I worked her head absently, scratching behind her ears, her favorite spot, letting my mind drift. The likely motive for the first crime. Blackmail. But why Boyd? His death made no sense—he was one of the people *being* blackmailed. Unless he knew something about the crime, was in on it in some way and was considered the weakest link? Threatened to tell someone. Sean knew more than he was saying. Though

I found him creepy, it wasn't grounds for accusing him of murder. And he and Boyd were friends. Hard to believe he'd murder a friend. Now, Mrs. Hurst. Maybe. The thought that there might have been two murders chilled me to the bone.

Or maybe Boyd had committed suicide the same way he'd might have poisoned Mrs. Hurst—some kind of bizarre twist of punishment and guilt? Nah, that didn't set right at all. Well, then, that only left Sean as the suspect. The realization made my head reel. Had I been in a vehicle with a murderer last night? *But there's no way he killed his best friend, right?* I just couldn't quite put all the pieces together.

I checked the bedside clock. I'd better hurry into the shower and prepare for the day. And hopefully this one would prove less exciting. *Please, please.* My heart rate sped up alarmingly, another thought firing in my brain. Granny would be home today and learn what was going on, and the crime, instead of being solved, had been compounded.

I jumped up, annoying Ling Ling with the abrupt departure from her rightful massage, a stark series of meowing complaints for my efforts following me all the way to the bathroom.

"Sorry, baby, got to get going, or that lawman might catch me unprepared." I showered in record time, not bothering to do more than apply a swipe of lip gloss and pull my hair into a neat ponytail.

"Okay. Will I do?" I asked Ling Ling, bending down and adding a few extra love pats.

She meowed in the affirmative, leading the royal way into my apartment's small kitchen nook, tail held like the standard bearer of our ancient clan. I needed to make time today to give her a serious combing—bits of white fluff danced through the air at each planted paw on the linoleum.

I reached into the cupboard for a tin of Fancy Feast, agreeing with our furry companion that chicken and gravy was the breakfast of champions. While Ling Ling got down to the serious business of picky eating, I put on a pot of coffee and made myself a quick bowl of oats.

After adding a sprinkling of brown sugar and cream, I consumed my breakfast, eating quickly over the sink in case of an interruption. And there was always an interruption because someone needed something. Not that I truly minded. Family was family, the most important thing in the world.

I scrubbed my bowl in the sink, dried it then tucked it back into the cupboard. There was no money for a dishwasher but that was no problem — elbow grease was free. I picked up my cup of coffee, surprised I'd had so much time alone, and made my way downstairs. The back of the café was empty as well, not a soul in sight. *Hmm. Odd.*

The front of the café was still deserted too, the lights off. I switched them on and went to the front window that looked out on the street, pulling up the horizontal venetian blinds by the knotted cord. It was quiet on Main Street, just a few stragglers making their way to their businesses. Of course, it was early. I took a sip of my coffee, contemplating the day while watching the activity. It boded well, I congratulated myself, that no one was running around yelling the sky was falling. Even though a part of me wondered if it had already happened while I wasn't looking. *Most likely scenario.*

Deciding it was too soon to open the café unless someone was banging on the door, I hurried back to the kitchen, Ling Ling at my heels. With Granny due home today, I'd better use wisely what could be my last few hours of freedom. Duck and dive the Mountie while trying to get at the truth. Something told me he'd not be all that unhappy to throw my behind in jail if the opportunity presented itself.

A candid talk with Emma was the first thing on my new agenda. I opened the back door and ran smack right into a wall. Again.

"We have to quit meeting like this," he quipped, his tone all jovial and nicey-nicey.

I mumbled something, a rise of anger and dread making my throat tighten. The last person I'd wanted to run into right then was Constable Ace Collins.

What had that been? A half-hour of uninterrupted bliss before the circus began? *Hardly fair.*

"Glad I ran into you, darlin'. We need to talk."

That made one of us.

"Care to go back inside?" he asked. Dressed in his Mountie uniform, fresh from the shower, he presented a formidable, all-too-nice-smelling package.

"Whatever."

"Do I detect a hint of reluctance on your part?"

"Not at all, Officer. I'd love to be questioned about something I had nothing to do with. Just makes my day." *Why am I being like this?*

He rubbed the nape of his neck, following me back into the café. He set his Stetson carefully on a chair, then ran his hand over his hair to smooth it. It looked unnecessary. In fact, everything about the lawman seemed a bit too posh. Why had I ever thought he was the right man for Star?

"Would you like coffee?" Etiquette runs deep in our family, even when we'd like to push people into an alley and pull up the drawbridge.

"No, I'm fine, thanks."

"Then have a seat. You're making me all antsy." Not to mention I had to crank my head to look up at him. I rubbed the back of my neck to ease the tension, his focus unnerving.

He sat down across from me, the expression in his eyes unreadable. I folded my hands on the table top and waited. He cleared his throat but didn't say anything. *What, no witty banter this morning? This* is *serious.*

"Are you here in an official capacity, Constable Collins?"

"I'm just trying to get to the facts of the case. Find out why the murder rate in this town, that has been nil for more than a decade, now resides at two in two days. I would think that would be of interest to you as well, Miss McCall, being a town supporter and all."

"Yes, of course. I will help in any way I can." Properly chastised, I pressed my lips together.

He nodded his approval. "Why did you take brownies to Boyd Thompson last evening?"

"I wanted to get on his good side, pick his brain. He has a fondness for my triple chocolate variety with buttercream frosting."

"Had," he corrected me.

I winced. "Yeah. Are you sending them in for testing? Along with the coffee pods?"

"Seems like the thing to do, yes. We'll know by later today. I put a rush on it. Sooner you're cleared, the better, unless your brownies prove it overwise. Anyone else have an opportunity to mess with them?"

My heart slammed. "No. I baked them fresh. Even ate some of the batter raw. And I'm fine."

"I can see that." He rubbed the back of his head, wincing.

"Something wrong?"

"No. It's nothing. Someone sucker-punched me with something last night, maybe a baseball bat or tire iron, when I was leaving Boyd's Wheels with the evidence I'd collected. I was going out of the back with the lights off. They tried to grab the bag, but I managed to hold on to it and drive them off. Kind of touch and go, but the strong arm of the law prevailed." He gave a lop-sided grin.

I sat up straighter. "You okay?"

"Yeah, I've had worse headaches."

"So, someone's worried that what you find will incriminate them. Now we're talking. Any surveillance at the back of Boyd's?"

"No." He shook his head. "Already checked. The perp was wearing a ski mask, if that helps."

"Lots of those in this town. You'll be buying one yourself come winter."

A soft knock on the back door drew my attention. "Excuse me."

I opened the door to find Helen Davis with a friend in tow — Elsie Arnold, her next-door neighbor.

"I hope we're not bothering you, dear. But we have a matter we'd like to discuss with you," Helen said, her expression serious. Elsie added an enthusiastic nod.

"Okay. Come on in. Would you like some coffee?"

Ace got to his feet, his chair scraping on the floor. "Ladies." He gave a charming smile that made both women light up like it was Christmas and Easter and Valentine's all rolled into one. He picked up his hat, addressing me. "I'll be going now. We can continue this later."

"Sure, anytime."

His eyes warmed at my words and he gave me a courteous salute with his Stetson. *There's something about a lawman in a hat...*

"My, what a gentleman," Elsie twittered.

"He does seem to have taken a liking to you, Charm," Helen added, a twinkle in her eyes.

"Ah, did anyone say yes to coffee?"

"No, we're fine, dear. But we'd like to sit and have a chat with you."

I gestured at the chairs around the kitchen table. "Will this do?"

"Fine." The two women sat, hanging their purses out of the way on the backs of their chairs. Both leaned forward, drawing me in.

"What can I do for you?"

"Seems that your visit of the other day had some rather good side effects on my health."

"I'm glad you're feeling better." I smiled warmly at Helen, noting her high color and the healthy sheen to her skin. Did she have fewer wrinkles, as though she'd gone in for a facial lift or something? It wouldn't be polite to ask, though, so I kept quiet, waiting.

"Now, I don't need a doctor to tell me I'm a hundred percent better." Helen sounded stronger as well, her tone suggesting she'd not be suffering fools gladly.

I nodded. Where was this headed? I glanced at Elsie. She was favoring her right shoulder, wincing when she rubbed it.

I glanced back at Helen, who gave a nod at her friend. "Elsie's hurt her shoulder in a fall and I think you can help her. Will you do for her what you did for me, Charm?"

"Ah, I don't know if I can. I'm really not sure what I did. Maybe it was all coincidence." I shrugged, though a part of me was ecstatic to have it confirmed that I had not harmed the woman with my intentions. I crossed my fingers. *Please let it hold, goddess.*

"No. It was far more than that. I *felt* the healing. And now I'm right as rain. It won't hurt to try, dear."

"And I do want to get away from using medical cannabis if I can," Elsie said, startling me and making the recent conversation with Tulip about making edibles to bring in more money come to mind. "For my glaucoma. It helps ease eye pressure," she confirmed. I tucked the information away for now.

"I didn't know you had eye problems and taken a fall. I'm sorry to hear that. Okay, I can try."

"Thank you, dear."

"What do I do?" Elsie asked. She was a tiny little woman, bird-like with pretty eyes. Her curly gray hair was styled rather clumsily, a product most likely of her bad shoulder.

"I just need to hold your hands while you think about what's troubling you." I reached to take her frail-looking hands, careful not to grasp them too tight. Her fingers were swollen and bent from arthritis and could be painful.

Helen smiled at her friend, giving her a nod of encouragement. "Do as she asks, Elsie, it can't hurt."

"Now, close your eyes," I said.

Elsie's cool, thin fingers trembled in mine. I closed my own eyes, letting my mind roam free.

An image appeared. Again, I followed a strange path through her inner body, zooming down nerves that branched and curved as if I was gliding on a bobsled down a given track, leading me onward. But instead of finding an invader, I found some purple-red bruising in a muscle that looked attached to her shoulder. I sent thoughts of it being healed and of the area losing its inflammation, feeling rays of power pulse into it at my direction. *Make it work perfectly*, I prayed to the goddess.

But it didn't end there. The journey continued, with a sensation of rising higher, to the beautiful sight that was her brain. *Ah, nirvana.* An electronic marvel that made me give a gasp I managed to stifle completely, not wanting to interrupt the beauty of discovery. And then I was on a long curving section that opened in the distance to an egg-like shape. An eyeball. The nerve appeared squeezed in one spot like a bent tube, and I tried freeing it, giving it back its rightful rounded shape. When it finally filled out, I felt such incredible joy that I was nearly overcome, tears running down my face unheeded.

And then with a rush I was back at the beginning, holding her twisted hands. Could they be helped as well? I gave them what little energy I had left, envisioning them straight and true. I gasped, suddenly wrenched free of her. I took a deep breath and opened my eyes, falling back against my chair.

The two women were staring at me, mesmerized, unblinking.

"Are you okay, dear?" Helen asked, her eyes dark with worry. "You're crying."

I swiped at my cheeks, surprised my hand was trembling. "I'm fine. Just need to catch my breath. How are you, Elsie?"

"Fine, I think. I'm feeling kind of energized." She moved her shoulder tentatively, a smile lighting her face. "It doesn't hurt at all." She beamed at me. "You healed it."

"I don't know. I hope so. Better have a doctor look at it though."

"No need. It's fine."

"What did you see, dear?" Helen asked, her bright blue eyes filled with curiosity.

The door opened and voices came through loud and clear.

"No! Absolutely not! Charm will kill us."

My sisters rushed in, squabbling as usual, their arms filled with trays of fresh-baked cookies. Right, the bake sale was today, although I wasn't sure how many people would buy something from our café.

"Phhht. Once it's done, she'll come around. Way more benefits than not, especially as things stand."

The both stopped dead in their tracks when they spotted company.

I got up, swaying a bit before I got my bearings. I waved off Helen's assistance.

"I will kill you *both* if you don't share. Right now!"

Chapter Thirteen

"Ah, we'll be going now. Thanks for your help, Charm." Helen and Elsie made a beeline for the door. My not-so-adorable sisters make room for the two women to escape.

"So, what were Elsie and Helen doing here?" Tulip asked, setting her burden on the counter beside Tulip's.

"What were you two talking about?" I stood strong, hands on hips.

"Nothing that matters. We're more worried about you. What's going on, Charm? Was the Mountie here? Are you under investigation?" Star rushed to my side, giving me a hug. Tulip came in from the other side and we stood together. I took a deep breath.

I swiped another annoying tear from my cheek. No matter what, family was family.

"Okay, what's the plan of action?" Tulip asked, pulling away.

"Why would anyone set us up? That's the hardest part for me to swallow," Star volunteered.

"Jealousy. You're good enough for Nashville, sis," Tulip said.

My mind churned. "So, what's the deal with the bake sale today?"

"Tulip's looking after it, I'm working the café and you're solving the mystery."

"Sounds doable." I smiled at my fellow triplets. "At least I've managed to rule out all the suspects except for Sean at the moment, but I just can't believe he killed his best friend. So I don't know what to think. I'm heading over to Emma's to get her take on it, if you have everything covered?"

"You bet." The look-a-likes nodded in unison.

"Thanks."

I hurried over to Thor and turned the key. Nothing. *No, don't fail me now.* I gave a little prayer to the goddess, stroked his dash and tried again. *Ah, there we go.* Rewarded with a powerful purr, we were off, heading down the alley.

Emma's house looked deserted, the tiny one-storey gingerbread cottage dark, blinds drawn. Maybe she'd slept in? She'd been pretty upset about her aunt.

I picked up the package of cookies I'd brought and strode to her front door. Banging loudly on the doorframe, I balanced the cookies in one hand and slipped Thor's keys into my pocket.

A second series of knocks brought no response. Where was she? Turning away, I glanced around, chewing on my bottom lip. Maybe she was out back? Emma loved to garden, saying it was the only place she found complete peace. Having an aunt like Mrs. Hurst explained everything.

I came around the corner of the house, nearly banging into my friend.

"Hey, Emma, I've been knocking for ages. You okay?"

She looked tired, as if she hadn't slept a wink, dark circles under her eyes.

"Yeah, just about to head in. Want some tea?"

"Sure." I followed her through the back door and sat down at her small kitchen table while she put the kettle on to boil.

"Terrible thing about Boyd," I said, watching her pull a couple of tea bags from a tin.

"I can hardly believe it. First my aunt, now Boyd Thompson. What's going on, Charm?"

I shook my head. "I don't know, but it's hard to take in, all right. And it looks like someone is trying to frame me."

"Oh my, I don't know what to say to that except you could *never* do such a thing. No one can believe that you would. It's crazy."

She sat down across from me, picked up a jar of our Saskatoon jam from last year and began nervously picking the label off it. Watching her fingers move made me flash back to the night we'd found Mrs. Hurst dead in her kitchen. The apricot jam jar on the table. I tried to picture it but failed.

"I need to make a call." I got up, raced to her phone, dialed the number for the detachment and waited.

"Snowy Lake RCMP."

"Constable Collins, please."

"Hi, Charm. Thought I recognized your voice. How's it going?"

"Fine, thanks for asking, Delores. How are you?" Delores works the day shift as a dispatcher.

"Good, considering what's been going on. My — oh — my, more than enough excitement to go around. I'll patch you through to Ace now. One moment, please."

"Constable Collins."

"Ace, it's Charm. I need to ask you something."

"Shoot."

"Maybe not a good choice of word," I teased, trying to hide my worry under my words. "The jar of jam found at Mrs. Hurst's with the cyanide. Did it have a label?"

"I don't know. Is it important?"

"Well, if it did, it was from an earlier batch. The one Mrs. Hurst took home in the morning — I hadn't had time to label it yet. Which means it broadens the field of suspects. Possibly a lot."

"I'll get right back to you."

"Thanks."

I put the phone back in place and turned to my best friend.

"What are you thinking?" she asked, pouring the freshly made tea into china teacups.

"I'm thinking this might have gotten a whole lot more complicated." Much as I wanted to get at the truth, if the jar had been from an earlier batch, the list of suspects could be enormous. I hadn't made apricot jam since last week. Checking every visitor, if Suzanna could remember them all, would take a lot more time. I prayed for some kind of log or security camera if the field got expanded. But the cash banking deposits were still our best bet. Three suspicious payments each month. Though with Boyd gone and being one of those blackmailed, according to Sean, it looked like it was down to two, if indeed she was hitting up others for money. My instincts screamed yes. But who were those people?

The phone rang. I rushed to answer it.

"Charm?"

"Yeah."

"It's Ace. You were right. The jar *was* labeled. So, it wasn't the one she took home that day. Which means someone else could have placed the poison in it at an earlier time."

"Thanks for checking."

"When did you make the last batch?"

"Let me think. Yes, seven days ago."

"Well, it'll made my job a whole lot tougher, expanding it by a full seven days' worth of visitors. I'll get right on it. Interrogation's one of my specialities. I'll drop by later to confer."

"Good, do that." I liked his confidence. And the idea of conferring. We'd come some distance in forty-eight hours.

I sat down, tapping my fingernails on the wooden tabletop.

"Sounds like the new Mountie's becoming a friend."

I gave Emma a quick glance and shrugged. "Well, we both want to prove I'm innocent."

"That's something, that, him believing in your innocence."

"Yeah, it is." I picked up the fragile teacup and took a swallow, barely tasting the fragrant brew, my mind was so focused on the problem.

I sat down the empty cup. "I'm heading over to see Suzanna. See if she can remember who visited your aunt this past week."

"I appreciate all you're doing to solve my aunt's murder." Tears swam in her eyes, making me jump up from the table and hug her tight. Her red curls gave off their usual fragrance of strawberry shampoo and I breathed deeply, the odor comforting.

"We will find out. I promise."

She nodded and I rushed to make it to my next stop. Suzanna worked at Doris Johnson's on her off days. I hoped to find her there.

Five minutes later, I pulled into the driveway of the Johnson family, as advertised on a painted rock in their yard, surrounded by flowers. *Nice touch.*

Banging on the door, I waited impatiently for someone to answer.

"Ah, Suzanna, just the woman I wanted to talk to. You got a minute?"

"Come in. Just getting started, but we can talk as I work, if you don't mind?"

"No worries." I slipped in the door and followed her into the living room. She went back to dusting the ornaments.

"Is there any record of who visits Mrs. Hurst on a given week?"

"Not really. Why do you ask?"

"Well, turns out it's important who visited her in the past seven days."

"Really? Why?"

I explained the situation.

"Okay. Let me think. She doesn't really get a lot of visitors any more — not like before. The day she died was more than most." She scratched her head. "Christine Blackmore came by, one of the days. Monday, no, Tuesday. I remember because it was my bowling league night and I always leave an hour early. Oh, and she was in a right mood. Angry as a pitbull about something."

"Really? Did you get any idea as to why she was so angry?"

Suzanna lowered her voice. "I think Sean was caught cheating on her again."

"Oh." That sounded plausible.

"Anyone else come to mind?"

"Hmm, like I say, she doesn't get many visitors. Oh, yes, Pastor Evans came by one day with Mrs. Smith to collect a donation." She gave a shrug.

"Really?" I filed away the information. "Well, I didn't know Mrs. Hurst ever did things like that."

"Not often. But she'd come into some money and wanted to purchase a pew for the church fundraiser to have a new roof installed. One of the nicest things I think she's ever done. Good timing. Maybe it will buy her some ease in heaven. Who knows, eh."

"Maybe. That all?"

"All that comes to mind. I'll give you a call if I think of anyone else. Ah, while you're here, Charm, could I ask you something?"

"Sure."

"I ran into Helen Davis today at the Grab-n-go. She was with her friend Elsie. They're both looking *so* good. They said it was some kind of treatment you offered them?"

"Ah, not sure about that." Flummoxed by the change of subject, I stalled for time.

"Maybe you could help out my brother? Thomas has been diagnosed with epilepsy. He has such terrible seizures, and they're getting worse. Do you think you could help him?" Her pretty face screwed up with worry as she pleaded her case.

"I don't know. I guess I could try."

"That's all I ask. Thanks, Charm, you're the best."

"Hardly." My skin heated from the unexpected compliment. "Well, I should be going. I've got to find out who killed Mrs. Hurst and Boyd Thompson before they come after me."

"No one in their right mind would ever think it was you."

"Thanks. I'll let myself out."

Thor shone like sanctuary in the mid-morning sunlight bouncing off his paint and chrome. I climbed in and leaned on his steering wheel to gather myself. My life had left crazy in the rear-view mirror and taken a turn into the multiverse. Everything had shifted of late. My life no longer felt my own. Pieces were breaking away and I desperately needed to keep them cemented together, to keep everything the same. Star wanting to leave, a new Mountie in town, two murders and a lot of people in my little hamlet I suspected of doing things I couldn't have imagined a couple of days ago. And strangest of all, some kind of weird new ability that made no sense and that I couldn't get a handle on. Was the word going to spread all over town? The thought made me ill. I just wanted to fit in, not be different. But wasn't that selfish, if I could help others? *Goddess, I don't know everything – give me a little guidance here.* I pleaded my case to have silence returned.

Okay. Just take it one step at a time, Miss McCall. I started Thor's motor and set a course for the Blackmores'. Christine had some explainin' to do.

I'd barely driven a block before I caught sight of a figure racing toward me on the road, windmilling their arms for me to stop. Tulip. I braked hard to avoid hitting her and jumped from the front seat.

"What's going on? I nearly ran you down!"

Out of breath, she leaned over at the waist, holding her sides. "Sorry. Need you. Big fight. Bake sale."

"Get in."

We clamored into Thor. I slammed my foot to the metal and made Main Street in record time. It was impossible to miss where the bruhaha had broken out. A large group of milling women gave the game away.

I leaped from Thor, leaving the driver's door ajar, and ran full-tilt to the knot of angry worker bees protecting their hive. I shoved my way through the press of women, trying to get to the heart of the problem. It was obvious immediately. Bikinis. *Not our usual bake sale dress.*

"No! Absolutely not!" Mrs. Smith, the banker's usually serene spouse, was confronting the two underdressed women, her face matching perfectly the color of her tomato-red dress. She caught sight of me. "Charm. Thank goodness you're here! Would you explain to these — these *girls* that no one wears their underwear to a bake sale and brings cookies made from pre-made dough purchased in a package from the grocery store!"

The way she turned up her nose with a sniff at the offering of the 'girls" not-homemade-cookies, I wasn't sure which was worse. Bikinis or pre-bought dough.

The two out-of-towners eyed me up and down as I stepped forward, their eyes defiant. I got it. They were being dished for who they were when there was no crime in that. It was just best not to rub it in others' faces — especially in Snowy Lake.

"Now, Mrs. Smith, they're just trying to help themselves. You've heard of bikini car washes? This is kind of like that."

"Help themselves! Yeah! To our husbands. You mark my words. They are up to no good. Why, in my day, we'd—"

"Looks like your day has passed, lady." The blonde one stood her ground, the brunette at her side hanging back a little. She looked like she'd been talked into it and just wanted an excuse to leave.

Crap on a cracker. Fighting words. I cringed. "Now, I think it would be best if you two would put on a dress or some pants or something. You might not realize it, but the sun in Snowy Lake is lethal to exposed skin. Very aging. Something to do with the huge amount of ultraviolet rays getting through the large ozone hole in the atmosphere right above us. And a hat or scarf wouldn't be a bad idea. Don't want to age a year or two in one day, now do you?"

The two twenty-somethings looked skyward, then gave a horrified look around at all the faces pressing in on them. "Yes. You're right. I don't want to prematurely age," the blonde announced, grabbing the brunette's arm and turning to leave.

Whew. The two women strutted through the reluctantly parting crowd. *Best show in months, probably since John Cooper and Erin Johnson ran down Main Street in their skivvies at the stroke of midnight New Years' Eve, drunk and waving a beaver crossing flag.* That reminded me that I had to get the list for the New Years' Day Polar Bear swim volunteers ready. That always brought in a nice chunk of cash for the town. Months early, but we could never be too prepared. It would be winter before we knew it.

"Well, I never." Mrs. Smith put her hand to her pearls, and a few women crowded around to offer their undying support.

"I'm sure you haven't," came one last parting shot accompanied by one last hand gesture from the blonde. She'd better be careful or she'd need to hire bodyguards to protect those gorgeous blonde locks. This crew could easily snatch her bald.

Well, my job there was done. I wormed my way back to the outside of the crowd. Tulip followed, still breathing hard.

"Didn't see that one coming," she said, swiping the sweat from her brow. "Emma have anything useful to add?"

"Not really, but I found out that the jam was from an earlier batch, making it accessible to more people. I need to talk to Christine Blackmore now. Have you seen her?"

"She gave a small donation, said she had no time to bake, about an hour ago. Not sure when she went after that."

"I'll head over to her place. You got this?" I nodded toward the bake sale.

"Yeah, thanks for helping out. You know, I've been reading more about edibles online. Cannabis has a proven track record for a lot of medical conditions, like chemotherapy nausea, weight loss and vomiting, neurogenic pain, asthma, epilepsy, glaucoma, bipolar disorder, Tourette's Syndrome, arterial blockages, Alzheimer disease, autoimmune disease, blood pressure disorders, Aids wasting, multiple sclerosis." She ticked them off on her fingers, rushing to finish her rant.

"I can't talk about it right now. Besides, it's already available for medical conditions. You know. Where's this coming from, Tulip?"

"Well, some people won't go to their doctor for a problem around here. You know how entrenched the history of doing for yourself is. So I thought we could fill a niche. Plus, it would control having it laced with something far worse for you or made too strong. Most people just want a little relief, not be blown away. They still need to work and live their lives."

"I gotta go. We'll talk about this later." And I'd put the kybosh on it then. *Not going to happen, not now, not ever.* Granny Toogood would never agree. At least I'd have her on my side, and probably Auntie T.J. as well, effectively outvoting my enterprising fellow-triplets. There was nothing to worry about there, though the extra money would have been nice.

I hurried back to Thor—who was now blocking traffic—and jumped inside. *Christine Blackstone, here we come.*

I made a swift U-turn on Main Street—common practice—and was shocked to see sirens blaring and a flashing red light out of the corner of my eye. *Oh, boy.* Maybe it wasn't so common anymore.

I put on my flashers, pulling to the right-hand side of the road.

I rolled down the window, all too aware that we had an interested crowd of spectators. And who came strutting up in all his lawman glory…

"Mornin', Miss McCall. May I see your license and registration, please?" His low-timbred voice resonated, making me wish for a nice cold glass of water.

I reached over and fumbled with the latch on Thor's glovebox. *Please, please let the official papers be in there where I placed them months ago.* Being stopped by a policeman—well, it had never happened. Ever. Until today.

Thankfully, they were right where they were supposed to be.

"Something wrong, Officer?" I asked, handing over the documents.

He raised his eyebrows under his hat, giving me a quizzical look. "I believe you like to read, correct, Miss McCall?"

"Ah, you know that."

"Then, pray tell, why have you not taken note of the No U-turn signs situated at *both* ends of Main Street?"

"Oh—that. Nobody pays it any mind." I chuckled with relief.

"Really? Well, time to let everyone know that times are a-changin'. There's a fine for pulling a U-turn where you're not supposed to. Pretty hefty one, as I recall." He tipped his hat back, giving me a steady look that mesmerized me.

"O-kay. I'll keep that in mind. Can I go now?"

"No. You broke the law. Wait here. I need to check your ID with the dispatcher."

"For heaven's sake! I just did a common practice. Why are you dinging me? And why aren't you out catching a killer instead of working traffic detail?" My Irish sense of centuries of being put upon reared. I made a gesture to open the driver's door and he stopped me with a look.

"I said, wait here. And as it happens, officers in this town are expected to do it all. Captain's exact words."

Sounded like something Captain Winn Duffy, the banker's brother-in-law, would say. "Delores will vouch for me. I've never had a ticket, never driven drunk, never been thrown in jail," I grumbled. Delores was not only the long-time RCMP dispatcher, she was an old friend of our family.

"Fine. Let me write that ticket and I'll be on my way then. There's a new way of doing things in this town, and it starts right here. No breaking the law — any law. Understood? It's nothing personal, Miss McCall. Could have been anyone made the illegal U-turn and I would have stopped them. If it helps, I wish it wasn't you." He pulled out his ticket book from his back pocket, in preparation.

"Could you be *charmed* into just giving me a warning, Officer? I hate to ruin my perfect record with a ticket. I make a mean pot roast." I batted my eyes, wanting to save myself an expensive ticket that I really couldn't afford. I'd be scrubbing floors at the detachment to pay for it.

"Are you trying to bribe an officer of the law?" Was that a twinkle in his eye?

"No." I shook my head emphatically. "I'd never do that either. But if you could see your way to cut me a break, I'd be ever so grateful."

"Like make me dinner or something?" He paused in writing out the ticket.

"Oh, you want *me* to make *you* dinner? I hardly think that's a fair trade." *'Don't give in too easy, sweeting, a man only respects what he has to win over.'* My granny's words, not mine.

"Oh, yeah. The fine will set you back more than a few groceries. Heck, I'll even throw in the steaks and cook them on the barbeque, if you have one?"

"Well, can't pass up that opportunity. Make it steaks for a dinner of — let's see, there's Granny, Star, Tulip and Auntie T.J., you and I. Adds up to seven." My inner goddess roiled at my idiocy while his face tightened, his Adam's apple moving up and down while he swallowed. "Nah, just kidding. Steaks for two, if you'll bring the wine?"

"Ma'am, you strike a hard bargain. But I've been raised a gentleman, so I'll go along with it. Say tonight? Seven p.m.?"

"Sounds good. What's your favorite dessert, Constable?"

He smiled for the first time, a thoughtful expression on his handsome mug. "Anything with chocolate."

"Hmm, one of those, eh."

He raised his eyebrows in query.

"One of the thirteen out of ten chocoholics."

He snorted.

"I know. Lame. Catch you later."

I left him in a small cloud of dust. *No point in pushing it.*

Taking a deep breath, I pulled into Christine and Sean Blackmore's driveway on Ring Road, about half a block from Mrs. Hurst's. Their house was just as impressive, but not quite as large. It featured an indoor swimming pool, which set it apart in our town. It was the only one, not counting the public wading pool open in the summer for Moms & Tots.

I'd have thought that a pair of families which rivaled the Hatfields and McCoys back in the day would live at opposite ends of town, but that was incorrect. The history between the founding families included a gold mine dispute that had never been settled, and a parcel of land with an iffy title. But this generation had mostly put it to rest. Other than a war of words on a few occasions, things had gone smoothly. And here was Christine actually checking on Mrs. Hurst to see if she was faring well. And why don't I believe that?

I scrambled out of Thor and hurried down the walk to the steps. The knocker on the front door was impressive. A lion with a huge mane. I gave it a couple of loud wacks and waited.

Chapter Fourteen

"What a surprise. I wasn't expecting to see you today." Christine's mouth, puffy from all the filler injections, turned down at the corners before she gave me the tiniest smile. She had that high-class trailer-trash look down to a T, in tight, tight black suede pants and a matching low-necked black lace top. She'd had so much work done that her expression was invisible. Seven years older than Boyd, she worked hard to appear the same age. Worked as if she was striving for a plastic doll look with an unmovable face. She was very pretty in an exotic way, though, her deep mahogany-colored hair styled into a mass of long wavy curls. Her ample money bought her a lifestyle I didn't envy—which might have surprised her, if truth were told—one of constant doubt.

"Well, I was in the neighborhood and thought I might talk with you about a matter of some importance. Mind if I come in?"

She shrugged but left the door ajar.

I walked inside, trying not to breathe too deeply. Her strong perfume was making my eyes water.

She perched on the expensive-looking white-leather living room sofa, making a limp-wrist gesture at me to have a seat. I sat across from her, though I wanted to sit right beside her. But she might have found that too odd and clammed up on me.

"What is it you want?"

She'd always been a woman of few words, until she got mad. *Then look out. The old adage you can't stop a woman when she's out of control goes double for Christine.* "I imagine you know about the murders?"

She checked her perfect nails, carefully inspecting for a flaw in the burgundy-colored tips, and didn't bother to answer. Was she not upset that her husband's best friend was dead?

"I was wondering if you could tell me about the last conversation you had with Mrs. Hurst?"

"Why? What's it to you?"

"My jam has been spurned due to this whole debacle, and I need to get to the bottom of it." I tamped down my anger.

"That's right." She finally looked me in the eye, a gleam suggesting she approved. *Good way to rule yourself out, Christine.* I should have sat next to her. It would have made it easier to choke her.

"And I need to find out all the facts."

"Don't you think Constable Ace Collins can handle it just fine?" It wasn't a question, but was accompanied by a smirk. "He seems very capable. And he's got a real nice hat. I don't imagine many women in this town wouldn't like that trophy on their mantel, and those extra-large-sized boots."

"I have a personal stake here. Please, for my family's sake, I need to get to the bottom of this." Begging pained me more than she knew.

"Okay." She sighed loudly. "Mrs. Hurst and I had one of our regular arguments. Like I told Ace..."

First name basis already. My heart skipped a full beat.

"...we've never seen eye to eye. She was such a difficult person to deal with." Her mouth finally moved a bit more, twisting into a grimace.

"What was the nature of the argument?"

"Same old. She loved to slander Sean, make all kind of accusations, stab me in the heart whenever she could. Evil witch."

"Would you have any objections to my doing a reading on you?"

"What? You know I don't believe in such silly things." The frown didn't quite make it through the fillers, but the eye scorn managed a direct hit.

I got up and sat beside her, surprising her. She squirmed back in her seat. "Then you won't care if I try, because you know I'll not discover anything, right?"

"Then why bother?"

"Please. For Granny Toogood."

I had her there. Her eyes softened for a moment. Everyone in Snowy Lake loved our granny. She'd taken in so many strays over the years, for a day or month or two if the case warranted it, making sure of everyone's welfare. No one did without in our town. Granny would have been up in arms. She even led the Christmas Hamper Drive every fall to make darn sure each family had a turkey and a country ham with all the fixings for the big day.

"Okay." She gave a louder sigh. "What do I do?"

"Just give me your hands and think of Mrs. Hurst. The last time you saw her."

She dutifully closed her eyes, offering up her paws with their fancy claws.

Holding her hands in mine, I closed my eyes, praying I would find something of import. The image that coalesced in her mind was of Mrs. Hurst loaded for bear and pointing a finger, her face an alarming shade of magenta. The usual confrontational stance, à la Hatfield versus McCoy.

"Think harder. The *very* last time you saw her, please."

"I *am*."

But behind the first image, another one pieced itself together. I struggled to see it as it wobbled in and out of focus. Mrs. Hurst lying on the floor. Dead. My heart thudded hard. Had Christine really done it? Murdered the poor woman?

"Okay, I confess. I saw Mrs. Hurst that final day." Christine's hands trembled in mine. "But I didn't kill her. She was already dead when I got there."

I held on to her hands, tighter. "Think about my apricot jam. When did you last see a jar of it?"

"What? You think I poisoned your jam? That's crazy!" She tried pulling her hands away, but I kept an iron grasp.

"Just think about the jam. Last thing I'll ask of you, Christine. It could clear you. We both want that, right?" I kept my eyes closed as I tried to push her into cooperating.

"Okay." The word came out on a gust of expelled air.

The jar she envisioned was tipped over on Mrs. Hurst's kitchen table, dripping down onto the floor.

"Did you touch it?"

"No." She shook her head so emphatically I felt the breeze.

"How come no one saw you there?" Ace needed to know this. ASAP.

"I came in the back after Suzanna left. Went out the same way."

"Why were you there? You hated the woman, remember."

"I had to give her something. Something she demanded from me." She hedged, trying not to give the game away.

"Was it money?"

"How did you know?"

"Was she blackmailing you?"

She wrestled her hands from mine. I let her, opening my eyes to catch her horrified expression. I actually felt sorry for her at that moment, more so when tears filled her hazel-colored eyes.

"She was a hateful woman. But I didn't kill her, Charm, you have to believe me. I'd never do that. I'd rather pay forever." It was as though the walls of Jericho came tumbling down,. I'd never seen a person's façade crack faster.

"What was she blackmailing you about?"

"Phhht. What wasn't she trying to take advantage of? Sean's affairs, my health problems."

"I'm sorry. I didn't realize you had health concerns."

"No, I'm fine now, but the damage was done. It was before I married Sean. She threatened to tell him about it."

"I don't think Sean would be so callous as to throw that in your face." Confused, I gave her a look of disbelief. A philanderer, oh yeah, but that callous? No way I could see it of a human being walking upright.

"He would if he knew that I can never have his son. The one he's always going on about."

"Oh. Infertility. And she threatened to tell Sean." Now *that* made sense. It was no secret that the man wanted children, probably the only reason he stayed married to Christine. Well, that and all that lovely family money.

"I don't know what I'd do if Sean left me. I love him, Charm, plain and simple. But I'd never kill anyone over it. You have to believe me."

"You could adopt. Or try in vitro. There must be some way."

She shook her head. "He wants his own kids. And my time's running out. He's starting to ask questions. Why is it taking so long? If I bring up in vitro, he's going to get suspicious. And my doctor doubts it would work. Everything's so scarred from an infection."

"But I don't understand how Mrs. Hurst knew about all this? Medical records are confidential."

"That witch. She knew *everything* that went on in this town. She bought and sold information like a commodity. Kept her filthy rich. I doubt anyone misses her."

"Her niece Emma does."

"Oh, I'm sorry. Yes, of course."

Her tune had taken a one-eighty, but I believed most of her story. It had the ring of truth.

"Can you clear me, Charm? What did you see? Did you see the murderer?"

"I can only see the murderer if I'm holding *their* hands." It looked like us psychic trackers had a new convert. I wasn't quite sure how to take it, but it was refreshing.

"Then you don't think I did it?"

"I'm not one hundred percent certain. But I didn't see you put anything into the jam."

Her hazel eyes lit up. "What if I think about Boyd and you come up with nothing? Would that help?"

"We could try." The breakthrough with Christine boggled my mind, almost like she was seeing me as a friend. I suddenly expected the Earth to quit spinning or gravity to be a no-show.

She grasped at my hands, dutifully closing her eyes. *O – kay.*

"The last time I saw Boyd..." she murmured, reinforcing my usual directive.

I took up her sweaty hands, feeling her agitation. I bent to the task of refocusing. It took a bit more time, as she was too agitated at first, but slowly an image emerged. Boyd in their living room, sitting about where I was sitting now, drinking a beer, laughing at something being said. Nothing conclusive.

"You sure that was the last time?" She could be trying to pull the wool over my eyes, as Granny liked to say.

"Yes. He came over for a barbecue a couple of days ago. He seemed fine."

"How's Sean taking his death?"

I felt her body lift in a shrug, even with my eyes closed. "Okay, I guess. You know Sean. Likes to hide his feelings. Real macho stuff."

"Machoism's alive and well in Snowy Lake, I'll give you that."

She chucked. A sound I'd never thought to hear in my lifetime. "Yeah, you got that right."

"You know you'll have to share all this with the police, right?"

She pulled away, and I let her hands go, opening my eyes. She stared at me in horror. "But they'll think I did it!" Her voice had gone screechy enough that I worried the overhead chandelier might be in jeopardy.

"Maybe not. No more than they think I did it, anyway. They need your facts to get to the culprit. Look into the blackmail angle. See who else was in the same position. We can't have a murderer running loose in our town, Christine."

She swallowed, her eyes round and staring. "Oh lord, could you go with me, Charm, help me explain?"

"I-I don't know," I stuttered. I hadn't seen this coming.

"Please. I need your help — as a friend."

Now I'm in the friend category. My life was filling up faster than a hot stripper's G-string at the Boots & Lace dancehall.

Against every bit of better judgment I possessed, I found myself nodding. "Sure. Do you want to take care of it now?"

She swallowed hard again, her eyes showing the tug of war within. She sat up straighter. "Yes, darn it, let's get it over with."

"Good choice." I smiled my agreement and got up. "Do you want to head over in my jeep?"

"Sure. Why not? Always fancied a ride in a Cherokee."

Who was this woman? Had I inadvertently placed some kind of spell on her? So many strange things had happened in the last forty-eight hours that there was no point in dwelling on this one. Especially since I applauded the change.

We two-stepped out of the front door and she closed it behind us, taking a moment to lock it. She caught me watching her, looking up from slipping the house keys into her pocket. "Don't normally do this, but with what's going on—"

"Couldn't agree more."

She hustled to my jeep and swung her long legs inside. Holding one hand to the doorframe, she leaned forward, more animation on her gorgeous face than I'd seen…ever.

"Like that gangster hunk said in the movie *GoodFellas*, 'Now take me to jail.'"

"Okay." I gave her a positive smile and hustled us over to the RCMP detachment, paying attention to all the road rules. I didn't want to be on the hook for a second dinner. *Or do I?*

Chapter Fifteen

The low-rise building that housed the small RCMP force flew the distinctive red and white Canadian maple leaf flag out front. The proud standard waved softly in the fresh breeze drifting in off the lake our town was named after. The flag stood atop a tall pole that was surrounded by a flowerbed of well-attended matching petunias, courtesy of the town's Hospital Guild ladies. My granny always insisted on leaving flowers at the base whenever an officer in Canada was killed in the line of duty. The thought came back to haunt me now. Suddenly, it was personal. I was beginning to know one annoying constable a bit too well.

I parked my trusty friend along the curved driveway, leaving room for other vehicles to get by. As I'd never been to the police station for anything formal, just Officer Appreciation Day each spring, knots began to test intricate new designs in my stomach. Why did I feel guilty when I had nothing to be guilty about? Cops probably counted on that instinctive response. *Right?*

Christine didn't jump out straightaway either. She paused with her hand on the door handle. I pasted a smile on my face, announcing unnecessarily, "Okay. We're here. You want to take lead?"

"Ah, sure. I just need someone to have my back."

"Okay, we go on three. One, two, three…"

We both moved in unison, closing Thor's doors with extra-loud bangs. I winced, asking his forgiveness.

"Lovely weather we're having," I said. I envisioned a treat of fresh-made brownies at the end of the impending interview to make my feet move quicker. The way my breath was hitching in my chest, I just might need Tulip's asthma inhaler before this day ended.

I opened the front door for Christine. "Go ahead."

She did, but stopped so short I ran into the back of her. She'd nearly collided with Captain Winn Duffy, on his way out.

"Christine, sorry, I almost ran you down there." He noted me lurking behind her. "Charm, what can I do for you lovely ladies?"

"I've come about Mrs. Hurst. I have some information that Charm thinks is important to Constable Collins' investigation. Could we see him, please?"

The rather ordinary-looking middle-aged man with the salt-and-pepper brush cut pursed his lips, his dark eyes gleaming with intelligence. A big man with a slight belly that rode his black belt, he was a no-nonsense cop by reputation. His expression remained cordial as he gave us an appraisal.

"Constable Collins is at his desk." He turned his hefty body half-around. "Delores," he shouted out. "Take care of these young ladies. They want to see our new Mountie, just like all the others. Apparently, I'm the old hat around here, even if I do have my own southern roots."

He turned back to address us. "Delores will help you. Now, if you'll excuse me, ladies, I'm headed out."

We scrambled out of the way. I led the way over to the dispatcher's desk, Christine trailing me.

"You here to see our new Mountie too, eh? Been quite a crime spree going on in Snowy Lake yesterday and today, besides the obvious." Her expression turned momentarily serious at the mention of the murders before she resumed. "Everything from dog nappings to neighbour parking disputes." Delores's expression could not have been smugger. A woman of a certain age, she'd been in her job for as long as I could remember. A motherly type, she virtually ran the detachment, like all strong women do. Her dyed brown hair was sprayed into a helmet, her makeup flattering. She was an easy woman to like. "And I'll be asking after your Granny as well. She holding out all right with all this ruckus about?"

"She's fine. Thanks for asking. I sent her with Auntie T.J. to visit her sister in Winterville yesterday. But we're expecting her back sometime today or tomorrow."

Delores nodded approval. "Best she stays away until these murders are solved. Gives me the willies, thinking such things can happen here. Winn's even talking about starting a Neighborhood Watch program. The Bear Clan that set up in Winnipeg a few years ago to patrol the streets to keep that city safer has even offered their help and expertise."

"That's good to hear." I added my approval.

"I'm here to tell some things I know about the murders." Christine finally found her voice, stepping forward.

Delores' eyes rounded and she nodded. "Stay here." She took off at a fair clip and shouted from the back of the detachment fifteen seconds later.

"Come on down. The constable will see you now."

We followed her voice, passing her in the hallway as she bustled to her desk in reception.

I gestured for Christine to lead the way into the office, finding my feet reluctant to take the final last steps. This was a little too official.

Constable Ace Collins sat behind a desk strewn with loose sheaves of paper and baskets of homemade goodies. As we came through the doorway, he was busy making piles. Were they all the complaints he'd been subject to for the past two days? *Got to hand it to the women of Snowy Lake. They know how to throw a welcome party.*

"Please, sit down." He gestured at the chairs in front of his desk, tucking enough of the paper away into folders and trays and setting the baking aside to make his desk somewhat presentable.

"So, what can I do for you?" He looked awesome sitting behind the desk, big and in charge. His presence fueled the room with enough electrical current that I half-expected to see the sparks flare into fireworks at any second.

"Christine has some things she wants to share with you about Mrs. Hurst and the day she died."

"Okay." He sat forward, leaned his elbows on the top of the wooden desk and tented his large hands. "I'm listening."

He gave Christine his undivided attention while she spilled her story, only asking relevant questions when the facts weren't clear.

"And now I'm scared, Constable. Am I in trouble?"

"It would have been better if you had come forward sooner, but since you've had a change of heart and are wanting justice done for the victims, we may be able to overlook the obstruction of justice considerations."

Christine fidgeted in her chair, which had to be as uncomfortable as mine. I swear they had cut the legs down lower on our chairs, the way the new Mountie loomed over us. Nah, that was just something rumored to happen on talk shows where the hosts had pumpkin-sized egos.

"Did you see Boyd the night he was murdered?" he asked.

"No, not at all." She shook her head so emphatically her mahogany curls swung and swiped me across the chin. I leaned sideways to get out of the line of fire, casually pulling a strand of loose hair from the corner of my mouth and letting it drift to the floor.

"The blackmail angle is important. I'll need to go through all her bank records and check."

My stomach somersaulted and landed somewhere out in the lake a quarter mile away. Well, if confession was good for my new friend… Maybe Ace wouldn't throw my butt in jail. *Yeah, right. And Ling Ling can't spell.*

"Ah, is there any leeway for some amnesty for me too if I make a confession? Or maybe a pardon later, after things calm down and cooler heads prevail?"

Ace swung his penetrating stare my way. "Go ahead, Miss McCall. Shoot."

I felt like a butterfly pinned in place. Christine reached over and took my hand. The gesture caught me unprepared and a tear actually escaped. I looked down at my lap, finding a piece of fuzz on my jeans of extreme interest. I added it to the bright hair on the floor.

"I have Mrs. Hurst's banking records for the past year."

Silence.

I risked a peek through lowered lashes. *Oh boy.* He was livid, his skin stippled in shades of varying shades of red. I admired his control as he pressed his lips firmly together, lips that I had enjoyed kissing less than twenty-four hours ago.

"I want those records on my desk. Today. Understood?"

"Yes, they will be."

His desk phone buzzed and, with a second glare in my direction, he answered it. "Constable Collins here. How may I help you?"

I nudged Christine, giving her a nod at the escape hatch, the open doorway. She gave a quick thumbs-up and we got to our feet in tandem.

Ace put his hand over the receiver. "Thank you, Christine, for coming forward." *What? No thanks for me?* "And I'll be expecting those stolen documents from you, Charm, within the hour."

My eyes narrowed at the offensive word, wanting to debate it hotly since I'd planned to return the records, but instead I let Christine propel me out of the room.

I stormed down the hallway, my boots ringing satisfyingly on the tiled black and white floor. I gave Delores a pasted-on smile to offset my apparent rush and made it out to Thor in record time. Christine got in the other side and leaned back in the seat.

"I think that went well."

"Yeah, really great. I got called a thief." I could barely get the word out, my chest walls squeezing in from all sides. *Can someone get asthma all of a sudden? Or maybe this is what a panic attack feels like? Or do I have heart problems?*

"Oh, I don't think he was all that serious about it, Charm. He's a very nice lawman."

"Phttt, yeah, right," I muttered under my breath, feeling put upon. "About as serious as a heart attack. He's got it in for me, I tell you. You know he was going to give me a ticket for doing a U-turn on Main Street? Can you believe that?"

"I think he likes you. He didn't actually give you a ticket, right?"

"Not the point. He stopped me, and I had to bribe him."

"Oh really, with what? A lot of women in town would like that secret."

"Dinner, what else?"

"Good one. What are you cooking?"

"Aw, well, he's bringing the steaks and wine," I admitted. "Guess I'm to make some sides as my contribution."

"Oh, Charm, the guy's got it bad for you!" Christine laughed out loud, not helping my mood at all. "Well, you'd best get me home. You have an errand to run, remember?"

"Yeah, and a murder to solve." I gave a deep sigh.

She nodded sagely, not looking at all like the old Christine. I had to admit, I liked her far better now. Maybe some day I'd be able to help her too.

I dropped her off at home few minutes later, then set my sights on getting back to my suite to retrieve the folder. The clock was once more blasting away in my head. *Tick tock. Tick tock.*

I pulled in behind the café and leaped from Thor's front seat, intent on my mission. I missed seeing Mrs. Smith in the alley until she was planted right square in front of me.

"I need your help! It's my daughter. She's in town and has lost her engagement ring, of *all* things. Do you think you could give her a reading right now? Help her locate it?" The words tumbled out of the woman, highly unusual for someone who prided herself on her composure. And it was beyond weird to accost me in the alley.

"Uh, I have something really important I'm supposed to do. Could this wait a bit?" I ventured. An image of Ace at his desk, mad as a buck about to stomp a competitor, drove me forward.

"Please, I wouldn't ask if it wasn't important," she begged. "I'll pay you double your usual fee if you'll do it right away. Everyone is just so upset by this. Her fiancé just can't know. He's such a catch too." She lowered her voice and added in a conspiratorial tone, "One of the Davidsons. She did *so* well by herself and then this has to happen." Our Mrs. Smith was fine after all—perfectly self-absorbed as usual, if I didn't take into account the harried look in her eyes. "Alison's already inside speaking with your granny. I just wanted to touch base with *you* and tell you how very important this is to our family. We can't have a whiff of this getting back to the Davidsons. My goodness." The woman shook her head. "Could you just imagine the scandal?"

Not really, but the woman was being sincere in her own way. But oh shoot, Granny was back. And the murderer was still on the loose.

Chapter Sixteen

I sighed out loud. "Okay, but I don't have much time. There's something I have to take care of that has a very, very sensitive timeline."

"Thanks. I'm certain that it won't take you but a sec."

"Let's hope so."

I followed Mrs. Smith inside the back of the café into the kitchen, noting how she managed to keep her hair so perfect all day long, while mine, I knew without looking in a mirror, needed a thorough redoing from all the running around. It had strands coming loose and moving about willy-nilly. Well, that had to wait as well. *Do a reading. Get banking records. Then have a tantrum.* And maybe not in that precise order…

"Granny," I said, embracing my favorite person in all the world when she came forward to greet me.

"Sweeting. You're looking a bit stressed." She tucked a lock of hair behind my ear, giving my cheek a gentle pinch.

"I'm okay." I hid my worry, giving her a bright smile.

"Hi, Charm," Alison greeted me, getting up from the kitchen table and walking over to join us.

"Alison. How are you?" A carbon copy of her mom, Alison gave me a meek look from under her perfect brown bangs and ponytail.

"I've been better. Seems I've misplaced my engagement ring and Justin—my new fiancé—is expected to visit later today. Can you help me?"

"I'll try. There's never any guarantee, but I have a good record."

"Charm can find anything," Mrs. Smith added her vote of confidence with an edge to her tone that suggested I'd better live up to her prediction.

Alison nodded. "Is here okay?" She gestured around the room. "You know, to do the reading?"

"Sure, why not?" It would be faster. *Tick tock. Tick tock.* "Let's sit at the table."

We sat and I took her cool hands in mine. "Okay, close your eyes and think of the last time you saw the ring."

She closed her eyes, her hands trembling a bit. An image of the ring on her left hand came to mind, not helping at all.

"Think of the last time you took it off," I encouraged her, worrying that nothing was coming up.

Alison shivered, a grimace creasing the smooth skin of her face. She was blocking the image for some reason. Very strange. Maybe her mother was more enamored of her daughter marrying a Davidson than she was?

"Oh, for heaven's sake, what do you see, Charm?" Mrs. Smith's impatient voice cut through the room, making her daughter open her eyes, the expression within their deep pools of blueness worried and upset. And was that a touch of fear?

"Please, give me a moment," I murmured. But the impatient mother pulled up a chair in her efforts to encourage results, and her settling in so close threatened to derail things. Alison tugged her hands away from mine, hugging them close to her sides.

"Alison," her mother chastised. "You must try harder. We must protect the family's reputation. If this gets out..."

I reached out and slipped my right hand over Mrs. Smith's, encouraging her to pull back a bit. A terrifying cold seeped into my hand when our fingers touched, one almost burning in its intensity. I lurched in my chair when an image sprang fully formed in my mind, blurring my vision. I closed my eyes, unable to see anything but Mrs. Smith doing the unthinkable. Sour bile rose in my chest. What to do?

I opened my eyes and found Mrs. Smith staring at me, her blue eyes colder than the thick ice that remained frozen year-round circling the Artic Circle. I forced my face into some semblance of order, not wanting the woman to know about the scene she'd just exposed of her hitting her daughter. And her slanderous thoughts about Star being too popular for her own good. That her daughter should have been given her gifts.

"Alison, sit up and cooperate," her mother demanded, taking her hands away from mine and tugging at her daughter's shoulder to grab her attention.

Did she know what I had just seen? She appeared to be more interested in the engagement ring than anything else. *Thank the goddess.* I didn't want to be in on such dreadful family secrets, or the disgusting envy of others. But, too late for that.

I reluctantly took her daughter's hands again. We were both trembling. My teeth ached from the effort not to allow them to chatter with the dismal shock.

I closed my eyes, trying to see what I needed to see. The sooner I could get them out of here the better. *Tick tock. Tick tock.*

The ring flashed forward in my mind, the large solitaire faceted diamond gleaming in the darkness before the scene lightened a bit, showing it lying under something.

"I see it. It's under a bed, tucked just between where the carpet is joined. It's caught there, between the threads. Oh, and the bed is one with pink ruffles and an overhead canopy."

I opened my eyes, relieved, but my body was still roiling from the ordeal. I could not imagine such a thing happening in our little town. In some ways, it felt as bad a murder. *Does it matter more if the spirit or the body is harmed?* Alison gave me a wan smile. I wanted to hug her close, not let her go. Was the hitting still happening? What should I do? What should I say?

"Thanks, that's my bedroom," Alison said.

"Oh, thank the good Lord above." Mrs. Smith was all smiles, the coldness of her demeanor covered up with satisfaction. But I knew I would never see the woman in the same light again.

"Alison, please, if you could give me your hands one more time."

Surprised, she did what I asked, offering them freely. I went back to the trance, seeking entry to any problems in her body. Finding none, I nodded. The hitting had not been recent. Maybe not for years. Still, it gave me a sense of disquiet. What should I do about it? "Thanks, it's all good now. Let me know how things go, okay? If you ever need a friend, I'm here for you."

Mrs. Smith gave me a mistrusting look through the wreath of smiles, tugging her daughter to her feet. A chill sluiced through me.

She pushed a few bills at me and hurried Alison from the café.

"What did you see, child?"

Granny took Alison's seat at the table, her kind eyes concerned for my welfare. I bit my lip, trying to find the right words. In the end, I just spilled it.

"June has always had a bit of a mean streak — needing to control everything and everyone around her," Granny said after absorbing the information. "Too worried about social conventions by half. It's been hard on her family. And I believe Alison has taken the brunt of it." She sighed and patted my hand. "But she's a big girl now. Time for her to make her own life. You said it hadn't been recent abuse, yes?"

"I don't think so." I shook my head, pondering.

"There's something else we need to talk about, sweeting."

"Okay." I glanced at Granny, a frown knitting her brow. *Oh boy, now what?*

"Helen came by the café just after your aunt dropped me off. Oh, and don't think I don't know what you were up to, missy, sending me away on a fool's errand. My sister could not act her way out of a wet paper bag."

I blushed. "I wanted to solve the murder — murders," I corrected. "Before you were touched by them. I didn't want you hurt."

"I'm a strong woman, Charm Mary McCall. You need me more right here — you all do. This affects our whole family and we will figure things out together."

I nodded, properly chastised. Granny almost never used my full name.

"Now, there's something else needs mentioning first. Helen has told me what you did for her."

I fidgeted in my seat. There was no time for this discussion right now, but I couldn't get up for the life of me, pinned firmly in place, revisiting my recent experience.

"It just happened." I shrugged and glanced at the clock. Forty-five minutes had passed. *Tick tock.*

"The experience with Helen, the gift of healing, that only comes with the firstborn of our bloodline. Your sisters, on the other hand, may receive different abilities. I have never shared your heritage with all of you, and that's on me. I had hoped perhaps it would skip this generation. Prayed to the goddess about it. Such heavy responsibilities come with it for one so young." She shook her head, her lips pressed together. "So much will be asked of you, child, once word spreads."

"What do you mean?" My breath froze in my lungs. A sense of impending information that would shift the entire direction of my life had me ready to leap up. *Escape.* I wanted to block my ears. Turn away. But some part of me needed to hear it. That part made me stay, glued to my seat. The ticking second hand no longer seemed to matter.

"We haven't always made our home in Canada, sweeting. Before we emigrated here, we lived in Salem, Massachusetts. In the seventeen-hundreds. Back in the time of the accursed witch trials."

"Witch trials?" Confused, I shook my head, the words falling out of me unbidden. "What? Are you saying we came from that horror?"

"Yes, our family was persecuted by their neighbors. At that time, it was too easy to point fingers. Superstitions and ignorance reigned in the New World. It was a brutal time to try to scratch out a living. It was far too easy to covet what good people had worked so hard to build — try to tear it all down or take it for your own." Her eyes glazed over as she spoke, reliving a personal horror. "A terrible black mark on history. I only bring it up now to explain your heritage." She stopped to take a deep, shuddering breath.

"What happened to our ancestors? Who were they?"

"Your eighth-removed great-grandmother was a renowned midwife and healer from the old country. One of the last witches to be accused. Mary Sarah Toogood. Fortunately, she managed to escape with the help of her jailer, who took pity on her while accepting a substantial bribe. We are her descendants. Her blood runs through us. It gives the first female born of each matriarchal family the gift of healing in various degrees of strength. Yours is very powerful, sweeting. Thank the goddess you were born in this century."

A relieved expression came over her gentle face and she reached out to pat my hands where they were clenched on the tabletop. Her touch soothed me, giving me space to think.

I hesitated. I needed to know so much more. But where to start? But Granny continued without prompting.

"The part I hesitate to tell you, that I wish I didn't have to share quite yet — well, this part is a bit more difficult to explain."

January Bain

"Harder than burning so-called witches alive at the stake?" The shock was wearing off, filling me with indignation for the plight of innocents. It didn't matter that it had been long ago. And unlike what the bad mobster guy always parrots in the movies, it *was* personal.

"Yes, because it concerns a certain aspect of your gift." Granny sighed heavily and shifted in her chair.

"What about my gift?"

"Do you wonder why I don't have it—being firstborn?"

Confused, I chewed on my bottom lip, thinking. "But you have other gifts. You're the kindest, biggest-hearted person I know. Everyone loves you, Granny. Everyone." I nodded emphatically.

She smiled, a twinkle gleaming in her beautiful eyes. "Not everyone, sweeting, but it's nice to be appreciated."

"I'll never forget that you took us in." I wiped a tear threatening to run down my cheek. My best guess was that the last two days were catching up with me.

"You three have been the biggest blessings of my life." She patted my hand once more. "Now, the gift only passes to the firstborn if they reach the age of twenty-one and remain chaste."

"Chaste." The old-fashioned word challenged me. I shook my head. "You mean stay a virgin?"

"Yes, and she only keeps the gift if she marries her one true love. And never goes with another. Ah—physically, I mean, as well as spiritually, of course." Granny didn't meet my eye. I was suddenly too hot and as red as a beet from blushing. Yikes, but this conversation had taken an unforeseen twist.

I bit down on my lip, harder. "Does that mean that you—" I couldn't find the words. This was my granny, not some sex therapist. We never talked about such things. Rule number three, in fact. No swearing, no speaking ill of the dead and definitely no sex talk.

"I married your grandfather at eighteen and then met a man who was my one true love many years later, but that is another story for another day. And something I must share with you all before I pass on to let you know that what comes after this life—that it's all good. But, suffice to say, my ancient history took me out of the running to be a healer in this lifetime."

"O—kay." I kept looking over her shoulder, to my favorite picture on this year's calendar of snow-tipped Rocky Mountains gleaming in the golden sunshine. The month was January, and it was now July, but I wouldn't let anyone flip the page over, finding the image satisfying. Why change what works? Letting my Granny know I was still a virgin was weird in the extreme and gave me a sudden wish to be sitting on top of that mountain enjoying the view. And even thinking of her passing on, well, my mind refused to even go there. Ever.

Another thought occurred to me as I kept my eyes averted, one of vital importance.

"If it's that crucial to keeping the gift, how will I know for certain if he's the right one? I mean, life doesn't come with a bubble caption over anyone's head saying, 'he's the one, right here, Charm, look no further. Step right up!'"

Granny let loose a good belly laugh. She wiped her eyes on her ever-present apron.

"Don't worry, sweeting, you're a strong woman—you'll know. And he'll most likely annoy you until you accept the truth of the matter."

Loud noises made me start and look over in the direction they were coming from. Constable Ace Collins stood in the wide-open back door, big as life. *Oh, boy, the blasted time.* I looked over his head at the kitchen clock. Twelve-thirty. I grimaced. A half hour past the appointed hour.

"Mrs. Toogood. Miss McCall," he said, removing his Stetson, his thick hair gleaming in the overhead lights. He gave a polite nod in Granny's direction.

"Constable Collins," Granny said, her careworn face softening into a smile. "You must call me Granny. Everyone does."

He added a genuine smile. "Certainly, ma'am, it would be my honor. Granny it is." He looked at me now, his expression shifting. The man could talk a person into admitting just about anything he wanted. *Darn unfair.* "Do you have what you promised me a half hour ago, Miss McCall?"

I jumped up, the spell broken. "Right away. I'll just go get it." I dashed from the room before anyone could utter another word and raced up the stairs. Grabbing the offending file from my night table, I turned and retraced my footsteps back to the kitchen.

I handed Ace the file and, trying to soften things, added a brief ever-so-sorry-smile to the package with an impromptu curtsy.

He took it from me, his expression inscrutable, but I noticed a slight twitching of his lips. *Ha, got you.*

I glanced at Granny and found her smiling broadly.

"I've marked all the suspicious entries for you."

"Of course you have." He gave the file a cursory glance.

"Are we still on for that barbecue later?" I asked brightly, rocking back and forth on my heels, my hands tucked behind my back. Hopefully the picture of innocence. Maybe I needed to change my wardrobe? Buy a modest, frilly dress or three? *Nah, so not me.*

"I'm game, if you are. Best way I know how to keep an eye on you. Because if there ever was a woman who needed watching, it's you, Miss McCall."

"What? I've been nothing but helpful to the case. If you think I'll stand here and accept your verdict, Sheriff, then you have another think coming!"

"It's constable, ma'am."

"Why you —"

"Sweeting, I think you're needed in the café. I'll see the constable out."

The sounds of loud conversation slipped through the heat of my indignation. *Now what? One of the strippers get a little too friendly with someone's significant other?*

Chapter Seventeen

I forced my feet to walk the short distance from the kitchen into the café. I'd had enough shenanigans this week to take me well into Christmas, my favorite time of the year, when everything in the world came to a standstill and people were nicer. Twenty-four hours of bliss. And months away…

I let out a deep breath when I realized it was just Old Charlie and Tom Ferguson having the usual war of words. The pair hadn't seen eye-to-eye since Tom had stolen Charlie's girlfriend decades ago at a dance. They circled each other like lumbering bears, vying for a weak spot. *Oh, brother.*

"What can I get for you two gentlemen?" *Ha, not even close, but flattering the customer is always approved of by the owner of the café.* And I just wanted to serve them and get on with my investigation.

"Tom's buying," Old Charlie said, a gleam in his eyes. "Owes me, big time."

"I don't owe you anything, old man. In fact, you should be grateful I don't just—"

"No one's buying. It's on the house." I set aside my agitation at giving out more free food, but I had no time for their silliness today.

"In that case I'll have a dozen of the triple chocolate ones. And no poison, thank you very much."

I blessed Old Charlie with a hard glare, pressing my lips tightly together to keep my thoughts inside my head. *Remember he's a hermit, lost all his manners years ago, maybe a marble or three.*

I handed the treats over to the old geezer. Turning to Tom, I filled a box with his favorite gingersnaps.

I managed a squeaker of a smile.

Tom pulled a twenty from his pocket and pushed it into my hand, looking shamefaced. "Sorry, Charm."

"Nah, I'm paying!" Old Charlie thrust another twenty at me, crumpled up. "I'll not owe you a damn red cent, Ferguson."

"I think for the swearing they both owe us, don't you think so, sweeting?"

Granny walked over, giving the two men a stern glance with the warning.

I accepted the offerings with grace and watched the two men exit the café, praying they weren't our last customers of the day.

"Good job, Granny," I said.

"Don't know why feuds in this town never seem to end." She shook her head. "I'll take over now. You have more important things to get on with. We need an end to all this speculation."

"Thanks, Granny." I laid a quick kiss on her check then rushed back to the kitchen, intent on seeking out

Pastor Evans to see if he could shed some light on recent events.

I was already seated in my jeep when something fluttered under the driver's windshield wiper fluttered, catching my attention. Wait just a darn minute. Was that a ticket? Mr. Hot Stuff *had* just left the building. *How dare he?* Reaching around the front windshield, I tugged the white piece of paper from under the blade, not caring if I tore it to shreds in the process.

I unfolded the now slightly torn paper, expecting a summons for some imaginary offense. I stared in disbelief at the words obviously cut from some magazine and pasted together to craft a crude message. I had to read it a few times before the words sank in.

STAY OUT OF IT OR SOMEONE IN YOUR FAMILY WILL BE NEXT

Every drop of blood in my body froze solid. I shivered uncontrollably. Clutching the paper to my chest, I tried to think of what to do. I couldn't go back in and tell Granny — she might have a heart attack. My sisters were both busy working the final day of the festival.

Yes, of course, I saw clearly what I needed to do. Who I could share this with. I started Thor's motor with shaking fingers, put the jeep into drive and drove down the alley without being aware of doing it, just miming the actions until I arrived at my destination.

I stumbled out of the vehicle in the curved driveway and lurched toward the front door of the detachment.

Delores took one look at me and rushed to my side. "What's wrong, dear?" she asked, her voice coming at me through the mind fog.

"This." My hand fluttered about of its own volition.

She plucked the paper from my hand and read it.

"I'm sorry. It's going to be okay, Charm. Come, we need to show this to Constable Collins. He'll know what to do."

At that moment, he appeared from his office, striding down the hallway toward us. He glanced from Delores to me. "I'll take over now, thanks, Delores."

She nodded, handing him the paper.

"Are you okay?" he asked me, his expression concerned. I gulped, nodding once.

I watched him read the offensive words, his brow scrunching. He muttered an expletive under his breath, then looked down at me. "I'm sorry, Charm. But I don't want you to worry. We're going to make sure *nothing* happens to you or your family. Do you have any idea of who could have sent this?" He handed the paper back to Delores, holding it by the smallest bit of one corner between thumb and forefinger. "Get this dusted for fingerprints, please." She scurried off with it.

I shook my head. "I've ruled out some of the suspects. But I really have no idea who could have…sent this." I took a deep breath, finding it near impossible to imagine such a thing happening in our part of the world. "We've never had any real enemies in town that I know of. Just silly stuff growing up. You know, like kids get into." To think one of our neighbors would do such a thing hurt to the core.

And if not us, who next? The facts of the case made it so hard to keep everyone safe. Poison was a deadly killer. It was hard to know where it would be hidden in time to avoid consuming it. I shuddered again at an image of one of my sisters unknowingly eating the wrong thing.

I forced my mind away from the horrible thought and looked at Ace. "What are we going to do?"

"First off, we're going to round up your sisters and take them to the café. I want everyone in the same place where it will be easier to watch over you." His well-modulated tone soothed away my anguish, made me see there was a plan about to go into action. One to keep us all safe. I took a deep breath.

"Okay." I nodded. Concern for the festival had moved to the back of the line. "I'll go over there now and get them."

"I'm going with you."

"But—"

"No buts. You will listen to me from now on. You want your family to be safe, right?"

Had I caused this with all my snooping around? The thought made my insides clench into a fist and hurt all over again.

"Yes, of course I do."

"Then let's go. We'll take my cruiser."

We hurried from the station and into the white, blue and red RCMP vehicle with its 'to serve and protect' logo. Today I was seeing the words in action.

"Who have you talked with today? Other than Christine Blackmore?" he asked, intently watching the road as he drove. My foot pressed down on the floorboards, wanting the police vehicle to fly over to the fairgrounds. I bit my lip to keep from saying it out loud.

"Today? No one really. Just Mrs. Smith and her daughter Alison and a couple of customers—Old Charlie and Tom Ferguson, but they were too busy arguing to pay me much mind. Then ended up overpaying. Silly stuff."

"What did Mrs. Smith and Alison want?"

"Alison had lost her engagement ring. Mrs. Smith was frantic about it." I chewed on my thumbnail, my throat tightening. "I was able to help. See where it was hidden in the carpet under the bed."

"What about since the first murder?"

"Too many to be useful. But I specifically went looking for Sean Blackmore, Fred Smith, Boyd Thompson, Helen Davis and then ended up seeing her friend Elsie." I took a deep breath and continued my list. "Mrs. Hurst's maid Suzanna, and her niece Emma, and of course, a ton of people at the festival."

"Any readings you think I should know about?"

I shook my head, relieved to see we were turning onto the fairgrounds. "Well, Sean admitted people were being blackmailed by Mrs. Hurst. Boyd, his friend, was talked into giving her a new vehicle for almost nothing whenever she snapped her fingers. You already know about Christine, his wife."

Ace nodded. "Yes, all too true. There are a number of people with a motive. I've gotten the information out of Mr. Blackmore as well."

My heart sank. He was telling me in his own way that he was right on top of things, that I didn't have to draw such negative attention to myself. I bit the inside of my mouth, the metallic taste of blood making me grimace.

Soon as Ace cut the motor of the cruiser, we jumped out, striding side-by-side to the Tea & Tarot booth. Everyone else on the fairgrounds became a blur — I was too busy looking for my sisters to care about anything else.

"Hey, Charm," Tulip greeted me. I rushed to embrace her, so vigorous in my hugging that she began to protest.

"Hey, what's up?" she asked, pulling back and looking me square in the eyes.

"Just happy to see you."

"O — kay."

"There's been a threat against your family, Miss McCall. I'm afraid I'm going to have to ask you and your sister to come with me."

"What! No. That's crazy."

"Where's Star?" he asked, glancing around the area.

"She went to freshen up. She just finished singing a few minutes ago."

"Where did she go?" he asked, his eyes constantly scanning the area. He was dead serious about protecting us. Me too. My head spun in circles, keeping watch on everything and everyone at the same time, which was crazy because the murderer was obviously a coward, hiding behind death threats and poison.

"Over there." She pointed at the ladies' and men's bathrooms housed year-round in a squat blue building surrounded by a small oasis of cement. One side of the structure was for the females, one side for the males and another section reserved for families only. It had been built as a permanent structure a few years back, for the fair and other community happenings, including sporting events popular in the different seasons of the calendar. Everything from soccer to football to hockey and curling on our outdoor skating ring were popular in Snowy Lake.

"I'll go get her," I volunteered. It was only a hundred and fifty feet away but seemed to take forever. Time had a strange way of slowing down when each second counted.

"No, you wait here with your sister. I'll head inside," Ace said, catching up with me at the bathroom's entrance.

"But it's the ladies'," I said, confused, Tulip right on my heels.

"A lawman has clearance for this kind of thing in order to ensure the public safety. You both wait here."

It was then I realized he was packing heat, unlike me, and if something was going on, he'd be able to handle it, that he was fully trained for such things. The thought sent fear tearing through me and I pressed a hand to my chest. This had become something far beyond anything I could have imagined happening, placing everyone I cared deeply about in danger. Until now, it had been a whodunit for the most part, but now, with my family under siege, it was personal. Darn personal.

"What's going on, Charm?" Tulip's eyes had widened in fright. A crowd began to gather around us, but I ignored the looks of inquiry.

"I got a note — stuck on Thor's windscreen. It said to stay out of things — that my family could get hurt if I didn't." The words felt icy cold on my lips. I shivered in the warm afternoon sunshine.

"Really? That's horrible." Tulip put her arms around me, and we stood there together, waiting for the lawman to do his job.

I didn't dare breathe. I had to know that Star was safe and sound. A few seconds passed, and my legs began moving on their own, right in the direction of the door marked *Ladies*. I pushed it open and ran smack into Ace, Star in tow.

"Ma'am, we've got to stop meeting like this," he said in a deadpan manner, making me give a shaky bark of laughter as I backed away from him. I tugged my errant sister into my arms, her body closing around mine the best feeling in all the world.

"You arresting the whole family, Sheriff?" a smug voice rang out in the crowd. I spun around to see who it was. Sean Blackmore. *Figures.*

Ace gave a huge sigh. "First, I'm not a sheriff, and secondly, no, I am not arresting anyone at this time. The McCalls are just being given an escort to make sure they stay safe."

"But they are under suspicion, right?" he pressed, earning him a super-sized frown from me.

"What's going on? Are you okay?" Star asked, drawing my attention away from the scoundrel and back to her. She was looking confused, chewing on her lip.

"I'm fine now. I got a note today that said someone has it in for us. You know—for the ongoing investigation. We got here as soon as we could." I gestured at Ace. Murmurs sounded in the crowd behind us, the word *threat* ringing out loud and clear from a number of people.

"You mean we're now the target? For *your* looking into the murders?" she demanded, hands on hips. "When we've got a perfectly good Mountie right here to do the job?"

"Charm was only trying to help by getting to the bottom of things, Star." Tulip spoke up.

"Fine. Whatever. Fat lot of good that did."

"But you know I had to do something, Star. The evidence was pointing at our family. I couldn't have that. Look what that could do to Granny—to our business," I pleaded my case, upset that my loyalty was in question.

She let out a deep sigh, a pout forming on her mouth. "Yeah, I know. It just sucks. Okay?"

"Okay, ladies, let's go. Time to check on your granny."

With that we got a fast move on and were soon packed into the cruiser, everything and everybody else ignored. The booth could go to that place down-under for all I cared at the moment.

We hurried into the Tea & Tarot as a pack, looking for our granny. Seeing her there, serving coffee to a customer with a genuine smile lighting her face, made my heart sing. We were all safe — for now. I'd rather be threatened a thousand times over then have anyone think to harm a hair of my beloved Granny or my sisters. Yes. I still had to solve this. It was the only way to keep them all safe. But I had to be smarter about it, much smarter. Not run amok and draw unwanted attention. And the sooner it was done, the better. The clock in my head began to tick again, double time.

"What's going on, sweetings?" Granny came over to join us. "Who's looking after the booth?"

"Don't worry about the booth. It will be fine. And if not —" I gave a dismissive shrug. "But something came up. Something far more important." I gulped, not wanting to share the next part.

Ace stepped forward. "There's been a threat, ma'am."

Her hand fluttered to her neck. "Call me Granny, please." I saw her throat work to swallow. My eyes began to water and I looked downward at the floor. It needed a good scrubbing again. I'd best get at it. It wasn't as though Star or Tulip were going to volunteer.

"Granny," Ace said, nodding respectfully. "I thought it best to have all of you in one place for the time being so that the threat can be followed up on properly. The evidence is being fingerprinted as we speak."

"A note?" she asked softly, her eyes rounding with concern. The few customers in the café hushed, time seeming to stand still. I hated that she had to know.

"It was very specific. It was intended to keep Charm from investigating the recent murders."

"I see. Well, that does prove we had nothing to do with them." She nodded sagely. I waited for Ace to confirm this.

"It would appear so. But we must wait for forensics to have their say."

"Appear so!" I was outraged at the weak response in defending our honor. "No one in this family could have done this thing, no matter what you or anyone else thinks." Though I couldn't vouch for myself doing something in the future, if anyone tried to harm a hair on anyone I loved.

"Now, sweeting. The man is just going about his sworn duty. He needs the space to do so." Granny tried to placate me. I loved her so much for her wisdom, but in this, she might be off base. Ace didn't need space so much as he needed a tighter rein to keep him out of my way.

Chapter Eighteen

"Sheriff, would you like some coffee, maybe a bite to eat?" Star asked, a coy smile on her face at deliberately calling him by the wrong professional moniker.

Harrumph. She sure got over her scare fast.

I glanced at Ace, who returned her smile with a knowing look of his own, clearly saying he knew she was playing him and that was just fine with him. *Whatever.*

"Well, Miss McCall, I wouldn't mind a cup of your legendary coffee if you've got the time."

I figuratively rolled my eyes. Darned if I cared. The two of them enjoying each other's company would just make my plans that much easier to carry out. She could keep tabs on him while I got busy fixing things. I ignored the strange ping to my heart.

The chimes over the door announced another visitor. Emma. Before I could greet her, she exclaimed, "What's going on? I heard someone's been arrested."

"No one is under arrest," Ace said, his tone mild. He sat down at a booth and let Star fill a white ceramic cup with coffee, adding cream.

"What's going on then?"

I grabbed Emma's arm and pulled her aside, explaining the situation.

"Oh, my goodness, this is terrible!" Her words were accompanied by a grimace of worry.

"No, everyone's okay." *Crap on a cracker*, her aunt wasn't anywhere *near* okay.

Her eyes filled with tears and we hugged each other. Tears prickled behind my eyelids again. *Fine state of affairs.*

"Okay, I need you to do a couple of things for me," I whispered in her ear.

"Anything for you, you know that. What do you need?"

"I need you to find Pastor Evans and ask him to drop in to see me."

"No worries. I'll get right on it, and the other thing?"

I explained the second favor and her eyebrows shot up into her hairline. "Are you sure?"

"Yes. Thank you."

"Charm." Ace pinned me in his sights. "Would you join me, please?"

"I'll call you later. I have some errands to run," Emma said louder, giving me a final hug before scurrying from the café.

I dragged both feet over to the booth and plunked down, crossing my arms over my chest. I gave him my best what's-on-your-mind-buddy stare, arching one eyebrow for effect.

"I can see I'm not your favorite person right now, but I promise you, I'm going to find out who murdered two people and who is threatening your family. You have my word on that. And you need to let me do my job."

I pursed my lips. "So, do your job already. Send someone else to watch over us."

"I intend to. But I will be back later to take the night shift. Until then, Constable Jim Newman will take over. Soon as he gets here, I'll be on my way. But right now, I want your word you will stay put."

No way. "What can I do cooped up here anyway?" I gave a small shrug.

He gave me the stink eye, his normally full lips pressed into a firm line. I pretended complete innocence.

He shook his head slowly. "Charm, you have too much of the imp in your character for your own good."

"I'll see that she stays out of trouble." Granny came over to the booth. Darn it, I didn't want that. Not with my plans.

"Thank you, Granny." Ace gave her a smile.

The café door opened, revealing Constable Jim. A nice man, middle-aged and married to Carol, the kindergarten teacher over at Snowy Lake Elementary. Jim was blessed with a calming manner that kept most rowdy drunks in line on Saturday night. And his bulky body, topped with a no-nonsense regulation haircut, demanded a certain respect. He hefted that large frame in our direction, joining us at the booth. He nodded at Granny. "Sorry for the trouble, Granny. It's going to get sorted."

She gave him a brave smile. "Of course, it will. As the wise say, this too shall pass. Would you like coffee, Jim, something to eat?"

Ace got to his feet. "I'll leave you in charge then, Jim. And keep a special eye out for this one." He crooked his head at me. "She has a tendency to go off half-cocked."

"And don't I know that," Jim added his unwanted two cents.

I sputtered. "I most certainly do not."

All eyes turned on me, every head nodding.

"I rest my case." And with that the world's most annoying Mountie left the building.

How long until the reverend arrived? I glanced down at the floor. *Yes.* Something to do to wear off all this excess energy.

I got up and dashed into the kitchen in search of a mop and pail. Today the customers would just have to work around me for a change. Not like there were many. Our stellar reputation was in tatters.

I set to my task with vigor, working up a sweat in minutes.

"Darn floor, always looking crappy no matter how often you wash it or how much wax you apply," I muttered. "We need a new floor." I spoke the words louder, to no one in particular. Everyone seemed to be staying out of my way at the moment.

"New flooring is expensive, sweeting," Granny observed, turning from the front window, one of her favorite spots to observe traffic. "Brace yourself, your aunt is about to make her appearance."

I groaned then sloshed more hot soapy water on the floor, scrubbing harder. Why was I blessed with the world's most annoying aunt? *Sorry, don't really mean that*, I spoke to the goddess, covering all bases. If anything happened to her, I'd never forgive myself.

The door flew open and Auntie T.J. rushed in, her expression one of wide-eyed horror. I saw what had kept her so long. She'd had her hair freshly tinted this morning, a deep rich auburn.

"Is everyone okay?" she twittered. She bobbled her head around, trying to catch all of us in her line of sight.

"We're fine, dear. Your hair looks lovely." Granny gave her a quick hug. "Jim's watching over us."

Jim nodded from the booth where he was consuming a third cup of coffee. Star was in charge of seeing to his needs while Tulip was restocking shelves. Not that we'd sold much in the past few days, but they did need a good dusting. I was grateful to see she was attending to it instead of working on her time-consuming blog.

In a way, we were in limbo, and having everyone gathered around, I wasn't going to complain. *A family comes together in crisis.*

I finished my task, checking the time. Four-thirty. Where was that minister?

Like the goddess had overheard me, I caught a glimpse of silvery hair floating atop a noble head moving past the front window. Reverend Evans. *Finally.* At least the floor was clean enough to eat off. *Maybe I should start on the walls next?* I eyed them suspiciously.

"Afternoon, Reverend," Granny spoke first, blessing him with a smile. She might have her own beliefs on faith and politics, but she never pushed them off on anyone else or expected there was only one right way for everyone. A centrist to be admired.

"Granny, nice to see you. Sorry to hear of your troubles. I'm certain everything will work out just fine."

"Yes, things work out the way they are intended to, Reverend, if we but let them."

"Very true. Charm wanted to see me?" He gave a quick look in my direction. Catching sight of me, he strolled over.

"Sorry it took so long. Constable Collins and I have been chatting."

I'll just bet you have. I gritted my teeth, forcing a smile. "Pray tell, what secrets have you two been sharing?"

"Hmm, about the terrible things going on in our little town." His expression sobered, the lines etched in his compassionate face deepening.

I swallowed, properly chastised. Our town did need all the help it could get. And Ace, okay, did seem to be good at his job, just that he didn't know the people like I did, or have the gift of extra-sensory perception. My mind went back to Granny's revelations earlier. At least now I knew who I had to thank for that and my newly discovered gift, the one still blowing my mind. I had an extra name to add to my nightly prayers to the goddess. Mary Sarah Toogood.

"Would you care for coffee?" I asked, gesturing towards a table.

"Sure. I'm parched." He sat down while I hurried to get him a cup of joe. "Been a busy day."

I sat down across from him.

"How are you keeping?" he asked, blowing on the coffee to cool it.

"Fine. Considering what's been going on."

He shook his head and took a sip from the cup. "Yes, times are trying right now. Constable Collins seems to be doing his level best to sort through all the facts. I wouldn't worry. The truth will come out."

All fine and dandy if one knows where to locate the truth. "Talking about truth, I hear you visited Mrs. Hurst on that final day. With Mrs. Smith?" I added a question mark to my query.

He nodded. "Yes. Mrs. Hurst gave a very generous donation to the church. Much appreciated."

"Yes, of course. No one else came by while you were there with her?"

"No. Unfortunately, Mrs. Smith was feeling poorly and spent the time in the bathroom."

"That was poor timing for her." My heart rate speeded up. "Anything else you can remember?"

"No, nothing."

"Good thing whatever she had wasn't contagious."

"Good thing is right. You know how quickly viruses spread in our close-knit community. Must have been food-borne in her case."

"I'm sure it was." The irony wasn't lost on me. "Can I freshen your coffee?"

"No, I should get going. Got a committee meeting in a few minutes. The roof of the church needs repair and we're looking at fundraising ideas."

"Anything I can do to help, you let me know."

"Thanks, I will. Wish I knew more about what happened to Mrs. Hurst. I'll be glad to see you clear of all this almost as much as our new Mountie. Seems he's taken a shine to one of the McCall triplets."

"Just doing his job, I'm sure. But I think Star's the one he's got his eye on."

"Oh really," he teased. "And I always thought of you as the clever one, Charm."

I dug in my heels, figuratively, giving him a cheesy smile, then watched him take his leave from Granny while considering the best way to go about things.

Hmm. I got up and approached Jim. "Is it all right if I go up stairs for a bit? I need to take care of something. It's a woman thing," I stage-whispered.

He flushed and gestured me out.

I hurried away. Time to get at the truth. I checked if anyone was hanging about the kitchen, picked up a box of the triple chocolate brownies as cover and slipped out of the back door. Feeling like a real private eye, I hurried down the alley, heading on foot for the Smiths' residence, hoping Emma had observed the reverend leaving the café and had done what I'd asked her to do and made the phone call.

Hardly believing my luck, and afraid to acknowledge it in case I jinxed myself, I scurried up to the back door of the two-storey house, pretty certain I had not been observed. A few loud knocks and the door opened, revealing the lady of the hour. Shoot, she was still here.

"Hi, I've brought some brownies to welcome Alison back. Is she home?"

Mrs. Smith frowned, looking down at the white carboard box. "This is a surprise." Apparently just not a happy one. "Should you be doing this what with all the talk about where the poison came from?" She arched one of her perfectly groomed eyebrows in my direction.

"Oh, I'm not worried about that at all. Not since Constable Collins has pretty much solved the case. I'm off the hook." I gave her my second cheesy smile of the day. Or was it my third? Mr. Hot Stuff *had* been by the café this morning.

"Really? Where are my manners? Do come in, Charm. I'm afraid Alison's not home, but I'll make us some tea and you can tell me all about it."

We sat in her dining room, and she waited until I tried the brownies before helping herself to one. *Funny woman.* But then I had waited for her to have a sip of tea first, so fair was fair, eh.

"So, you were saying that Constable Collins is near to solving the case?" She took a wee bite of a brownie, her expression one that I could only catalog as prissy. Her little finger was held at a certain crooked angle, like people who think their bathroom habits smell like roses.

"Yes. He was just over at the café. Very intent on doing his job." I nodded my blessing. "Alison find her ring all right?"

"Yes, thank you."

"That was too bad about the other day, you know, when you visited Mrs. Hurst the day she died, and you got ill. Are you better now?"

She frowned. "Yes, I'm fine." She took a sip of her tea and her finger resumed the position.

"Oh, I must have a touch of something." I grimaced. "Mind if I use your bathroom?"

"Of course, dear." She gave a royal nod of assent.

I got up and made my way down the hall, intent on at least checking out one room thoroughly while praying that Emma would get a move on. I shut the door and began rummaging through the cupboards. Not that I expected she could be this sloppy, hiding anything in the guest bathroom, but sometimes luck prevails. *Shoot, not today.* Not one thing incriminating could be found. I gave up and flushed the toilet for effect.

A brisk knock on the door. "Are you all right, Charm? You've been in there a while. And I'm afraid I have to go out. Emma needs me. She's in a bit of a state."

I shouted out, over a loud groan for effect, "You go right ahead, Mrs. Smith, help Emma. I'm afraid I'm stuck in here for the time being. Tummy upset, you understand."

Silence.

"All right then. Alison should be home soon. Just lock up when you leave, please."

"I will." I flushed the toilet again. The fan came on overhead, startling me. Mrs. Smith had hit the switch to freshen the air in the room. *Sweet of her.*

I waited a good five minutes, then crept from the room. I turned off the fan, listening for any sounds. The house was empty.

Time to get a move on. At best, I might get an hour from Emma's ploy, and that was only if Alison didn't walk in on me looking for evidence her mother had poisoned two people.

Hmm. Where would I hide poison I didn't want found? Most likely deep in a closet, right? I ran up the stairs two at a time and scurried along the landing toward the master suite. I soon discovered sleuthing is overrated when everything has to go back *exactly* as it was. If only I could have thrown things willy-nilly, I'd have been finished in record time. But I found nothing in the bedroom or attached bathroom. *Linen closet?* I pulled out towels and sheets and piled them on the floor but came up empty handed again. *Tick Tock.* That darn clock was firing up in my brain again.

Think, Charm. The poison, what were its attributes? Of course, its distinctive odor of bitter almond.

I raced back down the steps and into the kitchen. Where to search first? I spotted the pantry near the back door to the house. I hurried across the floor and grasped the doorknob, giving it a firm twist, but it wouldn't budge. *Who locks the door to the pantry? Guess.*

But I needed to get inside to check. I couldn't very well say anything about my suspicions without proof. I hesitated. Surely there had to be a key somewhere?

Sounds of the front door opening made my heart slam. I had to get out of here. Right now. It was never a good idea to make a possible murderess angry. *Calm down, just act like nothing's amiss, all right?*

I took my own advice and moved to sit down on a stool. It was tucked under the kitchen island with three others. I slumped down on it, holding my middle.

"Charm. You're still here." Mrs. Smith endowed me with an evil frown as she came in and spotted me, her tone extra sharp. I was adding the evil part, but I was certain that I saw a glimpse of it in her devilish eyes. *Funny how different someone you suspect of murder looks.*

"Sorry, I was just resting a bit. Still feeling rather poorly."

"Would you like me to call someone to come and collect you?" She moved to pick up the phone. *No, no, no.* The last thing I needed was to be found out by granny. That could lead to Ace knowing and that would be intolerable. *No more darn lectures, please.*

"No, it's okay. I can manage." I stood up and set the stool back in place under the island. "I should be going."

"Yes. You should." Her voice housed suspicions and I caught her glance flicking over to the pantry door.

"Is Emma okay?" I thought to ask.

"Yes, she's fine." Her tone was short.

"I'd best check on her too." I gave her a weak smile and walked by her, fighting the urge to run. The hackles on my neck rose when her dark spirit brushed against mine. Every instinct I possessed screamed danger.

Mrs. Smith followed me to the front door. A sense of her breathing down my neck didn't help. At the front door, I pretended to stumble and she reached out for me with one hand, grasping my arm. *Good.* And oh so scary. *Be brave*, I told myself, fear icing my veins. I closed my eyes to allow her thoughts to enter my mind as our bodies touched. Then I wished I hadn't. A dark image of rage, hatred and revenge became clear. *Oh my goddess. Let me out of here.* I reached for the door knob, my heart hammering so loud I was certain she could hear it. *Thumpa-thumpa.*

"What did you see, Charm?" she demanded, still holding tightly to my arm. I didn't want to move quickly. There was no knowing what she might do, but I knew what she was capable of feeling. Feelings are no proof of guilt, though. If they were, the new Mountie would be strung up by his thumbs.

"Noth—ing. I didn't see anything." My voice sounded like Minnie Mouse, too squeaky by half. I cleared my throat. "Got a frog in here." I rubbed at my neck for emphasis. "I gotta go."

"I'm afraid I can't let you do that until you tell me what you saw just now. And don't lie—you're not good at it."

"Just—just a bit of you being unhappy with your lot in life." Why? Fred doted on her, by all accounts, and Alison had done everything in her power to be the daughter her mother wanted her to be. But was Mrs. Smith's unhappiness enough to have her commit murder? Not once, but twice? That I still didn't know. I was having trouble believing it. *Who takes chances like that?* She had so much to lose. Of course, that just might have made her more dangerous.

"You're young. When you've lived as long as I have, you gain a new perspective. You discover things about others you wish you didn't know."

I glanced at her, trying to keep my apprehension from showing, noting the strange look in her eyes. *Don't give the game away.* "Much as I would like to converse more, I should be going. Before I have another attack."

But still she held on, ignoring me.

Then a voice rang out in the kitchen. "Mom, are you home?"

Thank you, goddess. I let out a breath.

Alison popped around the kitchen doorway, spotting us. She frowned, watching the odd tableau.

"Mom, Charm, are you okay?"

"I'm fine, dear. Charm was just leaving. She's not feeling well." She dropped my hand and I stepped back, opening the front door with trembling fingers. *Freedom.* It called my name something fierce.

"I'll walk you home, Charm, make sure you're all right." Alison hurried to join me. I couldn't speak quite yet. Had I just escaped the clutches of a murderess? Only the goddess knew for certain. But if she was, she'd move the poison now, hide it somewhere no one could find it and wait for her chance to do me in. I might just have made things worse.

Chapter Nineteen

"Are you happy, Alison?"

"Yeah, sure. I mean, I just got engaged to a great guy. Mom loves him." She was defensive, twisted the ring round and round her finger.

"But do you? I think that might be a tad more important."

She wouldn't look me in the eyes. "He's promised me a life far away from here. That's good enough. I never want to live here ever again. Once we're married, I'm gone for good." The words were accompanied with a side of bitterness.

"I'm sorry your life growing up was so hard."

"Well, what doesn't kill you makes you stronger, right?"

"Maybe. Have you ever thought of therapy? Talking it out with someone can help. If you ever need an ear, I'd be happy to help."

"Mom would kill me if I ever let loose any family secrets. You know her, no dirty laundry in public."

"It wouldn't be public knowledge. A therapist is sworn to confidentiality and I never tell secrets."

She snorted. "Well, tell that to your sister."

"Excuse me?" I was taken aback, confused. "What do you mean?"

"Oh, so Star doesn't share her secrets with you, either."

"Star. What did she ever do to you?"

"Nothing. You want to know, ask her."

"I'm asking you." I stopped walking and turned to her. "Why are you angry with Star?"

She bit her lip. "You remember when we used to sing duets together in junior high?"

"Sure. You were good. I never understood why you stopped."

She grimaced. "There was this radio program we had been practicing to sing on for weeks. JCAT. Then I got caught cheating on a test off your sister. She was partially to blame because she let me do it. I was grounded for a month and Star went on to sing on the program alone. She got all the kudos, won the grand prize. While I was left in the dust. We never sang together again. And I was just as good as her."

"I'm sorry. I didn't realize that. What did your mother say about it?" I had vague recollections of the event, mostly remembering how proud we had all been of Star to have won such a big contest so young.

"She's not too fond of Star, if you get my meaning. She thinks she stole my big chance. She even thinks Star set me up to get caught cheating, but I told her that's just crazy. No way she did that."

"No. Star would never set anyone up. It always bothered her you know, that you broke up. She loved singing with you." I told the white fib with fingers crossed behind my back, praying it was true.

"Really?" She grinned shyly. "Maybe we'll sing a duet together one day, eh." Her tone was filled with so much longing that I had to swallow over the sudden lump in my throat.

"Sure. Why not?"

We'd reached the alley that led to the café's kitchen door. "You can get go back now if you like, I'm feeling much better, thanks."

She frowned, hesitating.

"Really, I got this. The fresh air cleared my brain."

"Okay." She smiled. "Nice talking with you, Charm."

"You too."

I turned and hurried toward the Tea & Tarot, praying no one had taken note of my absence. Like that would ever happen.

I opened the back door against my better judgement, suspecting what awaited me. And there stood Granny, Star, Tulip, Mountie Jim and Mr. Hot Stuff, the latter glaring at me with enough energy to electrify the whole town during an ice storm power outage.

"Where have you been?" Ace demanded. "We were just about to send out a search party for you."

"I'm obviously fine and here now. I needed to see someone." I held my chin up high.

"And pray tell what was so important that you defied my orders to stay with your family safe and sound?"

"What is this, the inquisition? I just stepped out for a sec."

My sisters rallied round me, giving me looks of concern and support.

"Consider yourself in protective custody for your own good, Miss McCall. I'm taking you down to the station for questioning."

"What? No way." I crossed my arms over my chest, widening my stance.

"Sweeting, you need to listen to Constable Collins," Granny said. I glanced over at her and she was watching me, her expression serious. "You were told to stay here. I think it best you tell the constable all you know. You can be a lot of help when you want to be."

What could I say?

I marched along beside Ace as he walked me out of the café, head held high. *If you're innocent, you'll be set free, right?* I got a twinge of doubt I tried to ignore. But I'd followed wrongful convictions in Canada, and, truthfully, they did happen.

He remained silent for the short trip while I chewed off a couple of fingernails. He turned into the police station's driveway. I tried to think of delaying tactics, really not wanting to go inside, innocent or not.

"Did you know that Mrs. Smith has it in for Star?" I quickly explained what Alison had told me. "And have you had any luck with discovering what was going on with all the bank deposits? Anyone else being blackmailed?"

"You just had to go and do it, right, Charm? You didn't have the faith that I had your best interests at heart." He groaned, shaking his head. My heart fell into my shoes.

"I just couldn't sit around twirling my thumbs," I sputtered. *The freakin' injustice of it all.*

"Like that's ever going to happen. Now we've got more problems. The murderer is busy entrenching themselves. While I have been carefully collecting testimony and facts to find out the full story, you've been undermining the investigation with all your interference."

"But you do believe I had nothing to do with all this, right?" Though he had said so once before, my insecurity rose at being taken into the police station, adding a frisson of worry.

He gave a huge Mountie sigh. "Of course. But you played right into their hands, darlin'. And my guess is next someone will plant a container of cyanide in your apartment, if they haven't already done so."

"Then I need to help fix it! Get a search warrant for Mrs. Smith's place. I think you might find evidence in her pantry. She's locked it, which is really weird." My voice came out louder than I intended.

Thunderclouds were less threatening.

"I was only trying to help." I faltered.

"Right. And the sun's not coming up tomorrow."

"It could miss a day," I muttered.

I hazarded a glance at him. His lips were pressed so tightly together they were in peril of vanishing. Not to mention the tic flicking to its own rhythm under his right eye.

"Charm, I hate that you've left me no choice in the matter."

Chapter Twenty

Sitting in a jail cell sucked. Big time. I discovered this three minutes later.

"Am I allowed visitors?"

"Of course. All your family can come by."

"I'm hungry."

He sighed. "I'm taking care of that. Okay?"

"Will you be checking out Mrs. Smith's pantry? I searched all the closets, but I couldn't find anything." *Funny how jail makes you want to spill all your secrets. Well, maybe not so funny.* I'd watched that TV show about a woman's prison, and oh boy, the inmates spill their guts there.

"Have you considered a career in law enforcement, Miss McCall?"

"No." I shook my head. "Because then I would be hamstrung, doing things by the book. Right?"

He didn't answer but turned on his heel and strode off, the keys on his belt jingling ominously, leaving me staring at three bare walls and a barred door. Yikes.

This was a tad too real. A cold shiver ran down my back. What if Mrs. Smith did manage to plant cyanide at the café? Had I really made her that suspicious? But I had no proof she was the one—others had motive. Sean could have done it. Maybe the pair were working together? I shivered again. It wouldn't be the first time someone had murdered their best friend, though I still rejected it. The pair had been so tight since grade school.

"Charm, you okay?" Tulip pressed her face to the bars like we'd been separated for months instead of minutes. Star hung back, looking less concerned, even a bit angry.

"I'm fine." I got up and slipped my hands through the bars. Tulip grabbed one and held on tight. Star relented and took the other.

"Okay, okay. It's not that bad, ladies." Ace shook his head as he came into view, toting a basket in one hand and watching us play out the scene. "She's not under arrest, only being detained for her own good."

"We've put a file in the pie," Tulip stage-whispered, giving Ace the stink eye.

He rolled his eyes. "They've brought supper."

"Yup, meatballs, fried chicken, potato salad, corn, biscuits and pumpkin pie with whipped cream." Tulip was quick to point at the large basket he carried.

"Great! Then let me out of here." My mouth watered in anticipation. "But you still owe me a steak, Sheriff."

"*You* are staying in the cell for now. You're not getting the chance to slink off again. And you will get a steak soon, just not today. I've got my hands full investigating a murder, if you remember?"

I ignored the sarcasm and smiled at my sisters.

"Then we eat in there with our sister," Tulip said.

"Suits me just fine."

He unlocked the steel door, plunked the wicker basket down on the bed and left us to our own devices, securing the door behind him. Not ten seconds later a loud commotion broke out in the hallway.

"Where my friend Charm? I demand her!" Ivana's voice rang, loud and clear.

Ace escorted the angry Russian to the bars of my cell, letting her in with a loud sigh.

"I'll be back later. Settle down, all of you."

Ivana's gray eyes were dark with emotion. She gave Ace the middle finger and turned to me. "This not right! We get you free. Now!"

"I'm fine. Want some supper? Tulip and Star have brought a huge feast. More than enough to go around."

She hesitated, but the delicious odor of fried chicken must have convinced her. She plunked herself down between my sisters on the bed, accepting a full plate that I quickly dished out for her. She'd settle down with a good meal in her belly. At least I hoped so.

"Ivana thank you." She nodded gravely and tucked into the food.

Munching and sighs of enjoyment soon followed.

Another loud commotion broke out and we all looked up.

This time Ace was escorting Christine to the cell.

"You have another visitor." He let her in, locking the door securely again. "Okay, we've hit the limit for now. No more visitors." He was right about that. It was getting crowded in a jail cell meant for one, maybe two people. I wondered for a second where Emma was, surprised she hadn't raced right to the jail. That would be her normal MO.

"Charm is good girl. You let her out right now or my brothers —"

"Are you threatening a police officer, Miss Petrov?" His voice hardened to steel, and even Ivana looked taken aback.

"Not right," she muttered in a quieter tone. It was the first time I'd ever seen anyone other than yours truly take the wind out of her sails.

He gave all of us a stern look before leaving, but I did note the twitch in his eye had worsened. *Small towns are not like big cities, are they, Officer?*

A loud repetitive chorus of, "Set Charm free! Set Charm free!" resounded through the building.

What on earth?

I jumped up and stood on tiptoe to peer through the tiny grille window. The holding cell faced the front of the detachment, meaning I had a good view of the street. I caught sight of my long-time friends getting prepared for the traditional lighting of the torch, done just before they burned someone in effigy. *Oh. My. Goddess.* Like at all such events held in Canada, from postal strikes to incinerating personal garbage in the backyard, a burn barrel was already lit, smoke and flame drifting upwards in billowing clouds to kiss the sky. All they needed were pitchforks to complete the picture.

"It's the other members of Northern Lights Coven," Tulip needlessly explained. "They're working on getting you out of here. Casting a release spell as we speak."

"I can see that," I mumbled, unable to look away as my coven sisters lit the hastily concocted straw figure of a lawman with the torch.

"*Oh*, can I join the coven?" Christine chimed in. "Wow, I'd love to be part of it. I mean, being in one is *so* in style."

I gave a very, very deep sigh. It was lovely to have such an incredible group of friends, but I had brought a *little* bit of this on myself, I had to admit. It wasn't entirely Ace's fault. Perhaps I did need protection from my own exuberance at times.

"Of course you can, Christine," I reassured her when I spied her downcast look. My sigh had sent the exact wrong message.

"Okay, we need to come up with some plan to set things right," I mused out loud. It wasn't going to be easy, not with me being stuck in jail.

Chapter Twenty-One

"Don't worry. We'll have this wrapped up in no time with everyone on the case," Tulip reassured me. "Hello, we want out of here!" she yelled to get someone's attention. She kept up the din for at least five minutes, even banging the bars with a steel bread knife she had packed in the picnic basket. At least back on the outside, this group of supporters could be my eyes and ears.

"Okay, okay, hold your darn horses." Constable Jim made his appearance in front of the cell door, shaking his head at us while fiddling with the lock. The door opened wide and everyone trooped out. I tried to follow, pretending innocence, but he gestured me back. "Not you, Charm, sorry. I've got my orders to keep you under lock and key until Ace gets back."

I pouted, giving him my best puppy-dog eyes, but he just grunted and relocked the cage. *Not nice.* I grabbed the cell bars with my hands and pretended I could bend them like Houdini. My sisters laughed and even Jim gave a slight smile.

"Anything you need, Charm?" he asked.

"Nah, I'm good." I winked at my crew. "Catch you later." Maybe it was going straight to my head, but I admit, I was stoked with all the support pouring in.

But then time slowed to a virtual crawl, while waiting for something, *anything* to happen.

Footsteps echoed, coming in my direction. *Halleluiah.* I jumped up and waited by the cell door. Ace came into view, his expression inscrutable.

"Miss McCall."

"Constable Collins. Have you heard the latest?"

"Excuse me?"

"The exoplanet Wolf 503b orbits its star every six days and is twice as large as Earth."

"And it's one hundred and forty-five light years away in the Virgo constellation. Yes, I've heard. But I was a bit too busy explaining to my captain why an effigy of one of his officers was being burned out front of the station to garner any more facts."

Heat rose in my body. I couldn't quite meet his intense glance.

"Yeah, well, my coven does tend to get carried away. But in their defense, they were offering support. And once it was explained that I wasn't *actually* under arrest but only in protective custody, they backed off, right?"

"Harrumph." He stayed outside the cell and pulled up a chair to talk with me through the bars. I frowned.

"What? Big guy like you afraid to come inside?"

"We need to straighten a few things out. Again."

"What things?" I fiddled with the ends of my braid. As usual it had unraveled.

"Ever wish you could time travel?" he asked. He placed his large hands on his muscular thighs that were defined and visible through his uniform pants, sitting like President Lincoln does in the big stone chair in Washington. *Impressive.* A buzzing started in my brain.

"Sometimes," I hedged, sensing what he was getting at. "But more importantly, what *kind* of machine do you want to travel in? An infinite rotating cylinder, wormhole or cosmic string? You know that Einstein's general theory of relativity allows for it, right?" He nodded in confirmation, narrowing his eyes. "Or maybe you'd prefer to just have your data stream transplanted?"

"What I would prefer is to reset it back a couple of days before you drew such unwanted attention to yourself and your family."

I couldn't hide a wince.

"My family's fine."

"Yes. We're seeing to that. On another note, it turns out you were right about the coffee pods. The poison was inserted into them."

"Good. No, I don't mean *that's good* —"

"I know what you mean. And furthermore, we've had an anonymous tip. And a cannister of poison has been found hidden in a house in Snowy Lake. The person gave us permission to search."

"Mrs. Smith's, right?" This was perfect. Finally. Though I was surprised she gave permission. Maybe she was sick of hiding and had decided it was time to come clean.

He winced, not quite meeting my eyes this time.

"No, it wasn't Mrs. Smith. It was Emma Hurst."

"What? No way! Emma wouldn't hurt anyone! She's being set up. You said she let you right in to search, right? What guilty person does that? I dare you to get Mrs. Smith to do that. And have you checked her pantry yet? That's where the poison was hidden first. I'm certain of it."

"Maybe. But we have to act on what can be proven."

"It wouldn't take much to prove Emma's not guilty! Because she's not! I'd bet my bottom dollar Mrs. Hurst was going to plant that poison at the Tea & Tarot and choose Emma instead because it was easier with all the police presence of late. This is *your* fault!"

"My fault. How is this my fault?"

"If you'd checked out Mrs. Smith's right away, this never would have happened. You'd have found the poison there instead."

"I did go and see her as well and there was no poison in her pantry."

"What? See, that just proves she'd moved it already."

"Because you went there earlier and tipped her off, perhaps?"

We glared at each other through the bars, neither of us backing down a millimeter.

He sighed, slapped his thighs once and got up, pushing back the chair. The legs scraped noisily on the cement floor.

I panicked. "Aren't you going to let me out of here?" I had to get out and help Emma.

"Have you learned your lesson, Miss McCall?" he asked pointedly. I gulped, hating that I had to say something less than true to receive a free get out of jail card.

"Yeah..."

"You don't sound certain."

It was in my best interests to be gracious and let him off the hook, if I wanted to prove my best friend was innocent. I had to be the bigger person here. Well, figuratively anyway.

"I'm certain, okay? I promise to give more credence to what you have to say in the future."

"Raise your right hand and repeat after me. I, Charm McCall, promise to follow the laws of the land."

I dutifully repeated him word for word, my right hand raised, the left behind my back, the fingers knotted.

"And, further, I vow to follow the rules set out by Constable Ace Collins —"

"Wait a darn minute!"

"You want out of here tonight?"

I fought hard to keep my agitation at bay. "And furthermore I vow to follow the rules set out by..."

"Constable Ace Collins," he prompted.

I mumbled his name, adding the stink eye as a bonus, but careful to keep it directed away from his line of sight.

One dark eyebrow raised over his piercing browns near did me in. Something about him and the situation made me want to laugh or cry. I wasn't sure which.

"Okay, I'll drive you back to the café."

"Great." I waited while he drew a key from his leather belt and unlocked the door. I slipped through the opening, feeling his closeness. His presence was a powerful magnet, like the needle on a compass spinning around trying to find due North during an electrical storm. I wasn't sure if we'd be unable to pull ourselves apart if we touched or if we'd be locked together for all eternity. At the moment, I didn't want to know. My BFF was in trouble and I had to sort it out.

We drove the short distance back to the café in utter silence. What was there to say? He had my best friend under suspicion of murder while the real one lurked in our community. I was now certain it was Mrs. Smith who had done the dastardly deeds. And the very idea of such evil existing among us? *Oh goddess,* I prayed, *give me the strength to do what needs to be done.* The horrible crimes she was involved in — they struck at the heart of who we were, what we stood for. But how to prove she did it and not Emma?

I walked in the front door of the café but found it empty. Where was everyone?

"Anyone home?" I called out, hurrying into the kitchen, Ace on my heels.

The fragrance of fresh-baked cookies lingered in the air, making my stomach rumble. I'd been too upset at supper to do more than chase my food around my plate. I set about sleuthing them out. Why on earth had my sisters hidden them anyway?

In the back of one of the cupboards I spied a small covered container and pulled it out. I pried off the tin lid, admiring the pretty green leaf stamped on the top. *Aha.* Macadamia Ginger Chewies. Perfect. I took a huge bite, relishing the flavors. Whoever had baked them had added an extra dose of love to the batter. Probably Granny.

"Want one?" I asked Ace, who hovered nearby.

He shrugged. "No, thanks."

"Milk?" I asked, over a mouthful of cookie. They were so beautifully flavored and moist, I could have eaten the whole tin full.

I took his silence as consent and poured two tall glasses from the container in the refrigerator. I was about to start into a second cookie, handing Ace a glass of milk, when footfalls took our attention. Star came rushing into the kitchen. She spotted us and stopped dead in her tracks, looking at the open canister of cookies in my hands.

"Oh—oh," she said, grimacing. "You *really* shouldn't be eating those."

Chapter Twenty-Two

"Did you make theses cookies? They're fabulous. And where is everyone?" I asked.

Star flushed beet red. "I did make those with Tulip, but they're not for public consumption. And Granny, Auntie T.J. and Tulip are upstairs asleep in your apartment." She came closer and thrust the tin lid back on the container then held it out of reach.

"What's going on?" Confused, I stopped drinking the milk and set it aside.

"How many have you had?" she asked, her expression turning to one of worry.

"Just one. Why?"

"Did you have any, Constable?"

Now she was being proper. "He didn't want any," I explained.

She gave me a curt nod. "I need to speak with you — alone."

"What have you got yourself into this time?" I shook my head, then turned to Ace. "If you'll excuse us a minute, I need to speak with my sister."

He eyed both of us suspiciously but gave us space by walking back into the café. I waited until his boots rang out near the front of the store.

"Okay. What is it, what's wrong?"

"You remember I said I had a great way to make more money from our baking? How we could charge a lot more?"

"Yeah, I remember. And —" I stared at her as the full memory of the conversation came back to me. "No way! These are marijuana-laced cookies?" Horrified, I rocked back on my heels.

"You only had one, so you'll be okay." She gulped, trying to be reassuring. "You'll just begin to feel more relaxed soon, that's all."

"You left them in the café. Anyone could have found them."

"Hardly. They were in a back of a cupboard with the proper label of the plant leaf on the cover. Don't you know anything about such things? You're supposed to be so darn smart, reading all those fancy physics books." Her defensive tone wasn't helping. "All you have to do is go to bed and you'll be fine by morning. One cookie is barely enough to affect a person anyway. I used such a little bit in the recipe. You'd need two or three to have any real effect. Maybe it will make you happier for a change, get you to relax. You're kind of uptight, sis. Just sayin'."

"But I have so much to do yet tonight. Did you hear about Emma? Poison was found at her place and now she's under suspicion. And I am *not* that uptight!"

"But that lets us off the hook, right? And yes, you are that uptight."

"That's not the point. I don't want my best friend charged with a crime she couldn't possibly have committed."

"Duh, the truth will come out. Just go put your hands on everyone involved and solve the case already!"

"You think it's that easy?" I shook my head, then began to giggle. "Did I tell you what happened with Helen Davis? Did you know she has—had cancer and I was able to drive it right out of her body? Just zapped it right then and there." I snapped my fingers for effect.

"What are you talking about? I think you'd better sit down, sis."

She led me to the kitchen table and I plunked myself down across from her.

"Now tell me exactly what happened with Helen."

I explained the process, finding I had never been more eloquent in my explanation of anything in my entire life. "And then Granny said that the gift is given to the firstborn—you and Tulip might get some other kind of ability, by the way—and that you only get to keep it if you remain a virgin and sleep with just your one true love for all your life." I spread my arms wide then brought them in to hug myself, blessing my fellow triplet with a full-on grin. "And since I'm still a virgin—" I looked up and realized Ace had come back into the kitchen and was listening. *Oh goddess, no.* "How long have you been standing there, Sheriff?"

"Long enough." He gave me the strangest look.

Star jumped up. "I need some coffee. How about you, Constable?"

He shook his head. "I think you should take Charm upstairs and put her to bed. I'll make the coffee. It's going to be a long night."

"I'm fine. We need to come up with a plan to catch the real killer. And all my instincts say it's Mrs. Smith. We need to get her to come clean."

"How are we going to do that?" Star asked.

Ace spoke up. "By working together."

I looked up at him, standing bigger than life in our tiny kitchen. "What? Now you want my help?" I teased. Working together had such a lovely ring to it.

A hesitant knock on the door took my full attention. Ace strode over to open it, revealing a subdued-looking Alison standing there.

I got up and hurried over. "What's wrong?" I asked before she threw herself into my arms and began to weep.

"She made me do it," she said, her words barely understandable through the deep sobs.

"Who made you do what?"

"My mom. She said if I wanted the money for school and a large wedding and to keep our home, I had to help her. That someone was blackmailing us and I was her only hope to get what she needed."

"What did she need?"

Alison looked over at Star now standing beside me and clammed up. But it was too late, I'd seen the stark image shared between us, of Alison planting the cyanide at Emma's.

"Why did you do it? Why would you do that to Emma?" I asked. We needed her confession out loud to clear Emma.

"Because she said it was the only way. I'm sorry. She's my mom and I had to help her. Otherwise, you know how she gets." Her voice trembled with emotion.

Thank you, goddess.

"I'm sorry, Alison. Yes, I know." I turned and spoke to Ace. "See, I told you Emma had nothing to do with it. It *was* Mrs. Smith all the time. She killed Mrs. Hurst for blackmailing her husband and looting their savings and then Boyd for threatening to tell the tale, I'll just bet." I gave a confused-looking Alison a reassuring hug. "Don't worry. Constable Collins will protect you."

"No, no." She shook her head violently side to side, taking in my words. "My mother's not a killer. She's just worried about her family, making sure we're going to be okay."

But even as she denied it, cracks opened in her façade as we all stood there, giving her looks of sympathy.

"My mother wouldn't really hurt anyone, right?" She suddenly looked lost.

"That remains to be seen, Alison. But I need you to make a statement about what you do know. That's the best way to help your mom. Are you prepared to do that now?" Ace asked, his voice resonating with both strength and empathy. A good combination to calm fears, judging by Alison's response. Truthfully, I felt better too, my inner goddess relaxing.

She nodded, straightening her shoulders, her eyes reddened by tears. Star handed her a handful of Kleenex and she dabbed at her tears. "Yes, I can do that."

"I need to take Miss Smith to the station, Charm. I don't want to leave you and your family alone. I'll see if Jim's available."

"Not necessary. We're fine. You do what you have to and we'll lock up and head upstairs." *The bad stuff happening after a comment like that only happens in the movies, right?*

"If you're sure."

"Duh." I added a smile for good measure. I had never felt calmer or more assured of myself in my life. Which was kind of weird, now that I thought about it. "And, Officer?"

"Yes?"

"You never heard a word that passed between Star and me, right?"

"Of course not. Family business is private." But I did detect a twinkle in his brown eyes that made my heart rate speed up. *Later, eh.*

He escorted Alison out of the front door of the café, the chimes ringing in full-hearted agreement.

Another loud knock came on the back door. I gave a sigh then turned the handle to open it. *What now? A late-night cookie emergency?* Though I could see the cookies that Star and Tulip had dreamed up as having real possibilities of someone wanting to purchase them late at night. I couldn't believe I was thinking that. But very soon, cannabis was going to be legal. And if it did nothing but relax a person, maybe, just maybe, there was some merit to it? And as my sister had said, there were medical issues it was proven to help with as well...

"Mrs. Smith, what are you doing here?" The banker's wife looked none too happy. And a tad disheveled. Then I shook myself awake and out of the mental haze. This was *nothing* to be glib about. An actual murderess stood in the Tea & Tarot, one who might yet do us harm. My heart began racing as new worries flooded my brain. This had become way too real.

"Alison, she ran out on me. I thought she might have come here?" She pushed her way through the door, looking about frantically. Her dark spirit pulsed around me, her touch leaving a frightening sense of being unclean and in danger.

"No, she's not here right now." *Oh goddess, be with me now.*

"But she was, right? What did she say? You have to tell me!"

"Calm down. Granny's upstairs asleep. And Constable Jim is with her." Best to let her think we still had police presence. I licked my lips, my mouth gone dry.

She spotted Star and gave a hiss. "What did Alison say to you?"

"You'll need to talk to her about that. Constable Collins is with her at the detachment. You should go there," I encouraged her, anything to get her to leave and take her vileness with her. I put a hand out to direct her to turn around and leave, managing to barely overcome my horror.

"Don't you dare touch me!" she screamed. "You're a bloody witch, that's what you are."

"So?" I shrugged, trying hard to be brave and ignore the intense fear and hatred I was surrounded by. "Better that than a murderess." The lethal word slipped out without warning.

"How dare you! Who do you think you are!"

"What's going on?" Tulip came rushing down the stairs. "Granny's trying to sleep!"

"Granny, Granny, Granny! She's not a bloody saint. Any more than any of you are. Just think of what you did to my Alison, Star. Freezing her out of the competition and taking what was rightfully hers all for your own. You think you can sing," she scoffed. "My Alison has the voice of an angel." Mrs. Smith's face turned an alarming shade of pissed-off royal purple. Not the calm, smug banker's wife anymore. Her true self stood exposed. *But maybe we could get a confession out of her? People make all sorts of mistakes when they're upset. Be brave. And where's a good coven when you need it?*

"How dare you, you murderer!" I said. She rushed me as I spoke the condemning words, knocking me aside. It was then a gun seemed to magically appear in her right hand. *Oh, goddess, no.*

"Put that down," I said, my voice stronger than expected. It didn't feel real though, having a lethal weapon pointed at me. I could see she had no idea of what she was doing. It was just a threat—there was no way would she use it. *Right?*

She waved it about in a flashy manner, proving my assumption correct. She was a poisoner, a person better suited to the coward's way of dealing with things. "I mean to do this. You tell me what Alison said or I will shoot one of you."

An idea came to me, as I remembered what I had read about beating a lie detector. *If you believe, it will sound true.* "Alison mentioned you were helping plan the wedding. She was upset that you were taking over, making plans she didn't want."

She lowered the gun a couple of inches, perhaps hearing the truth of conviction in my tone. "Then why did the constable take her to the station? That makes no sense."

Think, Charm, think. Where was a good basic time machine when I really needed it? It didn't need bells and whistles, just to be able to send us back a few precious minutes. "Something about a confession? I don't know for certain. He took her out of here so fast, I really have no idea."

Her eyes narrowed. I kept my eye on the gun that now dangled from her hand. "Confession? Alison's confessing? No, she can't! I won't let her. She's getting married. To a Davidson!" An unholy light gleamed in her calculating eyes.

"You should go to her," I urged. "She needs you."

"You'd like that, eh? Let all of you off the hook." She waggled the gun about alarmingly.

"What's going on?"

Granny's voice resounded from the top of the stairs. Mrs. Smith's attention was taken away at that moment, her glance shifting to watch our grandmother coming into view. It was my chance, my only chance. I couldn't risk having our beloved Granny come down the stairs to confront a killer. I lunged for the gun, striking at the woman's arm with all my force.

She screamed in rage as the weapon flew out of her hand and struck the floor, followed by a loud sound that instantly deafened me. *Oh. My. Goddess.* My throat tightened and a cold sweat broke out all over my body. Loaded, the weapon had fired a shot.

I have to save my family.

I dived for the gun, wanting to grab if before the killer could. She reached it first and we locked together in a life or death struggle. My foot connected with her shin, making her use a stream of profanity that sickened me. Striking out at her, touching her—it was almost more than I could bear. Nauseous and wanting to upchuck, I gritted my teeth and suffered it all. *Better me than anyone else.*

She was so strong for a woman well past middle age, easily my match in the deadly battle, overpowering me, laying me out flat on the floor, and the triumphant look on her face glittered, a horrifying sight to behold. That is, until the back door burst open under the pressure of a wave of women, the surprise freezing her in place. It helped me to find an enormous storehouse of willpower I didn't even know I possessed. I slid free and on top of her in one last mighty effort, visualizing Hercules in my mind's eye, pinning to the floor the arm that held the gun and grabbing her other hand, shaking with the adrenaline.

"Is everyone okay?" I gasped, shooting a quick look around. Everyone was still standing. *Good sign, right?* Granny came down the stairs slowly followed by her sister, their eyes wide with worry.

"We're all fine. The bullet hit the wall above the sink," Tulip said, pointing in that direction, her voice tinged by fear. *No kidding.*

I took a scarf offered from the extended hand of someone nearby, using my teeth and chin to tie it together in a loop, not wanting to take my hands off the killer until I unceremoniously secured the still-frozen Mrs. Smith's hands behind her back, thrusting her into the corner near the back door, against the wall. All the fight went out of her then, making the job simpler. My breathing came heavily, my muscles aching, and I was beyond thankful it was over.

"Call nine-one-one. We've got our murderer."

I looked up and realised the *entire* Northern Lights Coven stood in our kitchen, silent, shoulder to shoulder, their faces focused. I…couldn't have done it without them. Not that I had any idea *how* we'd done it, and judging by their faces, neither did any of them. But —

The door burst open again and there was our Mountie.

"Stand aside. RCMP business." He made his way up to me, looked at Mrs. Smith still squeezed into the corner and closely guarded by those standing nearest her, and then at the bullet hole over the sink. He tugged me into his arms. "Are you okay?" he asked, holding tighter than necessary. It was quite nice and I snuggled closer.

"I'm fine. Just fine."

"That you are, Miss McCall."

"Aww, isn't that just *too* sweet?" Mrs. Smith muttered, finding her voice.

"Will you be all right while I book Mrs. Smith?"

"Of course. Go about your business, Constable."

The sea of women parted for him and he reached down and tugged the culprit to her feet. "Mrs. Smith, you are under arrest for attempted murder. Anything you say will be held in evidence against you. If you want a lawyer, one will be appointed…"

"Guess what?" Christine had pushed herself through to the front of the crowd and now stood by my side, looking excited.

"What?" Unable to take much more, I prayed it was good news.

"The strippers' bus is fixed and they're about to leave town."

"Really? Well, that's one good thing, eh?" Maybe things would settle down. *Please.*

"Let's give them a proper send-off," Christine called, to be heard over the din of those assembled. Instantly the coven cheered then streamed through the kitchen into the café and out the front door to line Main Street. I caught sight of Emma's red hair, a bright beacon in the middle of the group, and breathed a sigh of relief. She'd be fine now. I'd see to it.

"Hidey-ho, strippers, time to go!"

"Hidey-ho, strippers, time to go!"

I winced at the message and reluctantly took my place between Tulip and Star, to be part of the collective.

Just another day in Snowy Lake.

Chapter Twenty-Three

The big Greyhound bus belched diesel fuel while lumbering down the street and scorching the air with sulfur fumes, but otherwise looking sea-worthy. *Thank you, goddess.* It steamed by the town's women assembled for the impromptu send-off.

Not taking the message well, two of the strippers mooned the crowd through the windows, garnering extra boos and hisses. I narrowed my eyes at the odd rotten egg or piece of fruit hitting the sides of the bus and sliding down to plop on the street, simulating what came out of a cow's rear end when their tails were held high. *Some people*…and I didn't mean the strippers.

"So, can I join the Northern Lights Coven?" Christine implored, her face alight with the possibilities. She'd parked herself next to Star in the line-up.

"Ah, sure, if you want. Tomorrow's our bi-monthly meeting night anyway and it's our turn to host. Come on by. We'd be pleased to have you," I said, giving her a friendly smile. She had helped our town out and that meant a lot. She deserved membership as much as anyone.

The bus gone, the women began to disband. It was getting late, the street lights coming on and casting their blue light onto the pavements. Everyone was beginning to look otherworldly in the glow as they slipped back to their homes to pick up the lives they'd abandoned to recent shenanigans. Would I see Ace again tonight? Most likely not. He had a murderess to book and hopefully get a full confession from. *Good for the soul, Mrs. Smith.* I sent the message into the universe, hoping she'd catch it. One of the streetlights flickered and I knew then that everything was going as planned.

I put my arms around my sisters' shoulders, hugging them close, while the three of us stared up at the stars. Baby Ling Ling strolled up and rubbed her fluffy body against my leg, inserting herself into the picture. I reached down and stroked her fur coat, enjoying its silkiness while she purred and chirped with pleasure.

"I've rebooked Ling Ling's *Vétérinaire* appointment," Star mentioned casually.

Instantly the three of us were left to our own devices, Ling Ling having removed herself to parts unknown until the current threat passed.

"What? She's bilingual now?" Star quirked an eyebrow, making me snort.

"Apparently so," I deadpanned, straightening and giving her a quick wink.

"Think Mom will ever come back?" Tulip asked, taking me by complete surprise. I swallowed over the lump lodged in my throat at the memory which still haunted me in the dark hours before dawn, of being dropped off like we were just bags of trash. "Do you remember her, Charm? What she looked like? I can't see her anymore...and it scares me."

"That's okay. It's been a long time, sis." I tried to hide the sudden pain of a spear being thrust into my heart.

"Who cares," Star added, her voice strained and not in tune with her words.

"We'll deal with it if and when it happens. Together." I took a deep breath, needing to change the subject. "Now, who do I blame for the cannabis cookie caper tonight?"

"What are you talking about?" Tulip pretended to have no knowledge.

"She already knows about it. She had one," Star filled her in. "Don't blame me, it was an accident. She's fine. You're fine, right, Charm?" She suddenly looked anxious, giving me a once-over.

"I'm fine. We should look in on Granny, though."

"You do know she uses cannabis?"

"*What?*" I stopped dead in my tracks.

"Yes, for her arthritis. She didn't want to tell you because of your objections, and you know, the history in the family."

"Well, I guess if Granny uses it..." My voice trailed off. The woman knew her stuff so I couldn't very well object. She'd never steered us wrong before.

"So, we can sell the cookies?" Tulip's voice filled with exuberance.

"I guess. Once it's legal, okay? No more practicing until then. I don't want any trouble. Understood?"

"Great! We'll make a killing. Oops." Tulip covered her mouth in mock horror. "Oh look, dark fingers are stretching across the moon. Strangers are coming soon and bringing danger." She shuddered.

Tulip's prediction chilled me to the bone, making me glance up and observe my ancient friend. The luminous moon spoke to me on such an elemental level. She'd been here before I came and would be here after I was long gone. "I hope it's not too soon. I think I've had enough excitement for a while."

"You know, I heard something today at the Boots & Lace from Darcy and then Auntie T.J. confirmed it. There's talk of our town being used for a movie titled *Witches and Wolves*. A historical paranormal drama. Isn't that awesome?" Star's tone was beyond thrilled. "Maybe I can act in it? They might need extras."

"Maybe," I agreed, though I was taken aback by the odd title. I shivered. Not a fun mix in my opinion, wolves and witches.

"You know, you're not the only one who's recently discovered something awesome about themselves. Here, look at this!" And with that Star moved a few feet away, raising her hands to the night sky. A slight humming sound began, a gentle breeze stirred and she grew taller. *What the heck?* Looking closer, I realized her feet had left the ground. She was levitating. At least six inches from the sidewalk. I gasped in shock.

"How is that even possible?" I asked, not sure who I was talking to.

She lowered herself back down, a wide smile lighting her face. "I can't go very high yet, but I'm working on it. It feels like the energy comes from the earth and buoys me up—sort of like magnetic, but the opposite, repelling me upwards."

"How did you do that?" Tulip asked, her eyes round as saucers. "I want to do that."

"I don't know. It just started happening. Cool, eh?"

"I'll say. But maybe you'd better not be doing that in front of others just yet. At least until we know what's going on. Granny will know what to do."

"Okay," Star agreed. "But maybe they can use it in the movie. Wouldn't that be sweet?"

"They'll just think you're using a harness or maybe copying David Blaine, the magician," Tulip scoffed.

"Maybe so, but it's still really something. Can *you* do anything remotely like that?" The hurt was obvious in Star's tone. I'd have thought she'd have grown a thicker skin by now, hanging around this town. Or maybe it was her songwriter's soul that made her extra vulnerable.

Tulip buttoned her lip at my scowl. Who knew, maybe it would be her turn next to discover a little something extra? As if cloud reading and dream interpretation weren't enough. We were a quirky family, all right. The best one I could ever have imagined being part of, bar none.

I opened the front door for my sisters and heard Ivana's voice loud and clear and obviously highly annoyed. "Why Charm not invite Ivana to help send strippers running?" I groaned. Both Tulip and Star blessed me with looks of sympathy.

My sisters were scooting into the café ahead of me when I heard my name being called. I turned to look. And there he was. Constable Ace Collins striding down the street right toward me. How could I have ever mixed up such a handsome, intelligent man with Bigfoot? He was so much more than just a pretty face and hot bod.

"Hey, darlin', thought I'd check on you. Make sure everything's okay." He tipped his hat with respect, making me smile. It was so like him. He needed to be in charge as much as me.

"We're fine. And the town should settle down now. The strippers have decamped, thank goodness."

"Good." He nodded. "That's a relief."

"How did you make out with Mrs. Smith?"

"Full confession. She's making my job easier. I do feel sorry for Alison and Fred, though. They're both upset."

"Understandable. So…" For some reason I couldn't think of something witty to add. I got a whiff of his outdoorsy fragrance underlaid with a musk and my heart filled with anticipation. Was he *The One*? Like Granny said I had to wait for, or lose my gift? Only time would tell. And we could wait. Neither of us was going anywhere soon. It would be years before he was rotated out of Snowy Lake for another posting.

"Well, I should be going. You must be tired."

"I'm not that tired. Want some coffee? Something to eat?"

"I still owe you a barbecue, Miss McCall."

"Anytime, Sheriff," I teased. "I'm always around."

"I'm be countin' on that," he said, following me into the café.

Want to see more from this author?
Here's a taster for you to enjoy!

Manitoba Tea & Tarot Mysteries:
Movies, Moonlight & Magic
January Bain

Excerpt

"I've got it, Charm!" Star flew into the Tea & Tarot café, the ever-present star-pendant swinging wildly about her neck and a piece of paper clutched in her hand. The angel chimes holding court over the doorway accompanied her arrival, singing with enough enthusiasm to awaken the dead. Before I could move, she pulled me into a crushing hug, doing a spectacular impression of one of the black bears that our part of the world is renowned for.

"Slow down, sis. What's going on?" I pulled away to pick up the faded tea towel I'd dropped in the brouhaha.

"I got the part! You know, the movie? *Witches and Wolves!* Get with the program, sis. See? I got confirmation right here." She waved the crumpled piece of paper about as if it was a stock certificate. Maybe it was, for her. I had absolutely no interest in being in a movie, now or ever.

"What kind of part? Witch or wolf?" Tulip asked, shutting the lid of her laptop for once and joining us in the huddle. She and Star were gorgeous. Both blessed with blonde hair and tan-able skin while I looked like Snow White, only lacking the seven dwarfs, summer or winter. *Go figure, and us triplets.*

"Duh! Witch, of course. And it's a period piece, too, so we get to wear *awesome* costumes." Star gave a faux-waltz step, obviously in love with the idea. As the town's resident country and western singer and songwriter to boot, she was into looking good. Sometimes a bit too into it — she attracted more than her fair share of jealous stabs.

"What's it about?" I asked, squinting through the window at a couple who had just appeared walking down the street. They were looking rather chummy, if body language didn't lie. *Is that Constable Ace Collins? With a female?* I slipped on a pair of polar ray sunglasses to sharpen the image.

"A company coming to town to develop a tourist mecca by selling the outside world on the natural hot springs in the area having magical properties."

Hot springs laced with minerals we had for some weird reason, even though Snowy Lake perched on the Canadian Shield. Add in Skull Cave for the wolf clans, and the choice of location was now making a whole lot of sense. I shuddered. Caves gave me the willies. *A nightmare left over from childhood.*

But the sheriff — as I liked to call the constable — and an unknown female? Who was she? Tall and slender with her golden-brown hair tied up in a ponytail, she had the best tan. She also made it easy for the males of the species to appreciate those long, bronzed legs, in her short shorts. Maybe it was time to try the spray tan special that Susie was offering at the Clip Joint this month? My blue-white legs could use some help. *Desperately.*

Star, of course, kept droning on while I sidestepped to the front picture window for the best surveillance. "*And* it's the werewolves' territorial land, while the witches are upset they'll be exposed, so they have to build an alliance to fight the conglomerate. But not everyone's ready for a truce and all kinds of problems develop. It even features the use of arsenic by a suspected serial killer. They've got a poison expert on the set too, the daughter of the actress with the lead role—you know, Mimi Blake. Her daughter knows all about its uses. I forget her name. Oh, they need more billets for some of the extras. Can you think of people who might help with that?"

The pair vanished into Snowy Lake Hardware, with Ace holding the door open with a flourish for Miss Perfect Tan. They shared some comment that made her smile, and possibly giggle—I was too far away to be certain. The hackles on my neck prickled. A light fixture blew out over the first booth in a cascade of exploding sparks. I sighed. Now I'd have to scout the street to find the ladder to change the bulb. Seemed someone was always borrowing the handy-dandy climbing device.

"Sorry, what did you say about a serial killer and arsenic?" I focused on the part of Star's intel that intrigued me.

"Aren't you listening to me? I said a serial killer uses arsenic to kill off characters. Where's your mind this morning?"

Star interrupted her spiel to make a spinning twirl, her usual performance piece when she was over-the-moon excited. The phone rang and I hurried to answer it, hoping it was who I thought it was. *Yes.*

"Auntie T.J. What's the scoop?" I normally had the common sense not to ask, but today was different. I needed intel.

Her voice came over the house phone, all wheezy and breathy. Land lines were the only reliable mode of communication in Snowy Lake, where cell phones were a crap shoot. "Jennifer Morgan. She's a geologist with Altima Explorations. A graduate student from the University of Manitoba. Good grades, though not brilliant. She's here with a small team looking for precious minerals. Mark my word, a big gold strike is imminent. She lives close to his parents' duplex in Winnipeg—did you know they live side by side? Families are old friends. I'm waiting on more information that I should have shortly. I think her father and Ace's mother both work at that virology lab in Winnipeg. Will have verification soon." With that my aunt stopped to take a breath.

I kept a sharp lookout across the street. Fortunately, the telephone rested on the counter near the entrance where we sold all sorts of cookies and bakery goods alongside my favorite magical items, including the new Gilded Tarot by Ciro with its black and gold borders framing lyrical illustrations that whispered to me whenever I ventured nearby. The location was perfect, offering up a proper surveillance position. A stranger came into focus, drawing my full attention—he was so stiff-looking with his pressed beige chino pants, white shirt and black tie and an old-fashioned pocket protector lining up a series of identical pens. He was coming right towards the Tea & Tarot with a determined look on his pasty-white face. His short ginger hair was pressed into service with one section at the crown that wouldn't commit to the status quo sticking up with military defiance.

"I gotta go. Call me later when you know more."

"Roger that. Over and out."

I slipped off the sunglasses just as the angels tinkled a discordant note, announcing the visitor. He gave a harried look around, as though he had no idea how to go about what he needed, but needed it done—and done yesterday.

"Can I help you?" I got to him first. Easy enough, when no one else looked remotely interested.

"Yes, I'm here to check on catering. Do you do that?"

"Catering? Sometimes. What for?"

"I'm with Blue Vest Studios, the company producing the movie *Witches and Wolves*, and we need reliable catering six days a week at the movie set. You know, sandwiches, soups, salads, vegetable trays, desserts, that kind of thing. And especially anything chocolate. Can you do that?" He hurried his words, looking about with eyes that shifted so much I was concerned for his well-being.

"Well, possibly. And we specialize in chocolate, so you're in luck. You must try our death-by-chocolate slice. It's worth dying for with its hooey-gooey center of chocolate ganache and liquid caramel." I caught the gleam in his eye at my description. While I relished the idea of a catering job, I knew most of it would fall to Tulip and me as Star had a role and, no doubt, she'd play that up. Add her bi-weekly singing at the Boots & Lace Tavern and she'd work both excuses for the foreseeable future.

"Would you like to try a sample?" I asked.

"Yes, definitely." The gleam in his eye was blinding now.

I laid a square of the slice on a small plate, added a fork and handed it to him.

He demolished it in two spectacular bites.

"You do love chocolate." I smiled at his satiated expression. Illicit drugs couldn't have given him more of a sense of being in Blissville. "How many people are we talking about?"

"About a hundred and fifty."

"A hundred and fifty meals a day?" My horror must have shown on my face, because he twitched and his eyes spun around like cartwheels.

"Yes, but just simple meals. Nothing fancy. And we'd pay ten dollars a head. One meal will suffice, delivered around noon. Send enough and we can eat off the buffet for the rest of the day. We have refrigerators in most of the trailers. What do you say?"

Hmm. Ten dollars a head times one hundred and fifty meals. Sweet. But I would need to hire an extra hand or two. No way could we manage all that on top of our usual workload. I made some swift calculations.

"Make that eleven dollars a meal and we have a deal."

"Ten dollars and twenty-five cents. Then we have a deal. I'm Howard Smith, by the way, the resident accountant."

"Charm McCall. Ten-fifty. And I'll even throw in our gluten-free dessert, Cake of a Thousand Faces." The yummy cake was called by that quirky name because it could be dolled up any number of ways—its vanilla flavor went with just about everything else in existence. That, and we loved weird names that made people stand up and take notice. "A house speciality that substitutes almond meal for pastry flour. So, as long as the customer is not allergic to nuts, it works really well. Low-carb, high protein."

"Nice. Okay, that'll work," he agreed with a curt nod.

I sucked up losing the extra fifty cents and nodded my acceptance. An accountant would be concerned about costs. I got that, being the one and only bookkeeper for our small business. Cutting costs was essential to survival. Still, it rankled. We'd do the town proud with our catering—I'd make sure of that—even if it ate into profits.

He stuck out his hand for a shake and I was blessed with the dampest paw on the planet, accompanied by a zinger of an image. Howard cared about every penny because he was embezzling company funds, meaning there would be less to steal if I made a decent profit. Sometimes I wished Granny Toogood hadn't banned swearing—I had a few apt descriptors for this weaselly dealer. I also hoped she was feeling better. The doctor had advised a few days of rest and that had me worried.

Instead, I narrowed my eyes at him and he slid his hand from mine. Yuck. I dried my palm by rubbing it discreetly down the side of my jeans, half hidden by my Tea & Tarot apron.

"Can you start tomorrow?" he asked, his desperation leaking through, making his face shiny with sweat. *Probably because the only other quote he most likely got today far exceeded ours. Guaranteed.* The Husky Service on the highway did some catering, but they didn't come cheap. And their bakery goods came out of pre-frozen tubs and boxes. We prided ourselves on everything fresh baked, from scratch—my fingernails were reduced to rubble from constant work. *Proof positive.*

"Tomorrow! So soon?" All the nerves in my body slammed into high gear. There was so much to do to prepare for such a large undertaking. Could it even be done that quickly?

"We'd really appreciate it. Might even find you a bit part in the movie." It wasn't the incentive he expected—I just shook my head, giving his start date some thought. Sometimes it was best to jump into things, otherwise I'd never do it. I just prayed I could pull it off and do my family and our town proud.

"Okay, but minus the movie walk-on."

The relief on his face made me smile, despite his weaselly-ness.

The café door opened abruptly and in strode a young man dressed in expensive dark-wash jeans and a tight black T-shirt clothing a wiry, thin body, his face a study in annoyance. "Howard, I need to speak with you *right now*. Don't think you can just get up and walk out on me, mister." His hand on his hip pressed his case.

Howard's face darkened to a dull red. "Chace, this is not the time or the place. *Go*. I'll catch up with you later."

The man looked as though he was going to object before he about-faced and left. His one-finger salute, reflected in the front window before he pranced away, was not in the best taste. *Hmm*. Good thing Granny wasn't around to cut him down to size. In the nicest, politest way of course — she could make the worst villain tippy-toe around her. *Probably ask him if he needs the finger for anything other than being rude.*

"Please excuse my friend. He's not himself today."

"Oh, who is he then?"

Howard gave me a blank stare.

Baby Ling Ling sauntered in, grabbing my attention as she always announced her arrival with a loud greeting, or warning, depending on how her day was going. Our spectacular white Himalayan with her adorable squished-in face and apricot-colored ears, fluffy tail raised high, proceeded to choose her steps with the utmost care across the tiled floor of the café. I'd guess it was in case we'd had the bad manners to add a trap door since yesterday's saunter. She deigned to notice the new visitor, striding over and giving him a quick sniff. She jumped a couple of feet in the air with a loud howl, her fluffy white fur standing straight on end as though she'd placed her paw on an electrical charge.

"*Hiss.*" She made herself as big as a tiny eight-pound cat could make herself, arched her back and continued the hissing.

"Nice cat," Howard deadpanned.

"Careful what you say to her. Ling Ling's officially multi-lingual since our librarian, Miriam, added Portuguese to her weekly slate of free language lessons." I just couldn't resist, not liking his look of disdain. Or his cheapness that was certain to affect our bottom line.

His look of confusion was quite satisfying. He gave Ling Ling a wide berth and headed for the door.

"Okay, then, we'll expect you tomorrow? You'll get paid once a week, just come by my office and I'll cut you a check. Oh, and the camp's out by Spirit Springs." He paused, his hand on the doorknob, obviously needing confirmation.

"Yes, I know where the camp is, and the food will be there. You can count on the McCall family. We never go back on our word." I gave him a level look that he declined to return. A nervous twitch of his nose and he hopped out of the café.

"That guy has a blackish aura with streaks of gray," Tulip said, pursing her lips.

"Yeah, no surprise—he's working under a brain cloud." I didn't want to say the words *embezzling cocaine addict* out loud and sink the project before it started. "And since when did you start seeing auras?" And what was I going to do with the unwanted knowledge that the guy was stealing company funds? *A moral dilemma.* I shouldn't think that was business as normal, even for the movie industry.

She gave me a smug look. "You're not the only one discovering gifts since we turned twenty-one on July first."

"Nice. Hey, what color's mine?"

"Depends."

"What do you mean?"

"It's usually light with a halo of pink, silver or gold, but right now it's tinged with green. Never seen that color on you before. Interesting."

Movement across the street drew my attention, and out of Snowy Lake Hardware popped Ace and his fancy friend. Hmm. She was swinging that ponytail so much it was in peril of getting caught in something. *Not that that would be a bad thing.* I envisioned it catching in the closing door and…

"Who's that with Ace?" Tulip joined me at the window. "By the way, your aura's getting greener. Maybe you're jealous, eh?" She poked me with a sharp elbow.

"Ow! I'm not jealous. That's Jennifer Morgan, an old family friend of Ace's. Graduate student here on geology exploration," I said through clenched teeth. What else was going on? She lightly swatted Ace's arm in feigned anger play, making me wince. *A flirt to boot.*

They crossed the street and strolled merrily toward the café. I ducked out of the window and hurried to continue dusting the shelves. Tulip dallied.

"Move away from there, they'll see you spying on them," I hissed at her.

"So?" She shrugged, but thankfully moved toward her laptop again and got back to keyboarding. *Good, just write the blog already and pretend nothing's going on.* And what exactly *was* going on?

The angel chimes sang out the new arrivals with all the enthusiasm of a Baptist congregation. *I swear they know more about who's coming into our café than I do, changing their mood with each customer they announce.*

"Mornin', Charm, Tulip. I'd like you to meet an old family friend, Jennifer Morgan," Ace said with a respectful tilt of his impressive hat. Star had long vanished into the back recesses of the kitchen, probably to text or call everyone of the Northern Lights Coven about her shiny new job. I sighed. *Shoot.* I had to get to the Grab-n-go and buy supplies for tomorrow's catering or I'd be sunk.

I gave the pair a quick greeting, unable to keep from noticing how sweet-smelling our almost-brand-new Mountie was that morning. The fragrance of soap and a special mix that was all Ace's own rolled off him in waves, like pheromones at a picnic. If I was an ant, I'd be crawling all over him. I took a deep appreciative breath, remembering to give the new female a smile of welcome. If Granny Toogood heard that I'd lost my manners, well, suffice to say, there would be repercussions. Three things she can't abide, that special woman who took us in at the age of eight when we arrived unannounced on her doorstep—swearing, speaking ill of the dead and sex talk. But politeness, that was a given. Ace himself was no slouch in that department either, having grown up in the southern state of Kentucky before his parents moved with their three sons to Canada.

"What are you doing in Snowy Lake, Jennifer?" I asked, though it was a useless waste of time to confirm my aunt's information. She was always spot on. We all have our gifts in Snowy Lake. Mine is finding lost objects and a recent development I hadn't quite worked my mind around yet—some kind of weird ability to heal the human body—while Auntie T.J.'s was always knowing the news first.

"I'm a graduate student from the University of Manitoba. We're working with Altima Explorations, checking for alluvial gold deposits." Her voice had a serious edge to it, mixed with a lyrical quality.

"Ah, the kind deposited through water movements. But, of course, the best indicator is the fact that substantial gold deposits were found here in the past," I added, entirely grateful for my need to know a little something about everything, when her eyes lit up with interest.

"Charm's a major league bookworm," Ace said with an appreciative smile.

Great. I'd just placed myself into the boring-librarian category. Maybe it was time for dark-framed glasses. *Nah, I don't even wear contacts. I'm one of the lucky ones, so far. Never been sick one day in my life, touch wood. Annoys my sisters no end when they're stricken by a runny nose or fever.*

"She's a lot more than that, Ace. She runs a business and still manages to look gorgeous."

Oh no. She didn't just say that. The. Worst. Possible. Thing. A woman who looked like she did and was super-nice to other women? My barely begun romance was dead in the water. *Kaput.* All Ace and I had shared was one kiss, though. I sighed. *But what a kiss.* A treasured memory now, since it didn't look like any more would be forthcoming. It didn't help that Tulip made a circle with her forefinger and thumb at me, a gesture meant to emphasize my aura getting greener, no doubt.

A horrendous sound struck my brain. *Oh, jeez, not today.*

"Who's that?" Jennifer pointed out of the window, her eyes wide open.

I cringed. Auntie T.J., in full battle dress and playing bagpipes usually reserved for fending off bear attacks, marched by the café's entrance. At least the residents would turn a blind eye, knowing my family, though my auntie didn't make it easy wearing head-to-toe plaid.

"That's my auntie. She's—uh—driving away evil spirits. Just ignore her. So, what can I do for you this morning? Quiche? Coffee?" I asked brightly, pretending it was business as usual. "We make mini-breakfast quiches in pastry pockets, easy for our customers to take to go." I pointed them out to Jennifer. "How about you, Constable?"

"Sorry, no time, today, darlin'. I'm heading out to check that new movie set, to make sure everything's up to code," Ace said.

Jennifer's eyebrows rose at the casual "darlin'", but she continued to smile like a sunny pixie. At least her lips did. Her eyeballs appeared frozen over. "And I've got to get to work. Ace helped me pick up some supplies." She held up the small Snowy Lake Hardware bag she was carrying as proof of their prior engagement.

"Maybe a croissant or a cheese scone?" For some reason I couldn't let it go. She looked a tad narrow in the hips.

"Oh, do you make cheese scones?" she squealed. "My grandmother always did when we visited the farm each summer vacation. I love them!"

I inwardly groaned. *Great, now I've made the elder woman category.* "Yes, it's an old family recipe of Granny Toogood."

"Granny Toogood?" she inquired, turning to check out our glass display of bakery goods with a keen interest.

"You'll meet her soon. She's the matriarch of our family."

"I do believe I must try them." She pointed at a peanut butter cookie tray lined up with all the other array of choices. "And one of those as well."

"Ace?" I asked, giving him a wee nudge, making sure to use his first name this time.

"Nothing for me, thanks." Well, that was a first. What was the deal? *Suddenly watching your weight, big guy? No need for that, no sir, not with that lean six-pack, quarterback shoulders and thighs like a lumberjack who's been cutting down trees all day. Oh my…*

"Don't worry. We haven't laced anything with cyanide this week," I teased, filling the silence. "Besides, champagne works best." He'd get the tribute to Agatha Christie's *Sparkling Cyanide* and our last case where the murderess had placed the poison in our apricot jam. *The nerve of the banker's wife, making our wares suspect.*

"That's good to know," Ace deadpanned, though he gave me a wink. *Nice.*

Jennifer opened the blue and white starred bakery bag I handed her with its Tea & Tarot moniker designed by Tulip, diving into the cheddar cheese scone. "Oh, this is wonderful. So moist. Ace, you must try a bite." She didn't wait for an answer, but force-fed him. He accepted the morsel from her fingers, swallowing it. She turned to give me a sly victory grin.

My heart sank.

Home of Erotic Romance

Sign up for our newsletter and find out about all our
romance book releases, eBook sales and promotions,
sneak peeks and FREE romance books!

About the Author

January Bain has wished on every falling star, every blown-out birthday candle and every coin thrown in a fountain to be a storyteller. To share the tales of high adventure, mysteries, and full-blown thrillers she has dreamed of all her life. The story you now have in your hands is the compilation of a lot of things manifesting itself for this special series. Hundreds of hours spent researching the unusual and the mundane have come together to create a series that features strong women who don't take life too seriously, wild adventures full of twists and unforeseen turns, and hot complicated men who aren't afraid to take risks. She can only hope the stories of her beloved Brass Ringers will capture your imagination as much as they did hers when she wrote them.

If you are looking for January Bain, you can find her hard at work every morning without fail in her office with two furry babies trying to prove who does a better job of guarding the doorway. And, of course, she's married to the most romantic man! Who once famously replied to her inquiry about buying fresh flowers for their home every week, "Give me one good reason why not?" Leaving her speechless and knocking her head against the proverbial wall for being so darn foolish. She loves flowers.

January loves to hear from readers. You can find her contact information, website details and author profile page at https://www.totallybound.com